This book is for anyone who feels like they can't be themselves or be loved because of trauma, heartache, or any other reason. It's also for those who found someone who understood them without explanation and in the most unexpected place. Souls can be funny like that.

Protecting yourself takes courage.

So does being loved.

NOT THAT KIND OF *Icing*

STELLA STEVENSON

CONTENT NOTES

―――――

includes possible spoilers

This is an **open door** romance that portrays on-page consensual sexual intimacy and **strong language** suitable for readers ages 18+.

There are also mentions of **drug/alcohol use** and abuse. Cheating (not among the main characters), past **childhood neglect**, past **childhood cancer**, there are instances of **sexist comments** and one scene with **sexual threats/harassment** and **threats of violence**.

Overall this story is a happy one. It is a romance and everyone gets the ending they need, but there are still some topics that can be triggering for some readers. Always put your own mental health and well-being first.

🌶 Spice can be found in chapters:
15
22
25
Vegas 😏

―――――

QUARRY CREEK ARCTIC

Victor Varg

#25   R

2023-24 Season

GP	G	A	P	+/-
65	40	71	111	25

Career

GP	G	A	P	+/-
980	423	716	1139	187

Height: 6'5"
Weight: 206lb
Born: 5/5/1991 (Age: 32)
Birthplace: Kimmelwick, NY
Shoots: R
Draft: 2009, TOR (7th overall,) 1st round, 7th pick

ICING CALLS

There are often times during a hockey game when the defensive team is under so much pressure that the only way to relieve it may be to drill the puck all the way down the ice as far as possible into the opponent's zone.

It's not always the preferable thing to do as the faceoff will come back into the defensive end and the team which shot the puck down the ice isn't allowed to make a player change. However, shooting the puck the length of the ice is always better than being scored against.

NHL Rule 81.1 – Icing

For the purpose of this rule, the red center line will divide the ice into halves. Should any player of a team, equal or superior in numerical strength (power-play) to the opposing team, shoot, bat or deflect the puck from his nw half of the ice synod the goal line of the opposing team, play shall be stopped. For the purpose of deflected pucks, this only applies when the puck was originally propelled down the ice by the offending team.

For the purpose of this rule, the point of last contact with the puck by the team in possession shall be used to determine whether icing has occurred or not. As such, the team in possession must "gain the line" in order for the icing to be nullified. "Gaining the line" shall mean that the puck, while on the player's stick (not the player's skate) must make contact with the center red line in order to nullify a potential icing.

For the purpose of interpretation of the rule, there are two judgments required for "icing the puck." The Linesman must first determine that the puck will cross the goal line. Once the Linesman determines that the puck will cross the goal line, icing is completed upon the determined as to which player (attacking or defending) would first touch the puck. This decision by the Linesman will be made by no later than the instant the first players reaches the end zone face-off dots with the player's skate being the determining factor. Should the puck be shot down the ice in such a manner that it travels around the boards and/or back toward the end zone face-off dots, the same procedure shall be in effect in that the Linesman shall determine within a similar distance as to who will have touched the puck first.

For clarification, the determining factor is which player would first touch the puck, not which player would first reach the end zone face-off dots.

If the race for the puck is too close to determine by the time the first players reaches the end zone face-off dots, icing shall be called.

The puck striking or deflecting off an official does not automatically nullify a potential icing.

Whatever our souls are made of, his and mine are the same.

EMILY BRONTË

TRISTAN

WHY IS it that when grown men behave with the maturity of toddlers, it's always expected that someone else will come clean up their messes? In my experience, the more fame and money a man has, the more likely he is to have situations that need a little elbow grease—a patch job almost always contracted out to the nearest woman.

The worst part about today isn't that it's a Monday, although that's almost enough to ruin any good morning. It's not that I overslept my six o'clock alarm and wasn't able to finish blow-drying my hair. It's not even that I'd somehow forgotten to put coffee on my weekly grocery list and had to make do with a packet of instant. My morning coffee tasted like burnt hair mixed with the white coating on sour candies.

No. The reason for my bad mood is that once again a grown man with more money than he can manage did something incredibly stupid, and it's going to be my job to fix it.

Again.

I've worked for the Quarry Creek Arctic hockey team for three years and I've been in this conference room more than once. Usually, I'm here for the standard marketing meetings, the holiday gift exchange, or anytime someone brings donuts by the office. Technically, I'm not senior enough to be in this meeting. I want to be. I'd love to be the VP of Marketing. Maybe in five years. Or when the boys' club finally stops locking all the entrances, leaving only the tiniest crack in a basement window for me to force my way through.

"Remind me of your role again, miss?" Bob Seever, owner and CEO of the team, looks at me from under caterpillar eyebrows. All the other men in this room are wearing the same black suit with ties in different shades of blue, but Bob's suit is double-breasted with big brass button and wide pinstripes. It's hard not to find him eccentric and charming even though I want to point out that he, or rather, my boss, specifically asked me to come to this meeting. The email arrived only thirty minutes ago, I might add.

"Mr. Seever." My direct boss Chris steps in front of me and offers his hand to the man who signs our checks. "This is Ms. Grant. She's our media and content manager."

That's a title I've never heard before. I don't manage anyone because there isn't an actual social media team, just me. A twenty-seven-year-old BU graduate trying to guide over-large athletes into proper social media usage. It's pretty standard stuff. No genitalia on public, or private, forums—I'm looking at you, Spaeglin—no obscenities in any captions, and nothing political or divisive. Not on their public player accounts. I'd love for them to use proper spelling and grammar too, but beggars can't be choosers. And, to be fair, close to thirty percent of our players speak English as a second language.

Mr. Seever holds his hand out to me and I shake it, making sure my grip is firm but not crushing. His skin is soft under my fingers, his palms a little sweaty.

"Please call me Tristan," I keep my work smile pasted firmly in place. It's the smile my second-oldest baby sibling made me practice in the mirror after I bombed my first post-college interview. Although I maintain that had nothing to do with my smile. Or lack thereof.

"And forgive me." Bob's eyes crinkle in the corners. "What exactly is it you do?"

Do my best to keep us relevant.

Attempt to keep your players' internet personas family-friendly.

Draw new crowds into The Stand for our home games and to their televisions and devices to watch the away match ups.

"Social media," I say instead and drop my hand down under the lacquered top of the table to wipe down the side of my black skirt. "Photos, videos, and the internet. That kind of thing."

"Ah yes," he beams at me, eyebrows almost vibrating along his forehead. "I've heard reports we're doing very well on the inter webs. Have a lot of..." he trails off, snapping the fingers of his left hand as though the word will materialize in his palm.

I give him a moment to come up with it, but he doesn't.

3

"Our following has been growing exponentially in the last year." We have close to 350 thousand users subscribed to our channels and that number only increases every time I check it.

"I must confess I don't understand most of those sites, no matter how many times my grandkids try to show me. Although, with a professional like you on board, I guess I don't have to. I don't have an account myself."

He does. For the team.

I run it for him.

"Job security." I shrug and he laughs, a wheeze of sound that makes me want to fetch him a glass of water.

Bob turns back to Chris, clearing his throat a few times. "If you don't mind me asking, why is our Media and Content manager in this particular meeting? Surely our PR and legal teams won't want this to hit the media."

They'll want us—me—to control the narrative.

I think the words as loudly as I can, but my ESP appears to be malfunctioning. Not that I know what this meeting is about just yet, but I can guess the important things. I'm the only woman in the room. My job literally involves the team's community image. I'm about to be put to work. I can feel it. The knowledge tingles in my brain like a sneeze I know is coming.

"She's going to be our secret weapon," Chris says as my brain works overtime to figure out exactly what could have happened in the early hours of the morning. It was definitely something overnight if management called an emergency meeting before nine, but I haven't seen any damning news reports yet. And I have google alerts set up to ping for every guy on the team.

Probably a bar fight or a drunk and disorderly. Maybe an old gambling habit or an incriminating photo. Something that requires an image rehab. I can deal with that.

"I'm here to help," I say. It's what they pay me to do. I'll have to figure out something.

"I sure hope so." Bob nods, which in hindsight is concerning.

The head of the legal team clears their throat and asks everyone to take their seats, and although he's my boss's boss's boss's boss, Bob pulls one of the cushy chairs out for me and waits for me to sit down. Then he pushes me back in and takes a seat on my right. He winks as he folds his hands on top of the table and I'm trying very hard not to be charmed by him. Not when I know that this meeting will not go well for me or my workload.

There's a projector at the far end of the room and Curtis Haine's player promo photo is zoomed in until his face fills the entire screen. Number eleven and one of our top defenders, Haine isn't someone I know very well. I haven't had to take over his social media after he DM'd his dick to an uninterested model. I haven't had to tell him to archive photos of himself drinking beer out of a skate while wearing his practice jersey—I really hope it wasn't a used skate, but I'm pretty sure it was—and I also haven't had to remind him to make posts. Sure, policing the antics of the young and famous is tough, but for some guys, getting them to post anything is like undergoing a root canal. Sans anesthesia.

For a moment, I'm almost lulled into a false sense of security. If Haine hasn't been on my radar before, whatever happened can't be a public relations nightmare. Maybe he's sick. Maybe he's donated a six-figure sum to a worthy cause. Maybe it's someone in his family. Or an injury.

I know better than to have any wishful thinking. I'm usually more of a pragmatist, which turns out to be a good thing because I was wrong.

It's none of those.

It's worse. So much worse.

"We pulled some strings, and Haine's wife bailed him out about an hour ago." The man at the head of the table says. "We have legal on the case and we're hoping to keep everything as quiet as possible, but the list of charges is extensive, and the team is going to need to do preemptive damage control. The sooner the better."

List. Of. Charges.

As in more than one.

As in, this man was arrested and while he's already bailed out, it's bad enough that we're having a meeting. There have been player arrests in the past. Usually, I get an email memo and devise a plan of action for content and posting. This is an all-hands-on-deck-meeting.

"The PR team will talk to the players and the coaching staff. No one is to make any comments to any members of the press. We are focusing on our game play. We don't want the media getting any more information on this situation than they already have. We are a closed-lip unit."

Right. Lips sealed is standard operating procedure

until the organization chooses what side they want to take. Then we spoon feed the answers to the right people.

"What did Haine do?" One of the younger men at the table asks. He has the roundness of middle age, but the face of a fraternity brother. He's grinning like this is juicy gossip to be spilled over shots of Jameson. And yes, it's the question we all want answered, but it looks like everyone else had enough common sense not to ask.

The head of legal looks pained. It's the same pinched look—brows furrowed, lips pursed—that my parents wore almost my entire childhood. It's the look of someone who'd rather chew their way through a bucket of live earthworms than be where they are right now. He sighs, rubbing a hand across his forehead. I wonder if he's deciding what to share.

"Last night, Curtis Haine's car crashed into the side of a local daycare."

There's a collective gasp around the table and several people ask if the kids are okay. If they'd take one minute to think, they'd realize it had to be closed. Daycares hold business hours and if this had happened while the place was full of kids, there's no way we'd be finding out in a meeting. Haine would have been headline news across the country. He might have even made the BBC.

"Police responding to the scene reported he was under the influence."

"Drinking?" Bob Seever has been sober for thirty years. He can't expressly ban his players and employees from drinking, but it's well known that he does not tolerate alcohol-inspired stupidity. There's that pinched expression again as the head of legal stares down the head honcho.

"Among other things." The man at the head of the table looks like he might faint. "Both Haine and his female passenger were transported to Grace Hospital and are in stable condition."

I might not know Haine well, but his wife Shelly is a darling. She's got a real knack for her social media and has developed quite a following as a mommy and lifestyle influencer. The couple has two-year-old twins, a boy and a girl. They feature in posts frequently, often in Arctic jerseys. Shelly is a social media goldmine for the team. I hope they're doing okay.

"Should we offer childcare support while Shelly and Curtis recover?" Twelve sets of confused eyes turn to me. For a moment, I think that it's a gender divide. That not a single one of these suits understands the concept of toddlers—twins!—and then the poor man at the head of the table clears his throat again, his face almost magenta.

"Shelly... wasn't injured."

What he's not saying hits me like a hockey puck to a tender part of my body.

Shelly wasn't in the car. Curtis had another woman with him when he got drunk and/or high and plowed his vehicle into a place of business. While his wife was home. With their toddlers. That, and Curtis probably isn't going home once he's discharged. He's probably going to jail.

Asshole.

Actually, that's too good of a name for Mr. Haine. I hope that whenever he puts on a new pair of socks, he immediately steps into something wet. For the rest of his life. I hope he goes flaccid every time he wants to have sex. I hope he needs to imagine Muppets doing an Irish jig to get off. I hope...

Someone—Bob—is patting the back of my hand and it takes conscious effort to unclench my fists. I'm fairly certain that I've left little half-moon cuts on my palm from my nails. I take a deep breath to calm my racing heart and try to focus past the roaring in my ears. I'm at work. I can rage about Curtis the swine later, under the spray of a scalding hot shower. The kind that will flay the skin from my bones and the thoughts from my mind.

"That's actually where you come in, Tristan." Chris leans across the polished table and smiles at me like I don't know exactly what's coming. "We're going to need you to do some preemptive distraction. Get people buzzing about something else on the team via our social media pages, or about the players themselves. That way, we can minimize any damage this whole debacle might cause to our image."

Actually, that's not nearly as bad as I expected my role would be. It's pretty much my job, anyway.

"Seattle has had a lot of success roping in new fans," someone down the table says and my smile grows tighter because I'm not pimping out our players on social media just to distract from one louse's criminal idiocy.

"Sex sells." Once again I'm met with horrified looks from a group of middle-aged men who apparently never considered that hockey players could sell sex better than a playboy bunny. Albeit to a different crowd.

"No," Bob shakes his head. "We're a family-friendly

team, this issue not-withstanding, and we want our fans to remember that long after they discover the truth about Haine."

The meeting turns to other things they need to cover—the new hole in the first-string defense, whether they should call up the young hotshot from the minors, if debuting the throwback jerseys now would be a good idea—and I tune them out to start game-planning.

I'll have the best luck putting together an actual campaign as opposed to random posts. Something that can debut on the Arctic channels but also cross over onto player profiles, too. Maybe some player spotlights? A content liaison? I'll need someone family-friendly. Someone with high moral fiber. Someone who is easy-on-the-eyes—an unfortunate truth about content and marketing—decently well-known around town, and willing to work with me. The last one is the kicker.

Ólaffson would work with me, but he's too shy to be compelling or comfortable on camera. As our starting goaltender, he could offer a unique perspective on the team, so maybe I can use him for a post or two. I file his name away for later. Jack Spaeglin is young and handsome, but he has an unfortunate tendency to need reminders about what parts of his body the public does not need to see. I could ask Oakes. He's a veteran player. Dark hair and blue eyes make him fun to look at, but I doubt he'd say yes. The man never smiles.

I'm still making mental lists of whom to tap for this new project as the meeting lets out and I follow the suits into the hallway. We can do some insider interviews to entice young players, shout-outs for local businesses to draw in the community, maybe highlight some volunteer projects. A few of the guys work with the pediatrics department of the local hospital. A few others volunteer at the local animal shelter.

This could be a hit. If I can maintain creative control, then maybe I can blow Chris out of the water and leverage this gig into a more permanent marketing position. Something beyond babysitting social media pages and creating content that will get views. Something I'm passionate about. I'm already thinking about ways we can bring different segments into home game intermissions when I plow into a hard surface.

My face lands between two sculpted pectoral muscles clad in a tight athletic shirt. There's no reason I should know who I've run into. No reason I can picture his sandy hair and hazel eyes and perpetual grin. Players rarely come to the office buildings and the meeting is over. There is no reason for him to be here or for me to be crashing into him. I'm so disgusted with my own hyper awareness that I take a step back without checking my surroundings and slam into my boss, Chris. Great.

Way to look professional, Tristan.

"Careful kitty cat," Number Twenty-Five says, as Chris's hands steady my upper arms. "There's someone behind you."

Kitty cat. He always calls me that. And every single time I hear that name in his honey voice, I have the urge to claw him to ribbons, which bothers me because this pretty boy hockey player does not have any effect on any part of me other than my gag reflex. And not in a fun way.

"I noticed, thank you." I keep my voice steady through sheer willpower, and I hope he can hear the sarcasm coating every word. I do not tilt my chin up to see his face. I keep my gaze trained on his chest. My contract requires a certain level of professionalism, but it does not necessitate eye contact.

"You made it," Chris says from behind me, and my muscles tense to the point of pain. Because that almost sounded like he's *supposed* to be here... like my boss invited him... which can only mean one thing.

I would have gotten there, eventually. From the minute they asked me to create smoke and mirrors, I knew it would be this player who ended up in the spotlight. He's scandal-free. Some would consider him handsome, if they like height and muscles and straight Roman noses and angular jaws and hazel eyes that swirl with blues and browns and greens. If they find competence on the ice attractive and know he's one of our top goal-scorers.

We all knew it would be him because he does everything that's asked of him, by everyone, including me, but I had wanted to at least pretend to run through other options. And when I did choose him, I wanted it to be *my* decision. Not my boss's. *My project. Mine,* my brain snarls with the feral protectiveness that I lock away when I'm at work.

And yes, in the grand scheme of things, it doesn't matter if I landed on the captain myself, or if Chris hand-picked him for me. But why put me in charge of a project just to tell me how to do it? Because Victor Varg might be the best choice from among the players, but I don't know if I can handle being in close proximity with him for however long we need to keep this going.

I just might go insane.

I KNEW what I was getting into when I agreed to meet Chris at the head office. Well, maybe not exactly what I'd need to do, but I had a good idea that it would involve tiny, blonde Tristan Grant, and offering myself up to the marketing team as some sort of sacrificial lamb. Along with knowing this favor would include her, I also knew she wouldn't be happy about me crashing the party. Unfortunately, no matter how I prepare myself for it, the look of abject horror she wears as she bounces off my chest is still a jab to the solar plexus.

It shouldn't be.

I don't think Tristan likes anyone. It shouldn't bother me in the slightest that her nose crinkles up when we cross paths, as though she's smelling something awful. Rotten eggs, turpentine, the inside of my practice bag—it doesn't matter how often everything gets washed, it will reek until the day it gets incinerated—every time she sees me her glacial eyes narrow and if looks could kill, I'd be nothing more than a grease spot on the floor, smoking just a little as she burns me into nothing.

It shouldn't matter.

Except for Ms. Grant, I'm well-liked. I know it sounds egotistical to admit something like that, but arrogance has nothing to do with it. I pride myself on being the guy who gets along. I work hard to not make waves. There are two things I do well. The first is slapping a tiny disc of vulcanized rubber down a sheet of ice. The second is putting people at ease. I've had a lot of practice with both.

I'm not sure anything would help Tristan. Her blood pressure must be astronomical. She's always so tense that I'm convinced she's vibrating. Not so anyone would notice, but like her muscles are shaking from being poised to strike at any minute. Does she ever get any down time? Take a minute to breathe?

Chris Markham, the head of the Arctic marketing department, gestures to the open conference room that all the suits just left, and we follow him in like dutiful puppies. Well, maybe not quite. The minute her boss's back is turned, Tristan scowls and I swear I hear her snarl like the little cat she reminds me of.

The first time I ever saw her, she was doing something similar. Making that same dangerous sound as she poked long, sharp nails into the chest of one of the rookies. Her words were low as she informed him that if he sent photos of his trouser snake—her words—to anyone unsolicited again, she'd rip it off with her bare hands and have it taxidermized and installed as the new team mascot. I watched the kid flinch. A whole foot taller than her without his skates and she had him cowering with one expertly placed poke and a hissed threat. All without breaking a sweat.

"I already had a game plan," she's saying as I step in behind her and let the door close. "I had a list."

I'll bet she did. It wouldn't surprise me if Tristan Grant has lists to keep track of lists. Color-coordinated and written in pen. No room for errors. She shoots me a look over her shoulder, one that says she thinks I'd draw doodles on her precious lists. Or crinkle them into balls and practice three-pointers into the trash.

"And I'm sure, given enough time, you'd have talked to Varg anyway, but time is something we don't have, Tristan. The sooner we can kick this campaign off, the better for everyone."

I can't help but grin at her and there go her eyes, narrowing into slits of palest blue as her nostrils flare.

"And maybe by the time I tapped him, I'd already have some content plans to pitch," Tristan says.

"Don't worry, kitty cat," I say, and her jaw flexes as she grinds her teeth together. "I don't have practice until two. I'm all yours for the next several hours. Take your time."

"Of course." Her tone is drier than the soft pretzels the arena sells on game day. "Anything to make *your* day easier."

"We *appreciate,*" Chris leans into that word until Tristan's shoulders twitch. "Your time, Victor. The Arctic wants to create additional buzz around the team and draw in some new fans. You'd be helping us out."

There's more going on here. I'm not dumb enough to miss the tension in Tristan's body, or the practiced shrug that Chris sends my way, but it doesn't matter what they need from me. Cooperation with the marketing and PR teams is part of my contract. Not that I need to be strong-armed. Part of being on a professional hockey team means being in the spotlight. It means being a role model for younger players, someone to help bring the community together, to raise money for the right causes. It's important. Someone from the team has to do it, and I don't mind.

"I'm your guy," I say and drop into one of the cushioned chairs.

"It doesn't have to be only one player." Tristan's hands are folded around a leather folio, but I can almost imagine her with them propped on her slim hips, tapping those shiny black spike heels on the floor. *Tap tap tap*. I'm pretty sure the only thing stopping her is her sense of professionalism. "I thought we could bring in a few of the guys. Maybe rotate."

Chris shrugs, as if the idea isn't awful. "Who were you thinking?"

She lists a couple of names, and her boss shakes his head. "You know as well as I do we need someone charismatic, attractive, and well-known to pull this off. This series needs to be personal. Focusing on one player gives a more intimate picture."

I'm not sure I like the word "intimate" in this context, but it can't be worse than the promo photos we took in just our hockey pants and skates. My shirtless chest glistened across the I-9 billboard for months and I had to send my mother out to get groceries to avoid being accosted in the produce aisle. And the dairy aisle. Every aisle. I don't mind signing autographs, I don't mind posing for photos with fans, but when a single trip to the store turned into a three-hour ordeal with several attempted squeezes of parts of me I'd rather not have squeezed... well, it's an experience I'd prefer to avoid.

"You need to hit the trifecta here," Chris says. "Looks, personality, and fame." He gestures at my whole body. "Varg is our guy."

"Right," she says, circling the wrist of her left hand with long, tapered fingers. Her knuckles go white as she squeezes and then releases, never letting her notebook so much as budge from where she has it tucked under her arm. "Welcome aboard, Varg."

It's on the tip of my tongue to say something tongue-in-cheek, to call her kitty again and watch her clench her jaw, but she's already at the end of her tether. Even I can tell. I meet her gaze and wink instead. I swear the color of her eyes shifts from the palest blue of a clear winter morning to the gray that precedes a blizzard. The wink was a mistake, except I don't regret it at all. Tristan Grant looks like nothing in the world would rattle her, but up close.... Up close, she's not as unflappable as she tries to seem.

"I'm needed at another meeting," Chris says with a pointed look at a very expensive watch. "I trust you two can take it from here?"

I'm not sure why that comment makes Tristan close her eyes and suck in a deep breath, but we should be fine. I have no intention of making this difficult. Well, not *too* difficult. Not for Tristan. She might pop like a Christmas cracker full of confetti. Just explode into tiny pieces and scatter in the slight breeze from the room's heating system. Contrary to what she clearly thinks of me, based on the glares and the pointed looks and the jaw clenching, I'm not trying to cause problems. I'm here to help. I just don't think Tristan wants help. From anyone.

"We're good," she says to her boss, "I'll send you a summary and proposal by end of day, and if you approve, we can get started right away."

I wait five seconds after the door closes behind the marketing executive to ask, "So, I wasn't your first choice, kitty cat?"

In response, she slams the leather folio down on the tabletop and drops her head to take a breath. Her white-blonde hair swings forward, curtaining her face until I can't see her, but I imagine that she's mouthing the numbers one through ten.

"Who was?"

Tristan straightens up and I watch her put herself back together. Chin comes up, shoulders shift and square, chest moves with a deep breath, one long blink, and then she's looking at me—looking through me—as she says, "Oakes."

"Robbie Oakes." There's a tickle in my throat that I refuse to clear. It's a bad time to have the overwhelming urge to cough. It feels like we're in some sort of standoff, and I refuse to be the one to stand down. Obviously, Tristan has the same thought.

"Robbie doesn't talk," I say. He might be my best friend, but that's putting it mildly. Robbie curses and Robbie grunts, but rarely does he do more than that. Especially not for social media.

"Trust me," Tristan says, her gaze dropping down my chest and over my hips and legs. I'm proud that I don't squirm under her perusal. Even more proud that I don't flinch when she says, "It's one of his strengths."

He'd have been a horrible choice for a social media campaign, no matter how much I love the grump. Robbie barely keeps up with his own. I've taken to reminding him to post so that he can avoid the pint-sized blonde's shit list, but even then, it's photos of his meals, pictures of him in his game-day gear, or working with the local youth camps. Even surrounded by nine-year-olds who hero-worship the guy, Robbie still doesn't smile.

"He's not as pretty as me," I say, and Tristan's eyes snap right back to mine. I don't know why I'm baiting her, but I wait for a reaction. For something that indicates she doesn't mind the way I look—that's not arrogance either. I just have a mirror and my job is literally to be in peak shape. She shrugs, an effortless roll of her shoulders under her cream-colored sweater that gives less than nothing away.

"A lot of people find the tall, dark, and stoic thing attractive."

Do you? I don't ask the question shoving against my brain, but I'm surprised by how much I want to.

"Tell me about this project," I say instead, and she sinks into the seat next to me.

Tristan studies me like I'm a bug under a microscope. Pinned down under glass so that I have to sit still for her perusal. I feel her gaze slide from my eyes down my nose and over my mouth. She doesn't linger, I'm sure of it, but my grin turns up the corners of my lips just the same. Her eyes continue to drop over my chin—I didn't shave before my early morning skate—over my throat and centers on my chest. I almost flex under her stare, but she isn't admiring my muscles. She's looking at the howling wolf logo over my heart.

Her pale brows tip together, a small line furrowing between them, and even when I cross my arms over my chest, she still doesn't shift her gaze.

The interesting thing about lies is that the best liars are also the best at catching them when others fib their way through any situation. That's how I know Tristan isn't telling me the truth when she repeats her boss's words about team and community building, fan base, ticket sales, etc. I wouldn't call myself a liar, but I have a lot of practice in putting on a facade. Faking my way through difficulty. She doesn't have a tell because it's not that kind of lie. It's not meant to be malicious or impressive, but there's a shimmer there just the same. A shiver of something she's holding back.

"What's the real reason," I interrupt some tangent she's making about marketability, because it doesn't matter, I'm going to help her out—no, the team out—no matter what, but I want to know what's going on.

Tristan's face goes blank. No glare, no tension in her jaw, just devoid of anything. For a moment I expect her to double down, to swear that it's just about taking a new direction with the team's social media, but she doesn't.

"I'm not sure what I'm allowed to share," she says

instead, her voice dropping to just above a whisper. I have to lean forward in my chair to hear her at all.

"But it's something," I say and after a too-long pause, she nods her head once. "So this campaign is a distraction of sorts." Another nod. "And is it a good idea?"

She's frowning again, leaning into me as much as I am into her. If this was anyone else, anyone who didn't spend ninety percent of their time disliking every atom in my body and the other ten percent forgetting my existence, I'd wonder if this was leading somewhere. Somewhere that would have me tangling my hand in the cool silk of her hair and tugging her mouth to mine. That's not what's happening here. Not when most of our encounters include eye rolls and clenched fists. Hers, not mine.

She looks shocked, though. Like I could reach out and tip her right out of her chair and onto the ugly gray carpet. Her lips are parted, and she swipes her tongue over the bright red curve of the lower one. I know from personal experience that lipstick doesn't taste great—not bad enough to deter a good time—but enough that I'm sure Tristan didn't choose to wet her mouth. This isn't some practiced move or distraction. It's a tiny glimpse under the veneer she shows the rest of the team, the rest of the world.

She seems stuck, so I repeat the question, "This distraction you need me to provide. Is it for the right reasons?"

"Yes," she says, and like a fog clearing from her brain, she leans away from me. "It is."

"Okay." I lean back too.

"Okay?" Tristan repeats as though she doesn't believe it's that easy and I shrug.

"If you say it's the right reasons, the right move, then let's do it." I smile because she looks doubtful still.

"You don't even know what I'm going to ask you to do," she says, and I want to ask why she's so distrustful. Why does she assume that I'm saying anything other than what I mean? But in my experience, telling someone to trust you isn't enough to make it happen. That only comes with time. This is only my second season with the Arctic. As long as I wear the baby blue and white, I'll continue to show all my teammates that I'm someone they can count on. I'm not someone who's going to cause trouble. If it takes years to prove myself... well, then it takes years.

"So ask me," I say. "I'm still your guy."

I won't say no.

"I was thinking it would be a social media takeover." Tristan explains, and I'm half paying attention to her words. The rest of me is watching the spark reignite as she lays out her plans. "Different segments hosted by you and uploaded to the team accounts and yours."

"Do I get a say in the content?" I ask because there is only one topic that I won't talk about. I won't exploit my family for any reason. No matter how good.

Tristan looks across the expansive table and shuffles the pages inside her folio. She has some notes jotted down, and it hits me that her handwriting is not the perfect print I'd assumed it would be. It's a messy sprawl of slanted letters, some looped together. I like that it's unexpected. I wonder if she hates it. If she practices slow and perfect notes and then loses it all as an idea hits her.

"Normally," she worries her bottom lip with straight, white teeth, "I'd say that you get ultimate veto power over any topics you aren't comfortable with, but given how you were invited to this impromptu meeting before I even knew there was an assignment, I can't promise that Chris and other marketing execs won't be involved in content and creation."

And dammit. Tristan can be a hard ass when she wants to be. She makes grown men cower and rethink their goals in life when they do stupid shit online, but even she respects boundaries. The one and only time I've refused to do something she asked of me, I didn't have the mental fortitude to tell her an actual "no." Instead, I hid from her for as long as I could. Even then, she got the hint. I like this team, I like this organization, but I do not trust all the higher ups to put my own needs—my family's needs—above their own.

"I don't foresee it being a problem," Tristan says, and this time I'm treated to her megawatt, do-what-I-need smile. "We can stick to favorite restaurants, local haunts, any charities you support..." the smile grows even wider. "You do a lot with the children's hospital, right? Didn't you and your mother get a visit rotation going and raise a bunch of money for their new pediatric oncology department? We could dive into what you've been doing there. Why you feel passionate about the project. Drum up a lot of interest and donations to help the kids and their families."

And there's the problem because what I do for Grace Hospital doesn't just affect me. The story isn't mine to tell, no matter how big the dollar signs would be or how much press we could drum up. I want to be helpful. I want to give back to the organization that has welcomed me in with open arms, but I owe my brother—my twin—more. It's his story to tell. It was his diagnosis. His leg. His loss. Not mine.

I don't know how to say no to Tristan Grant. I don't want to, not when she needs me. But I owe my brother more and I can't sign on to this without talking to Erik first.

IT SHOULDN'T SURPRISE me to find my sisters, Hayley and Madison, waiting on my couch when I get home. Couch is a bit of an overstatement. It's more like a loveseat and even my two slender sisters barely have room to sit hip to hip, but I don't mind. Not only am I the only blonde sibling, but I'm also the only one under five foot nine—try more than half a foot under—so I fit on it just fine. Purple velvet couches are scarce, even without a hefty sum of money.

"Where have you been?" Hayley demands, arms crossed over her chest and silver bracelets sparkling in the glow of my vintage stained-glass lamp.

"It's like you don't even care about our well-being," Madison adds, so in sync with Hayley that you'd think they were the twins instead of her and Max.

"Work," I say and drop my keys into the lumpy clay dish by the front door. "Palmer too busy to come over too?"

"She had a date," Madison says and checks her manicure. The bright pink polish is chipping around the edges, and she scowls as she notices.

I toe off my heels. I spread my toes wide on my plush green rug, digging them into the soft pile. Stilettos should be categorized as torture devices, but I'm already one of the few women in my organization. I need to be taller than crotch height if I want to be taken seriously.

"We called you," Hayley says.

I don't respond to personal messages at work, but I keep my phone on me. I need constant access to all the team's accounts, and my phone is a quick and easy way to do that at a moment's notice. So yes, I've seen the twenty-three missed calls, listened to the five voice messages, read the fifty-two texts and decided that there was no emergency that couldn't wait until I got home. In hindsight, that might have been a mistake.

I've spent the whole day running myself ragged. I had to stalk the media reports for news of the Haine scandal—there was nothing yet—get the guys up to date before they head out of town for a set of away games and come up with a Plan B for my new project. Plan A is still Vic, but he shut down a bit at the end of our conversation and I didn't get a definitive yes before he had to go. That felt much more like a definitive no, especially after how on board he'd been before he hightailed it away from me.

It felt like a no because Vic never says no. He always says yes. And this time he didn't. I didn't realize how much I had counted on him to come through for me. Even Chris had assumed he'd say yes. I think we all did.

It's very possible that my boss will force Vic to take part in this project, even if he's changed his mind, but if he's not comfortable... if there's a reason he needs to say no.... I'd rather have another option to pitch to marketing than force him to film and post something he doesn't want to. Chris won't like it, and I'm sure I'll feel the bite of that disappointment—I have in the past—which is why I need a kick-ass other option.

"Are you guys hungry?" I ask my younger sisters as I head into my kitchen and pull open the fridge. Unfortunately, healthy Tristan went shopping, and tired Tristan doesn't have the energy or patience to cook any of the meals I'd planned. "Pancakes?" I pull eggs and oat milk out and put them on the counter.

"I need to lose ten pounds," Mads says.

"Do you have chocolate chips?" Hayley asks.

I pull out a bag of semi-sweet chips and plonk them on the counter along with flour and baking powder.

"Don't start with me, Madison," I say, and she rolls her eyes. "If you aren't hungry, don't eat."

"I'll have one." That means she'll eat somewhere between two and five. I'll double the batter.

Pancakes were one of the easiest things to master when I was twelve. They require very few ingredients, very little thought, and just a smidgeon of patience. Breakfast foods, in general, are easier to master than others, as long as we're only counting basics. My younger siblings ate a lot of pancakes, scrambled eggs and toast for multiple meals a day. Cereal too. And apples. Bananas are cheaper, but apples last longer than most other fruits.

I measure the dry ingredients and crack two eggs into

the bowl. My griddle is preheating. I don't ask about the emergency. If it was something life-altering, there would have been less complaining, and I'd have heard by now. Instead, I wonder which one of my sisters will crack first and tell me. My guess is Hayley. She's not a gossip, but she likes to share information, make sure everyone is on the same page. She doesn't like secrets.

The tops of the first three pancakes are just starting to bubble and burst, and I have my spatula in hand when she can't hold it in anymore.

"Max has a girlfriend."

"She has to go," Madison adds.

It's possible that Mads knows something I don't—the twin bond is no joke—but it's more likely that my sisters are just being protective of their "baby brother." Protective like a band of feral wolves, or a mama grizzly bear. It doesn't matter that Max is nineteen, and that even the youngest, Joey, treats him like the baby. That's what happens when you're the only boy among five girls. Six if you count our mother. And Max and Mads were only four when Dad left. Young enough to have their world rocked, but not old enough to understand the war zone our home morphed into.

"She does." I leave the statement ambiguous, like I might agree with them and I might be asking a question. I don't want to poke the bears just yet.

"She's awful," Madison says.

I drop perfect golden cakes onto two plates and place them on my quartz countertop. Hayley reaches for one stack, and I push the other dish toward her. I only put chocolate in her cakes.

"Why is she awful?" I ask as I pour more batter onto my trusty griddle. Might as well make and freeze some extras for the next time my siblings break into my home or when I don't feel like cooking anything.

"Well, we don't really know her," Hayley starts at the same time Madison says, "She just is."

"Do we have a name?" I ask Hayley since she's more likely to tell me without volume issues.

"Stephanie Howell," Hayley says around a bite, and Madison lets out a sound somewhere between a cough and a huff.

It is very possible that this strange girl is the antichrist. It's more likely that my sisters will dislike almost anyone who gets even a crumb of our brother's attention. I understand the urge to close ranks, to keep him close and his heart whole. There's a tendency to be distrustful of relationships after what we saw as kids, but the same protectiveness that drives my sisters to hate everyone Max even looks at is the same protectiveness that has me wanting to stand between him and our siblings.

Maybe because I feel like he's my responsibility. They all are.

Maybe because just like he's the only boy and the odd one out, I often feel separate from my siblings. There are five years between me and Hayley. Ten between me and Joey. Every one of my siblings is at least a half a foot taller than me. Max is almost ten inches taller than me. Add my white-blond hair—all my other siblings share the same dark waves—and I have always wondered if dad's affair wasn't the actual thing that ended my parents' marriage. If maybe I, born a scant seven months after their wedding night, was the first bump in the road.

"I notice neither of you cares about Palmer's date." I flip my own cakes and raise an eyebrow at my sisters.

"Palmer can take care of herself," Madison says, and yes, I've seen Palmer throat punch a guy for touching her ass without her permission, but Max is no slouch either. He's six feet of teenage metabolism and muscles from his days on a baseball diamond. He's playing on a scholarship right now, pitching, and he might not be the team's starter, but he's still only a sophomore. And he can handle one girl. Although maybe not the combined fury of his sisters.

"How long have they been together?"

"This is their second official date." Hayley takes the syrup from me and drenches her pancakes. I swear the girl could live off sugar alone.

I pin my gaze on Madison, who doesn't seem to notice. I've made grown men cower with the strength of my nonverbal disapproval. I've made more than one cry. I've honed the look to perfection, but my little sister just stares right back. I wonder if it was getting caught playing the tooth fairy that made me less intimidating. I'm pretty sure the sight of anyone in mesh wings and glitter would make them a lot less scary, but it cramps my intimidation tactics with my own flesh and blood.

"Madison," I say her name like a warning. One she ignores.

"We need to drop a house on her." My sister does not

care at all that I'm turning my scary-bitch level up to maximum.

"No."

That gets her attention and Mads drops her fork, letting it clatter to her plate in a way that grates on my eardrums. I don't let myself wince. I've spent the last three years perfecting my unflappable, unwavering, don't-fuck-with-me attitude. Unfortunately, Madison is a lot like me. To be fair, I love that she takes after me, just not when she aims it back in my face.

"We hate her," From Mads it sounds more like a dare. Challenging me to disagree.

"We don't even know her," I say. "Maybe we need to give her a chance."

A few more dates. A couple months at least. Maybe this relationship won't go anywhere, but maybe it will. Either way, Max deserves a chance to figure it out for himself.

Madison is still glaring at me as Hayley spears a pancake off her sister's plate.

"She seems okay." Hayley refuses to meet Madison's eyes at the confession. "I ran into her getting coffee the other day."

"See?" I say to Madison, "She seems okay."

"If she steps one toe out of line..." Madison stuffs another bite of food into her mouth, her eyes narrowing as if I'm the one causing problems. I meet her gaze head on. If Stephanie Howell sets one toe out of line, Max will break up with her.

"Then we'll break her kneecaps and run her out of

town." I tell my sister, and she grins, her cheeks full of food.

"And you wonder why she's so bloodthirsty." Hayley pushes her empty plate away.

"We don't demand blood sacrifices right away." I shrug. "We hope for the best…"

"But prepare for the worst," they finish the sentence with me and it's my turn to smile. God, I love these gremlins.

"We don't just hate people the minute we meet them." I tell my sisters. "Give them a chance to disappoint you first, okay?"

I gather the plates and take them into the kitchen, dumping them all into the sink. I let the water run until it's scalding hot and start lathering up my sponge with soap. I have a dishwasher, but I still need to get most of the stuff off plates and bowls before I can load them up. Especially sticky chocolate and syrup residue. I expect my sisters might let themselves out while I do the dishes and tidy my small kitchen. It's become second nature to care for all my siblings. Just like it's become second nature for them to accept it. In theory, it's something I should work on. I should let them be more independent, fight their own battles, but not yet. I'm not ready to step back. What would I even do?

Madison heads back to the living room and I assume she's gathering her things, but Hayley stays and asks about my day. I can't tell her much, but I give her the rundown on the new project, making sure that I leave Vic's name out of the conversation. I force myself to smile at the right moments. I want this to sound like something I'm excited for—because I am, I really am—and not something I'm upset over. And okay, I'm a touch resentful that I was given this job, only to have my boss already have gone behind my back to plan before I had a chance to do anything of value—and yes, I know he's my boss and can do what he wants with the marketing department—but I'm handling it. I'd appreciate the vote of confidence, seeing as I've never let them down before. The one time last season doesn't count.

I'd handle it a lot better if I'd gotten Vic to say yes, but I'm still handling it.

"Did you pick a player to work with yet?" Hayley props her chin on her hands. "Mads and I can give you our unbiased opinion on who would draw in the most viewers."

"It won't matter." Madison slides back onto her stool, pulling one of my Arctic sweatshirts over her head. "We all know that despite the lectures, the guy she needs is the only one she won't ask."

I know who they're talking about. Everyone with eyes and a working brain knows who they're talking about, and I still ask, "Who?" Just for laughs.

"Obviously Victor Varg." Madison sighs his name like she's talking about Gibson Hawk, heartthrob rockstar extraordinaire and lead singer of Cast & Prey. It's only force of will that stops me from rolling my eyes.

"Why won't she ask him?" Hayley asks, and I want to stamp my foot. I want to scream at the fluorescent lights in my ceiling. I want to pull my hair out at the roots, because

I'm a goddamn professional and I would have asked him. I would have.

Eventually.

Probably.

Maybe.

No, I would have. I would've sucked up my pride and asked him to help with the campaign because he is the best choice. I don't know if I'm frustrated that everyone seems to have made that decision for me, or if I'm pissed off that despite everyone being sure he'd never say no, the jerk didn't actually say yes.

"She hates him," Madison says, and Hayley nods like this was information she knew but had forgotten. Which is ridiculous since it isn't even information that *I* knew. I don't *hate* Varg. I just…. I prefer… I don't…

"I thought we had to wait for people to 'let us down,'" Hayley raises her fingers and scrunches them around her face, mimicking floating quotation marks. I don't appreciate it one bit. "Before we decide to hate them."

"Oh, *we* do." Madison's smirk makes me want to grind my teeth together. "But not our perfect big sister. She has a different set of standards."

I turn my attention away from my sisters and back to my dishes. They're clean now. I could dry them off and put them away, but I open the door to my tiny dishwasher and load the plates and cutlery into the bottom rack. My movements aren't graceful, and I bang two of the plates together, lucky that nothing chips as I add detergent and slam the appliance closed.

Two sets of honey-brown eyes are staring at me when I

turn back to face them. Identical shit-eating grins aimed in my direction.

"It's been a long day," Hayley says, covering her mouth and the fakest yawn I've ever seen. "I have a neuro exam coming up and need to do some more studying."

"And I'm going to go binge-watch bad reality television until I pass out," Madison says, and then they're up and moving toward the front door as if they can't get away from me fast enough.

Hayley pulls the door open and Mads turns around before she follows our sister into the hallway.

"What's the name of that place where we got our nails done?" She glances down at the chipped polish on her fingers. "I need a new manicure but couldn't remember where we go."

"JJ's on second," I tell her, pressing my own hands flat against the quartz countertop. "You have to call them, Mads. They don't take walk-ins."

My little sister twists her mouth to the side, not quite a pout, but not thrilled with the news that she'll have to pick up the phone and call someone. Spoiled brat. And I'm the one who spoiled her.

"Fine. I'll call them in the morning. It's what, like twenty dollars?"

"You can grab sixty from my wallet." I tell her and her face morphs into a sweet smile as she reaches for my purse and grabs three crisp bills.

"You're the best, Tris. I love you most!" She calls as the door slams closed behind both her and Hayley and I lean forward to press my forehead to the cool stone.

I don't let anyone at work walk over me the way I let my babies do, but I can't help it. It's always been my job to take care of them. To spoil them. To love them. I spread my fingers wide, feeling the chill seep into my skin. They're still in college, still focusing on their educations. I can't shove them out of the nest while they're preparing for the rest of their lives.

But I do have the urge to call them back and tell them they were wrong. I didn't hate Vic from the start. There was a time when I liked him. When I looked to him first. Then I gave him a chance and he left me stranded. Chris has made his choices clear. Vic's the best option right now, for this project, but I'd be a fool if I wasn't worried that he'd let me down again. I'd be a fool to trust him again. Forgive, but don't forget.

I'm no fool.

"KEEP YOUR HEAD UP, Spaeglin. God fucking dammit."

I pop my mouth guard down and chew on the rubbery end to avoid laughing as the rookie gets slammed at the blue line. My co-captain doesn't drop his head into his hands, but it's a near miss as the kid lies sprawled across the ice, arms spread wide, helmet askew. He held onto his stick even as his skates left the ground after the rough hit from Gage.

"Someone should check his head." We've all been through the concussion protocols enough times that we can distinguish between an emergency that requires calling an ambulance and one that just needs a trip to the ER. "We're already down Haine for the foreseeable future. Can't afford to lose the rookie, too."

Robbie grunts but makes no move to go over the boards to check on our teammate.

Normally this kind of thing wouldn't be our responsibility, but practice ended a good hour ago, and I know for a fact that the trainers didn't stick around. Marge, the sweet lady who handles our accommodations when the team travels, has a cake in the main office for her sixty-fifth birthday and the staff descended on it like starving hyenas. There's a handful of players who stay behind after practice is called. Coach put the fear of god in us during our first official team meeting—don't even think about getting injured doing dumbass shit—but I think he knew better than to tell us not to skate. It would be like telling us not to breathe.

There's a reason guys like me, Robbie, Spaeglin, Ahlstrom, Maroni, Ólaffson, and Gage have made it as far as we have. Part of it is talent. I don't say that to sound arrogant, but balancing on blades thinner than an inch wide takes a certain amount of natural skill. Part of it is luck. Most players are big guys, and I don't just mean muscles. We're tall. We're built solid. Sure, you get the occasional teammate who stands under five foot nine, but you're just as likely to have a teammate over six foot seven. Zdeno Chára had to get a special exemption from the league to play with a longer-than-regulation stick. He's six foot nine. The National Hockey League only offers exemptions to players over six foot six. Even I'm an inch shorter than the requirement.

The rest of what gets us to the ice? Passion. For skating, for the ice, for the speed, the hits, the energy of the crowd... A lot of grueling hours go into training to be any kind of professional athlete. Talent and size alone don't change the love we need to have for the game. So, no, Coach knew better than to ban the team from the ice during off hours—he played almost a decade with Ottawa, Dallas, and Buffalo, so he knows—but we're not supposed to be doing anything dumb. Like playing two v two just because we can.

"Oakes," I eye the kid still splayed out on the frozen surface. "He could be unconscious."

Robbie grunts and his dark brows pull together as he leans his weight on the butt end of his stick.

He points out over the ice just as Spaeglin's arm twitches, gloved fingers closing around the shaft of his stick. The kid crunches up to sit, a feat difficult in hockey pants and pads, and shakes his head like a dog that just dove into a questionable body of water to chase a stick.

"Getting up doesn't mean he didn't have his bell rung," I say as the rookie levers to his feet.

It doesn't look like he's all that steady, but even from forty-five feet away I can see the kid's blinding grin. If the idiot took out his mouth guard out, he's just asking for future implants. I don't care how good our dental plan is, and okay; I care, but I'm not losing any teeth I don't have to.

"He's fine," Robbie says, as Gage loops around to offer a fist bump to the teammate he just flattened

"Slow to get up," I say. "You know as well as I do, Mark would have him run through at least the twenty-four-hour protocol for that alone."

We don't have a game for two more days, but missing practice isn't great either.

"I'm good," the nineteen-year-old sends up a thumbs-up from the center line. It's hard to make out through the bulk of his black glove, but if he has a finger in the air, I doubt it's the bird.

"Taking a quick nap?" I ask, just to see if I'm right and we need to call in the trainers.

"Nah," Spaeglin shakes his head as he turns a little pivot on his blades. "Just running through what I did wrong to get nailed like that."

"There's a joke in there somewhere," Tyler Gage shrugs, "but I can't think of it right now."

"You weren't even the one who got his bell rung. Missing some brain cells Gagey?" Spaeglin's laugh cuts across the rink, tinny and metallic in the expansive space.

I make a note to check him out when he heads my way. Or if he falls over.

"We should end the drills," I say, and Robbie grunts again. "Before someone ends up on the injured list."

It's only our years of friendship that allows me to translate the sound into an agreement. The almost sixteen years we played for separate teams don't matter. Friendships formed on the ice at the age of seven have the foundation to last through time.

I wave my glove at my teammates to grab their attention. When no one looks, not surprising, Robbie bellows out an "oy" that has four heads turning our way. This is the reason he wears the "A" as alternate captain. Despite over a decade apart, coming back to the same line was like no time had passed at all. A team. A unit.

"Let's call it a day."

Gage, Maroni, and Ahlstrom head to the nets to pack them away, but Spaeglin skates right for the bench. He's fast on his blades and he kicks up a flurry of snow at the boards as he cuts sideways to stop. He's grinning through his half shield, mossy eyes clear enough that I'm confident the hit left no lasting damage.

"I'm fine Cap. It was just a love tap."

It was more than that. It was the kind of hit that would get replayed on the Jumbotron during a game. Maybe even make the ESPN highlights. Getting caught with your head down at center ice is a rookie mistake. The kind that can lead to injuries and time off.

A snort from Robbie and Speaglin's grin grows wider. "It's not my fault Gagey's obsessed with me. My grannie hits worse."

Off the ice, the rookie isn't small. He clocks in at six feet tall and just under two hundred pounds. On the ice he's just under average, but there's a slightness to his build that leaves him open to a lot of attempted damage on the ice. He's fast. His puck-handling is good. He worms his way in and out of opposing players like he's made of water. Spaeglin ends up the target of a lot of hits, so yes, maybe Gage's hit was nothing special, but usually Spaeglin stays on his feet like a damn weeble. What's that stupid jingle again? "Weebles wobble but they don't fall down?" Something like that.

"We're going to get off the ice before you end up benched," I say and the kid shrugs like it's no hair off his chest either way.

Spaeglin has no hair on his chest, which is probably why he's so unconcerned about brain damage or missing ice time. Either that or he still feels invincible. We're not even halfway through his first season with the pros. I wonder if he's graduated to chewing handfuls of ibuprofen like they're tic tacs every morning. He's probably still riding high on being drafted, seeing his whole career stretch out in front of him, watching his phantom future self hoist the cup over his head as he takes lazy laps on the ice beneath a screaming crowd. We've all had that dream, but at some point in every pro-athlete's time on the roster, we start to see it as a race. Get to the finish line before breaking down. Push hard enough for results, but not injury.

I also need him off the ice because I have a blonde to locate. It's been almost twenty-four hours since I left Tristan sitting in the conference room at the main office. Since I said no and watched the delicate features of her face wipe clean until not a single ounce of emotion could slip through. There had been a flicker right before that moment. A moment when she seemed to know what was coming and her eyes flashed, but it was gone before I could spend too long examining it. My gut instinct says it was disappointment. The kind that is expected but doesn't change the split-second nausea when the floor drops and the fall begins.

It's not that I wanted to say no—I don't like to say no when I know I can fix something--but I didn't want to say yes either. I'm a hockey player. Social media, marketing, PR, are all the extra bits that I wish didn't come with the territory. Unfortunately, they do. I know the team enjoys using my face and my body for their campaigns. We're professional athletes. Our bodies are honed to perfection or we aren't doing our job, but I know my face is attractive, too. There's a reason I was dubbed the NHL's "pretty boy" for a few seasons. I'm not trying to brag, but I know how many women I've been able to tumble into my bed with the right smile. Although I'm sure the money and the fact that I have all my teeth don't hurt those prospects.

I also know the real reason the Arctic uses me for most of their marketing, the reason Chicago did the same, and Minnesota before them. I don't say no.

Do I want to give up my off days or free time to go flirt with the local news anchor? Not really, although I make sure not to show it. Do I want to strip down to my jock and oil myself up for photos? Not even a little, but someone on the team has to. And that's just it. No one on the team enjoys these extras. Maybe in the juniors there were guys along for the ride, more interested in the fame, the money, and the glory than in the game; but by the time we enter the draft, that's not possible anymore. If it follows some guys into their first seasons, well, there isn't time to focus only on notoriety and hero worship. Those are the guys who get traded away and end up circling the drain on minor league teams.

And since none of my boys wants to do these events and interviews and photo shoots either, then it's my job as captain to step up. It's the fastest, easiest way to keep the bigwigs happy while letting my teammates focus on the puck and the ice and the endless drills. If it helps connect us to the community? If whatever I do or say brings more people to this sport that beats in my veins like a drum? Well, I'm not sorry about that one bit. That's my job. Victor

Aaron Varg. Right wing for the Quarry Creek Arctic, a top ten goal scorer for the league, loving brother and son, and keeper—and creator—of the peace.

But now it's been a whole day, and I know Tristan Grant is twitching with not knowing if I'm in or out of her campaign.

"Or he could keep his head up and not get flattened because he'll see his opponents coming. That sounds easier." Robbie says, but he's already removing his gloves and gathering his water bottle from the inside of the boards. That's good. It'll look a lot less suspicious if we all leave together than if I leave while the guys are still working. I'm never the first one out. It would raise eyebrows, and for reasons I can't even begin to unravel, I don't want the guys to know about my meeting with the pretty little blonde.

"Varg." My name cuts through the arena, echoing in the space as her voice clambers off the boards and all the eyes in the vicinity swing to me. "We need to talk!"

I watch every bonus point I might have received for seeking her out on my own vanish as Tristan Grant stomps her way down the tunnel. Despite the rubber flooring for our skates, her shiny black shoes still make noise, announcing her entrance. She's not dressed for the rink, not at all. I don't expect her in a down parka, but I expected pants at least. My brother's fiancée piles on the layers whenever she comes to watch games, but the rink isn't exactly cold. And I don't just mean because I sweat buckets on the ice.

Aside from the spiked heels, and the snug-fitting black skirt, and the half see-through sky blue shirt, her silky hair twists back into some intricate knot at the base of her neck. Under the rink's bright lights, it gleams almost white. She's only about twelve feet from me, but I can see the flash in her ice eyes, the red slash of her mouth pressed into a thin line.

Spaeglin laughs. "Someone's in trouble."

The sing-song words are reminiscent of elementary school playgrounds, but he's not wrong. There is a little frisson of caught-by-teacher and it's inappropriate to go there with Tristan Grant, so I squash the thoughts. I do not need to picture her slapping a ruler against one palm, ankles crossed as she leans her slender hip on the corner of a big wooden desk and tells me I've been a bad boy. We work together. I'm fairly certain she hates my guts, although that doesn't hurt the fantasy one bit. It's hurt none of the fantasies I pretend not to have about this woman. I shake my head to clear the images as she grips the edge of the boards and steps up to the bench.

"Jack," Tristan says, and the kid honks out a sound like he just choked on his own spit.

"Ms. Grant." Spaeglin is red faced and sweating, and I know it's not just from practice. "We were just running some drills."

"And now we're done. Out," Robbie calls out to the guys who wrestled the nets away. They grab sticks and water bottles and pile over the boards to leave the rink. My teammates all dip their heads as they pass Tristan, and it's not sexist—I don't think—to say that I'm impressed by how she's earned the respect of a gaggle of oversized men. Robbie claps me on the shoulder as he leaves us alone. I think there's a squeeze there too, but it's hard to tell through my pads. I appreciate him clearing the ice for me, except there's a slight chance this woman is going to eviscerate me and leave my body bleeding out on the ice.

"Hey kitty cat," I grin at her because I like the way it makes her bristle. I can almost imagine fur standing up along her spine as she narrows her eyes at me.

"Victor." She's on the bench now, arms crossed over her chest and foot tapping. I'm not even looking at the way her breasts are pressed up and out, just showing that I think my earlier teacher fantasy was an aberration. "I'm already a full day behind on this new campaign and I need an answer before I fall behind."

I know what she's asking for, and I was going to seek her out once the guys were done, but I can't help but shake the hair out of my eyes and let my lips split into an even bigger grin, "An answer to what?"

I swear I see her eye twitch, but she's back to frosty before I can be sure. I shouldn't enjoy riling her up like this, but I do. She's wound so tight, clutching a million different threads in a white-knuckled fist, controlling every action like a puppeteer wielding an army of marionettes. I want to knock her off-kilter. I want to see her take a deep breath and smile and I don't even know what else, but something. I want to see her genuine reactions. Not the ones she's trained herself to have.

"You know what." She says the words like she thinks I'm an idiot and there's an airy pocket of something filling my stomach.

Tristan is small on the best days, only a few inches over

five feet. Usually, she comes up to my shoulder. Today I still have on my skates and full gear and she barely reaches my armpit. I take my helmet off to see her better and drop it on the bench behind me. I have the urge to sit her up on the top of the boards, just so we can be closer in height. Except I don't think it would help.

"Can you sit down or something?" For one moment, her straight white teeth bite down into her red-painted mouth. "I don't enjoy talking to Howl."

I look down at the wolf logo on my light blue practice jersey. With my black hockey pants, I wonder if she's noticed that we match. I drop onto the bench, and she glances away from me as the wood shakes under my weight. I should mention it to maintenance so they can get it replaced or tightened before one of the team ends up ass over elbow on the dirty floor.

"Thank you," she spits the words out between clenched teeth. "I need to know if you're in or out, Varg. I need to make contingency plans and prepare a pitch for Chris if you don't want to do this. He's set on you, so it'll take some work to convince him of a new idea, and I don't have a lot of time to waste."

If I wasn't already sure that something was going on with the team, I am now. It's something to do with Haine, but I know better than to press her for details she can't or won't share.

"I'm sorry I left you hanging," I say because I'm not one of those guys who refuses to own up to the problems they cause and I am sorry that not having an answer from me added to her stress. But I also know that I'm aggravating her by drawing this conversation out longer, and I like the electric tingle I feel when she closes her eyes and sucks a deep breath in through her nose.

"I'm in," I say as her lips form an O and she exhales. "I was going to come find you after practice."

Narrowed eyes.

"Practice ended over an hour ago."

"Some of us run additional drills after. I swear I was on my way to you once we finished." I hold back the "kitty cat" that's on the tip of my tongue because I'm trying for serious here. I didn't mean to leave her hanging. It took time to track down Erik last night and talk to him about what this could mean for him, for us. And when we were scheduled to get to the rink and suit up by eight, I assumed she wouldn't want to meet beforehand. Now I think maybe she would have met me at four in the morning if it was to give her an answer.

"I couldn't say yes without doubling checking one thing, not after you said that you couldn't guarantee what would stay private." I must be imagining the way her shoulders drop just a fraction of an inch. "My family and my brother have always been a subject that is off the table with the media. That was his choice and his request. I understand things are a little different after last season and the team's role in his relationship and his engagement, but he still had a right to know what this could mean for him. He had a right to decide if he was comfortable with what might be shared."

Normally, siblings aren't a big draw for stories about athletes. Not unless they're doing something borderline illegal or making their own headlines. But Erik is different. We're twins. Twins who played together. Twins drafted to the juniors together. Twins who expected to go to the NHL together. And then we didn't because Erik got sick. He got sick and lost his left leg below his knee and our dream crashed and burned.

I know the guilt I feel about making it on my own is survivor's guilt. It took a long time and a very expensive therapist for me to understand that. My brother is alive. I didn't survive over him. But my dream did. So yes, we keep the media out of his private life. He only recently started coming to games again. Only recently stepped back out on the ice. I don't want to mess any of that up for him. No matter how much I want to help the woman in front of me and the team I adore.

"Erik," Tristan says his name, and I know I see her soften this time. "Of course." Another bite to her plush lips. "I can understand that. Is he okay with the proposal?"

I nod. It was a long, long talk last night, and the plan is to avoid his diagnosis and past as much as possible, but he's okay with me taking part. Hopefully, he won't come up at all. Tristan's glare falls and I wonder if it's because she respects my reasons, or if it's because I told her yes. I think I can even see a hint of a smile at the corner of her lips. I want to breathe life into it like a nascent flame.

"I have the team schedule but send me your availability for the next two weeks, and I'll set up a meeting for us to get started. Send me any ideas you want to focus on and we'll start filming shorts as soon as possible. Thank you for agreeing." Tristan turns away from me, and all the bubbles in my center start to fizzle and pop.

"Come on, kitty cat." I get to my feet as she turns away. "You knew I'd say yes. I always do."

Tristan turns to look at me over her shoulder and just like that, her face shutters again. I don't know where I went wrong. I once had to hide from her because I didn't know how to say "no" when she asks me for anything. I don't like saying no to anybody, but especially not to Tristan Grant.

"Not always," she says and then she's swallowed up in the dark of the tunnel and I'm left alone wondering when she decided she couldn't trust me.

OF COURSE *he suggested the rink for the first video.* I huff out a breath and tug down the hem of my dress. I'm no stranger to the temperature here. I handle the cold just fine—Palmer says that the natural chill I radiate leaves me unsusceptible to the cold—but I know the layers to wear when I'll be near the ice. I'm not cold today, but I had a meeting with Chris and Bob added to my schedule at the last minute and had to race from the conference room downtown to The Stand. It doesn't matter if my schedule is filming or editing. I'm expected to dress like a paragon of professionalism when meeting with the wealthiest man in the city and my boss. And of course, I didn't have a single pair of clean dress pants to wear today.

So here I am, forcing my hands down by my side and walking through the tunnel towards the gleaming ice, wearing a cream-colored shift dress that falls way too high above the knee and a pair of thin pantyhose. Not cold, just praying to a higher power that Victor Varg will not attempt to put me on the ice. Knowing my luck, that's exactly what he has planned.

"Nice boots, kitty cat," Varg says, a smile crinkling the corners of his hazel eyes.

I look down at my feet, and despite the teasing lilt to his voice, I don't regret changing into the fuzzy shoes I always keep in my car. Better than trying to chase this man down on the rubber mats in my normal heels. Varg's wearing the heather gray sweatpants issued to every Arctic player, his number in white on his left thigh. His hands are in his pockets and I wish he was wearing the team sweatshirt too, so I wouldn't be staring at the bulge of his biceps under a thin warm-up t-shirt. A shirt that's molded to the dips and curves of his broad chest.

"Comfort is key, Varg."

His eyes start at the boots and slide up my legs to the hem of my dress. I feel his gaze like a caress, and I steel myself not to let him see me fidget under his scrutiny. Even though he's so tall I force myself to keep my eyes on his face. Varg's lips part and I see his shoulders shift before he meets my stare head on.

"I can see that." His voice is lower, a deep rasp that makes me cross my arms across my chest just in case my nipples like the sound too much. Traitorous bitches. This man may be attractive to most of the residents of Quarry Creek, but not to me. He can't be. And I can't let him know he is.

Our eyes are locked, neither of us moving an inch, and the tension is thick, like swimming through a vat of heavy cream.

"You didn't give me much to go on for today," I say to break the silence, and Varg grins at me like that was purposeful. It probably was. This man lives to get under my skin. I like order, control, schedules, and clear expectations. I've seen Varg in action. He's easy smiles and quick laughs. Not one to make firm plans, but always up for an adventure. I'm itchy just thinking about his *laissez-faire* approach to life.

"I thought we could film a few behind-the-scenes things for the series. Maybe some how-to videos of different drills, some skating tips, that kind of thing." He ducks his head. "I know I held up the start of this project, so I thought if we got a few things sorted out, you could have a couple of videos ready to go at once. And then we won't have to worry about our away game later this week."

That is... not what I expected.

Not from everything I know about Varg flying by the seat of his pants. I was sure I'd need to make us a schedule, write out film plans, be on top of him to show up and participate. But this... I blink slowly, trying to center myself in the conversation.

"If that works for you." Varg is looking at me, waiting, and I say, "Yes," because shock has stolen all my other thoughts and words. I swallow and add, "That's really thoughtful. Thank you."

This smile is different. The left side of his mouth quirks up, showing off the hint of a dimple in his cheek. How have I never seen that before? But no. One moment of prior planning doesn't erase the last time he let me down. The last time I ended up.... No.

"I thought we'd start with a rink tour." Varg says and now he's looking over my head and out across the ice. "I thought a personal approach might be nice over the tours given by the organization. Some stories about the players."

It's a good idea. We'll book more tours if we start off this way.

"Then I was going to go through gear and how we dress for games—"

"We need to keep this appropriate for the kids, Varg." I say, and he frowns again.

"I would never... I didn't mean like that." One hand moves to cup the back of his neck. "A lot of people don't know about the layers we wear or the padding, but we don't have to if you think it's a bad idea."

Dammit. It is a good idea. I have the urge to apologize. I feel like I've hurt his feelings, which makes no sense. Everyone knows hockey players get their fair share of action. There's no way Varg doesn't get more than the average player. Not with his face and body and teeth. Not that *I* would be in on that, but a lot of women would be. Or men.

Whoever.

Just not me.

"Let's film it," I say instead, and purse my lips to avoid smiling at him or something equally inane. This man is infuriating, and I don't need to give him any extra ammunition. The more he knows he gets to me, the more he'll poke at my weak spots until I disintegrate. "I can make sure we cut anything questionable when I edit the footage."

I put my bag down on the players' bench and pull out the small vlogging camera I use for most videos. I busy myself with starting it up and quadruple checking the battery life, the storage, and the settings. I did all this last night. And this morning. And before my meeting. But I don't want to look at Varg right now, and I don't want him to know that I'm avoiding looking at him.

I hate that this man turns me back into a middle schooler. I don't think I was this bitchy even then. I didn't have the time or energy to care so much about what someone else was thinking or planning. I had myself and my five siblings to take care of. I didn't have time for rivalries. I've perfected the art of being in control. Dressed perfectly for every occasion with hair and makeup flawless since appearance is a sort of armor. Always over prepared with lists and contingency plans because there's nothing worse than being frozen in a crisis.

I learned that at twelve, the first time that mom forgot to pick us up from school. Joey spent the days with our neighbor, but the twins were already in pre-K and there I was, a seventh grader, aware that I needed to collect them, Hayley from second grade, Palmer from first, and get us all home without anyone knowing that we were unsupervised. I'd already met the social worker and had looked her dead in the eye as I told her that everything was fine. It wasn't even a lie. Everything was fine. It wasn't like any of us were being hurt; we were just... forgotten. By mom. And dad. But that was fine because I was there and I would not forget any of us. Not for a moment.

Now, fifteen years later, I want to lie and say I don't

know why this one man gets under my skin in ways no one ever has, but I can't. It's the stupidly gorgeous face, the solid muscles, the easy grins that prove he's had a comfortable life. An easy life. Sure, he's worked hard to get where he is. I know that, everyone knows that. But I doubt he's ever felt his life spinning so far out of control that it seems impossible to fix, knowing he was the only one willing and able to try.

Then there's the fact that the man is pathologically agreeable. A volunteer needs to visit a kindergarten career day? Varg's there with his gear on and a bag of pucks for the kids to take home. One player needs help to move a family member? Varg's there with a rented truck and a smile. No one smiles while helping others move. That's not a thing. No one can like that many people. No one can be that available. Doesn't he have commitments? Doesn't he get angry?

The irony is that his constant yeses drive me insane, nails down a chalkboard, shivers deep in the marrow of my bones. But the one time I needed him, he didn't come through and I paid the price for it. The worst part is that he couldn't even tell me like an adult. He just went radio silent. This man is the emergency contact for most of the guys on the team, since he is always available. Always. Until I spent forty-eight hours trying to hunt him down, only to be met with... nothing. He couldn't even do me the decency to say "no" to my face.

"I thought we could start in the players' lot and walk through what it's like to show up for games."

"After you." I follow him to the side entrance of the

rink. I step out onto the asphalt and raise the camera to my eyes.

The tour goes well, even if I have to remind Varg, multiple times, that I will not be in the footage. I'm just a camera person, not his co-host. I can edit out most of the slip-ups as we make our way through the halls and he takes us into the locker room. It might come out even better as he breaks the fourth wall over and over again, talking to me, or the camera, or the viewer. I just have to bite my tongue to stop myself from responding.

I do well until we get to the locker room. The circular space has each player's name in silver lettering over solid wood cubbies for gear and uniforms. I'm surprised to see his full kit hanging on the hooks, clean and smelling fresh. The entire room has a vague bleach smell trying to cover the funk of testosterone and sweat, and someone clearly thought a pine-scented air freshener would make all the difference. It doesn't. I swallow thickly, trying not to take in more than I have to.

"It smells pretty rank in here," Varg says to the camera, "and that's when the room is empty of sweaty players and gear." His mouth tips up into that lopsided smile again and my fingers flex against the camera, but I hold it steady. "Even my camerawoman is trying to breathe through her mouth."

I shake my head and glare. I don't want him to refer to me at all, but he just shrugs his big shoulders and turns to haul out his pants and pads. I let the camera keep rolling so I don't miss anything as Varg lays each piece of equipment out along the wooden benches. I pan the camera over the items, making sure I get a good look at the light blue jersey and the howling wolf. I also spend an extra moment on the appliqued "C" over his chest.

"You might want to turn around kitty cat," Varg says, and I bring the camera with me as I look up and smooth, tanned skin is all I can see.

He's pulled his shirt off and it's hanging in his cubby, and I have a white-knuckled grip on the camera as I suck in a nose full of damp funk. I've seen Varg shirtless. Everyone has. He was on a billboard for a while in just his hockey pants, but it's different being this close to him. Deep grooves bracket his defined ab muscles and the divot between his pectorals. There's a faint smattering of sandy blonde hair in the center of his chest, and a darker trail starting under his belly button and dipping down under the waistband of his sweats. His hands are there, pulling at the white cord cinching the cotton to his hips.

"I guess I'll turn around then. Protect my virtue." There's a lilt to his voice as he turns, and I'm looking at the corded muscles of his triceps and trapezius. Muscles I only know the names of from quizzing Hayley for her anatomy class. He has a tattoo, the heads of two black and grey wolves. One snarling, the other tucking the angry one protectively under its chin. Then the pants loosen and slip down the firm curve of his glutes and I'm dropping the camera and turning myself around.

"What are you doing?" I hiss, balling my hands into tight fists until the edges of my nails cut into the skin of my palm.

"We agreed to run through how I dress for a game," Vic

says and there's a rustling and shuffling sound that I refuse to think about.

"We *agreed*," I lean into the word to show my distaste for his surprise nudity, "to keeping things family friendly."

Another chuckle and I will not acknowledge the swoop of my internal organs at the sound.

"I can't put my gear on over my sweats," Varg says. "And to be fair, I did warn you. Twice. Not my fault you didn't listen, kitty cat."

"Commando is not family friendly." I squeeze my eyes shut, but it doesn't block out the firm contour of his ass or the twin dimples at the base of his spine. I also don't want to admit that I hadn't heard his warning. If I had, I would have stepped out of the room or turned myself around before the show. Maybe.

"I wear a jock, kitty cat." The damn nickname makes me clench my teeth together. I'll show him kitty cat when I claw him and leave him bloody in my wake. The ass. Dammit. Not ass, I'm not thinking about certain parts of his body. The jerk. "Were you hoping for a peek?"

"I have no desire to see little Varg. I doubt he's worth the time." I say with a snort, and sudden shame floods my body from top to bottom.

"Play nice kitty. Bet I could change your mind," Varg says, and I can feel the heat in my cheeks as I turn off the camera and struggle to breathe through the tightness in my chest.

I can't let him get to me. Not about this. The Arctic organization has a strict non-fraternization policy. Sexual flirting might be a bit of a grey-area, but it's a far-cry from the professional I am. This line of conversation isn't appropriate, and despite the absolute truth that there is less than nothing between Victor Varg and me, there are people in the organization who might not agree. A hockey organization is a boys' club. A club that doesn't always approve of having women on board. I can't do anything inappropriate with the players or other employees, but not only am I standing here with a naked hockey player, he's flirting with me and I'm not shutting it down the way I should. On camera.

If anyone saw this.... It could mean my job.

"Stop." I'm not proud of the way my voice shakes just the tiniest bit. It's rage doing that. Rage at myself for forgetting.

There's more rustling, a muffled curse, and then I can feel the heat from Varg's body as he steps up behind me. I expect him to reach out, but he doesn't, and I turn my head to look at him over my shoulder. There's a respectable space between us. The whole bench plus a few extra inches, but I could have sworn he was a breath away from my back.

"I'm sorry, Tristan," he says, and there's a furrow between his brow. "I didn't think. Sometimes when you're around I—" he looks away and I watch his Adam's apple bob as he swallows. "I didn't mean to make you uncomfortable. That was never my intention."

His voice is low and serious, and I know he's telling the truth. I know it. No matter how much he aggravates me, I'm safe around Victor Varg. At least physically. That wasn't the problem.

"You didn't," I say, "But you can't flirt with me like that." *And I definitely can't flirt back.* I don't add the last part, but it's right there, battering my brain until I can't avoid the fact that I did.

There's another swallow, and then Varg says "I won't. You have my word."

There's a wrenching inside of me that wants to explain. It's my contract. It's technically his too, but we both know he wouldn't get traded away over something like this. Not when he leads the team in goals and assists. He has his socks and hockey pants on, but he's still shirtless and I take a step back. I square my shoulders and snap my spine into place.

"Let's film, Varg." I lift the camera again and line him up in the shot. "I don't have all day to get through this."

The grin I get as I hit record is the one everyone gets, it's lazy and broad, and I can't help but feel like there's something missing.

thearctic.hockey
The Stand, Quarry Creek

117,003 likes

thearctic.hockey why do they call them "pants" when they stop above the knee? #teamshorts ... more

vics_chicks666 don't ask me the color of nothing...

11.2k

View all 2,341 comments

 Add a comment...

"TALK ME THROUGH THE PLAN AGAIN," Tristan says as the door to the shop closes behind her and her icepick heels clack across the wide-plank floors. I can feel the stretch in my cheeks as my smile splits my face.

"Hello to you too, kitty cat," I prop my elbows on the shiny wooden counter. Her eyes narrow at the nickname, but it's not a full glare and the corner of her lips quirk as if she thought about smiling back for a fraction of a millisecond.

"If you want to blow our limited time on small talk, be my guest." Her wide blue eyes blink up at me as she pulls her phone out of her bag and starts tapping on the screen. I absolutely do not notice that her vivid red nails are the same shade as her vivid red mouth. Just like I absolutely do not spend a single second stuck on the word "blow." "It's not my free time we're wasting. I'm paid to do this."

Technically, I am too, when you consider that part of

my contract stipulates playing nicely with the marketing and PR departments, but I keep that thought to myself.

"Saying hello isn't small talk." I shrug. "It's the bare minimum for polite social interactions."

Tristan's eyes flick up from her phone screen at that, her fingers stilling their tapping. Her knuckles go white as she tightens her grip on the baby-blue case.

"Hello Varg."

I drop my head into my hands, pulling at my hair so she doesn't see I'm laughing.

"Now can I know the plan for today?"

Our first few videos didn't break the internet, but they garnered some attention. I knew Tristan was good at her job. I knew she had single-handedly turned the organization's social media accounts into something to watch, but even I was in awe when I saw the edited clips she posted. Not that I looked for them. I didn't have a chance. When her final proofs hit my email, I was lacing up my skates in Miami and about to hit the ice. I barely had time to send her a thumbs up response before I had to funnel out into the other team's tunnel. The first video went up during the first intermission, and by the time I made it back to my phone after a resounding win and a quick shower, my mother had sent the links to me too.

So had my brother, his fiancée, Quinn, and her best friend, Jen. Even my sister and her wife had emailed saying they'd seen the clips. Each message came with a healthy dose of affectionate ribbing, but also recognition of Tristan's skill and I can't help but hope that the powers that be are also noticing her hard work. My tour of the

Stand had included the offer of a personal tour for one of our followers. We picked an afternoon face-off that still had unsold tickets available, saying we'd pick one lucky attendee. Within forty-eight hours, the arena was sold out, and the team had gained several thousand new followers.

My numbers had grown too, not that I care too much about notoriety. I prefer to be known for my speed on the ice, for my points per game, for my reputation as a leader and team player. Those are the things that pave the way to the best contracts, the best teams, the best chances at the cup. And that's what I'm doing here. Showing my commitment to my team, to my city. Taking the job no one else wants and doing it with a smile. Keeping the peace as best I can.

I spread my arms wide and look around at the wood paneling and leather stools. The framed black and white photos of Quarry Creek from bygone decades, the jukebox flickering like an inebriated street sign in the corner. Nothing about this place fits and everything does all at the same time. The blue checked curtains and the maroon velvet booths. It's an interior designer's worst nightmare, standing-in-front-of-the-whole-school-naked level horrifying, which is why it's perfect.

I look at the shimmer of blonde hair that Tristan has twisted at the base of her neck, the razor-sharp pleats where her silky shirt tucks into a pair of painted-on navy slacks, the delicate bump of her ankle bone where it's visible between the hem of her pant-leg and the sheen of her heels. Every single piece of Tristan Grant is selected and coordinated to say she's more put together than anyone else could ever dream of being, and seeing her standing here in one of my favorite places... well, maybe I have faith that she might just love it the way I do.

"Ms. Grant," I say with mock seriousness, dipping my chin to pretend that I can look her in the eye, "Welcome to Magic Mangoes."

The snort escapes her along with a look of horror I assume is in reaction to the momentary loss of her ice queen persona. I know what she's thinking. It's the same place my brain had gone when Ragnar, our goalie, first dragged me in the front door during my first week in Quarry Creek. It's the same thing that's further exacerbated by the fact that the interior of this place looks nothing like what anyone would expect it to look like.

Tristan narrows her eyes and her right heel twitches as though she wants to tap her foot against the worn floor.

"This better not be something inappropriate," she says and I'm pretty sure she'd castrate me if it was. Right here. With her bare hands.

That shouldn't be a thought that I find interesting, but it clearly is because I lean into her and decide to poke the sleeping bear. "Get your mind out of the gutter, kitty cat." She bristles just like Loki does when Erik brings out the cat carrier. "Magic Mangoes is Quarry Creek's finest juice and smoothie bar."

I swear I can see the cogs spinning in her brain, clicking together as she ruminates on what I have just said. Her brows pinch together, a tiny divot between them, and the middle of her bottom lip puckers as though her teeth have sunk into the soft-looking curve. I can also see the moment the meaning sinks in because her eyes flash and the wrinkle in the middle of her forehead smooths out, replaced by tiny lines at the corners of her eyes. Smile lines. I may not see her do it often, but there's the proof that she knows how to smile.

"Okay Varg," she dips her chin as if bestowing an honor upon my household, "You got me. We both know I wouldn't have guessed that."

"Were you thinking strip club?" I turn an eye on the tiny stage where the owner hosts periodic poetry and children's book readings.

"The lack of a pole only stumped me," she admits. "I can't imagine those aren't bolted to the floor. They need to be... sturdy."

"You'd be surprised," and I grin, thinking of the time Spaeglin insisted on hitting a club on his first away game. Only to find out there were no great options close enough to patronize.

"Go to a lot of clubs, Varg?"

It's one of those questions that she thinks she already knows the answer to. I can see it in her smug smirk, and she's not entirely wrong, but not for the reason she's thinking.

"I tag along when the guys go. Team building is important to me."

She snorts through her nose and turns her head away. As if I've just verified some belief she had about pro-athletes in general, and me in particular.

"If the guys told you to cut off your hand with a rusty chainsaw, would you do that too?"

"Well no," I tell her, "I need my hands to play hockey and that sounds like a recipe for infection."

The look she gives me would drop a lesser man to his knees, but I'm a sick puppy. Heat is curling down through my chest, pooling in my stomach and dripping lower. She's so fucking fun to needle. I wonder if I could list this as a hobby every time someone asks what I do for fun besides skate.

"That's the only reason?" I'm pretty sure Tristan Grant has fantasies about smothering me. Or throwing things at my head. And I know I love to piss her off, but I don't know why I'm so successful at it.

"The NHL isn't friendly to amputees." My mood sours as I think of my twin and the dreams he lost, along with his illness and his leg. "But we aren't here to talk about depressing shit. We're here to make people like us."

Deflect, deflect, deflect. Smile and joke and don't make things weird or uncomfortable.

"Like The Arctic." Tristan corrects me, but she's frowning again. Not glaring, just giving me that look like she's trying to tear apart my layers and see the inner workings of my mind and body. It's scarier than when she tries to act mean or tough. I hold my smile steady, refusing to break.

"It's okay sweetheart, we both know it's really all about me."

I don't even think about the pet name before I say it, and I know that's where I've made a fatal mistake. She's used to kitty cat, if I'd stuck with that I'd have hit the tone I was going for—light, carefree, ridiculous, out-to-annoy-the-fuck-out-of-the-pretty-social-media-manager—but sweetheart... that's a new one. And there's no way Tristan won't recognize that she's thrown me off-balance.

I clap my hands together and she jolts at the sound.

"We're here to make smoothies." I tell her and turn away to pull out all the ingredients I've prepped.

"Smoothies." She repeats the word as if she's never heard it before, but not like she thinks it's a bad idea.

"Blended fruit, vegetables, and sometimes dairy products."

"I'm not opposed to the idea." Tristan steps forward and her eyes skate across the assorted berries, the bunch of bananas, the leafy greens, and container of Greek yogurt. I also have chocolate, jars of nut butter, coconut oil, and a million kinds of milk. "I just don't understand how it's going to bring in the attention we need."

"Trust me, kitty cat," I say as I grab the cup for the fancy industrial blender. "Just come over here and have some fun."

She looks at me and I swear I can see the mental list she's creating—pros on one side, cons on the other—before she's shrugging out of her fitted blazer and looping it over the back of the closest stool. I turn to locate the cutting boards I'd stashed behind the bar, and when I'm facing her again, Tristan is setting her camera up on the tiny tripod she uses for filming. She puts it up on the bar, aimed in my direction, and it doesn't escape my notice that she's trying to make sure she's out of the shot.

The first smoothie is one of my mom's favorites. Mangoes, fresh pineapple, frozen banana and Greek yogurt. I talk about each ingredient as I slice and add it to the blender, letting our future viewers know about the shop's commitment to fresh, organic ingredients without the exorbitant price. I add a handful of baby spinach leaves and a splash of orange juice and then set the whole thing to whir together. The machine is too loud to talk over, so I let my gaze rest on my film buddy.

The very edge of Tristan's pink tongue is resting against her upper lip. Her eyes are on my hands, not my face, as I use a rag to wipe down the counter. I watch the muscles in her throat shift as she swallows and there goes that heat again, simmering in my blood and setting my nerves on high alert. She looks away as I stop the blender and pour the smoothie into a tall glass. The spinach has turned the whole thing a light green color, and the banana and yogurt have left a creamy texture. It's a good smoothie. Popular. Tangy with just the right amount of sweetness, and I lift the glass to my mouth and take a healthy sip, letting the creamy liquid cool my body and my blood.

There's more than enough to fill a second glass, but I can't help sliding this one towards Tristan like a bartender showing off. She catches it, probably self-preservation so she wouldn't wear the drink, and eyes me. Tristan tries not to talk while we film. She'll give me occasional hand gestures or point at things with her head and eyes, but she tries to limit the things she'll need to cut out. From where she's seated, the film will look like I sent the smoothie sailing towards the viewer. She probably assumes it's a gimmick or a showboating maneuver, so I can't resist opening my mouth and saying.

"Try it, kitty cat."

Her eyes flare at me, but she maintains her composure and says nothing. Even as she lifts the glass and brings it to her own lips. I watch as she tips her head back and sips, then smiles as she lowers the drink. She nods at me. It's like I can read her mind. *Good Varg, but pretty basic.*

"That tropical twist is a favorite of my mama and my future sister-in-law, Quinn." I say as I reach for another blender. I'll do all the dishes after, but I don't want to pause our filming to rinse. "Now I'm going to show you my favorite."

I've made this smoothie so many times I could do it in my sleep. I blend the oats alone first until they're a flour-like consistency before adding milk and full-fat yogurt. Bananas, protein powder—cocoa powder works well too, I tell the camera—honey, and peanut butter go in next. I set the blender whirring as I drizzle chocolate syrup down the sides of a fresh glass. I turn the blender off and fill the glass up to the top. There's enough for another serving, but once again I take a taste before sliding the glass across the wooden bar top to Tristan.

This time she holds my gaze as she lifts it, turning the cup so she drinks from the same spot I did. For a moment, I swear I hallucinate her pink tongue dragging along the rim as she closes her eyes and lets out a guttural moan. I shift in place as the blood in my body rushes south. Her eyes fly open and pin mine in place.

"Sorry," she says, setting the glass down with more force than necessary. "I'll edit that out. I didn't mean to... be audible."

I don't have a teasing quip ready to go. I don't have an explanation for why I can't seem to form a single sentence. Instead, I hear my mouth say, "It's fine," as though the most PG of moans, and the middle school act of her mouth touching a spot mine just touched, didn't just flatten me where I stand.

"I didn't expect you to make something so delicious," she admits and then her cheeks redden, "Not that I don't think you have good taste, I guess it just didn't occur to me a professional athlete wasn't on some strict meal plan."

"I am," I say, "but during the season I eat roughly six thousand calories a day. Game days involve a lot of pasta, and I eat a metric ton of fresh fruits and vegetables, but these bad boys are a great way to get some healthy fats and protein in."

For a moment Tristan stares at me and then she laughs. The sound is husky and rich and I want to hear it again the minute she stops.

"The other day my sister told me she couldn't eat a pancake because it had carbs. I can't imagine the look on her face if I told her you eat six thousand calories a day."

"Sometimes more," I say. "If I lose muscle tone, the nutritionist might up my intake." I want to ask about her sister. I want to ask why Tristan was making her pancakes. Not that I think it's weird, but because I can't imagine cooking for my brother, although we've only recently found our way back to each other. I want to ask if her sister is younger than she is. If she has more than one. I want to ask a fuck-ton of personal questions I don't yet have the right to ask.

"I don't think you have to worry about that," Tristan says, cheeks flushed again.

I remember the way her eyes dipped to my chest and abdomen when we filmed our first set of videos. Her gaze tracing over the dips and definition of my hard-earned muscles. And I want to tease her about liking what she saw. I want to call her out for staring because god knows I stare all the time, but that feels weird. Not something I should do while our camera is rolling, even if the footage can be edited out. Because it's one thing to rile her up to watch her bristle, and it's another to blatantly flirt with her after she's asked me not to.

"You can find this delicious concoction, The Varg," I tell the camera, "exclusively at Magic Mangoes on Fourteenth Street. Some of my teammates have their own go-to smoothies on the board here too, so you'll have to stop by and try the Ólaffson, the Ahlstrom, the Oakes, the Spaeglin, the Gage, or the Maroni and decide which you like best." I lean in and stage whisper, "After the Varg, that is."

Tristan is staring at me wide-eyed, "You're going to quadruple this place's business." She says, as though that wasn't the entire plan. "And you brought the other guys in and made yourselves look down-to-earth and relatable, not just million-dollar athletes snorting coke and fucking hookers."

"Well, most people have facets," I tell her, "And the coke and hookers wait for the off-season."

She rolls her pretty blue eyes.

"I'm serious, Vic. This was a brilliant idea."

"I told you to trust me," I remind her, trying not to dwell on the way my intestines squirm under her praise. "You wanted us to be engaging and attractive, to connect with the community and appear wholesome and family friendly. Plus, I like Jim and this place is criminally underrated, décor and all."

"It does have a certain... aesthetic, doesn't it?" Tristan looks around the shop again, but this time there's a lot less horror in her eyes. "I'm sorry I doubted you. I assumed you were only doing these videos because you had to."

"I wasn't. You needed a player, and my contract demands I be available to marketing and PR when needed." I say because it's true. "But I could have left all the planning to you and shown up with a pasted-on smile, or let another player take the job, and still fulfilled my end of the deal." I wait until she looks up at me. "I said yes because I think it's a smart idea to connect more with the fans. I said yes because I enjoy being someone people can count on. My teammates can count on. The organization can count on." *You* can count on me.

I don't know what I did before, but I'm going to make it right.

I pour the rest of the smoothie into another glass and hold it out toward Tristan. I wait while she stares at me, her brows furrowing in obvious confusion this time.

"Come on, kitty cat," I say, "Don't leave me hanging." I jiggle the glass a little and a bit of chocolate smoothie sloshes over the side. "Whoops," I say and bring the cup to my mouth to lick up the drip, then I hold it back out towards Tristan. This time she seems to get what I'm after and she lifts her own glass, clinking it against mine.

"*Skål!*" I say, before taking a huge gulp.

"*Slàinte mhath,*" she says and for a moment, I think her eyes dip to my mouth before she takes her own sip.

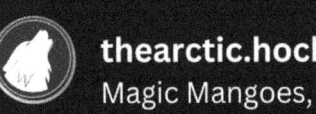

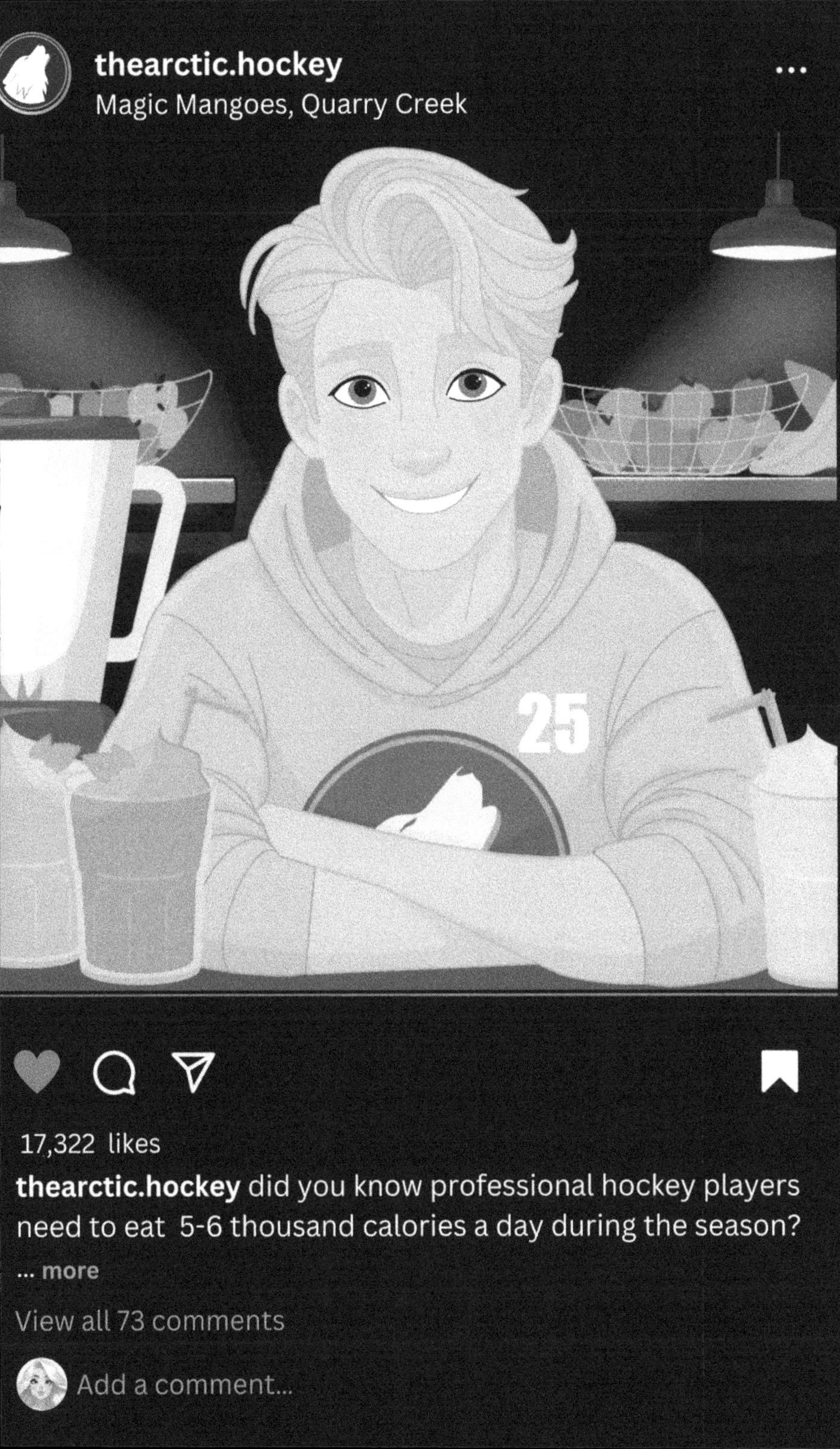
thearctic.hockey
Magic Mangoes, Quarry Creek
25
17,322 likes
thearctic.hockey did you know professional hockey players need to eat 5-6 thousand calories a day during the season?
... more
View all 73 comments
Add a comment...

I TURN off the engine to my sleek white SUV and stare at the building straight ahead. It's a single story with neatly trimmed hedges and a handful of daffodil sprouts just beginning to worm their way out of the dark soil. I rub my sweating palms down the length of my black slacks and pull in a deep breath, closing my eyes against the bright afternoon sunlight.

It's not the thought of seeing Varg that has my stomach tied in knots and my pulse hammering at the base of my throat. In fact, that gorgeous, infuriating man has zero impact on my pulse whatsoever. I think. No, it's not the hockey player that is shackled to me for the foreseeable future. It's the sign over the wide glass door. The one with the big blue heart and the distinctive canine and feline profiles facing each other inside the shape.

And it's not that I'm *afraid* of animals, I'm just not used to them. From a distance I think dogs and cats and hamsters and bunnies are fluffy and adorable, but up close I have no idea what I'm doing and I've watched enough nature documentaries to know that animals can smell fear and uncertainty. The Arctic might provide decent health insurance, but I'm not exactly in the market for mauling-related stitches.

The knock against my window makes me jerk in my seat, slamming my head back against my headrest and clutching a hand to my chest. Okay, so maybe Victor Varg has a slight effect on my heart rate, if the fact that I think I'm dying right now is any sign. I try to cover my nerves with a forced smile and open my door.

"I was beginning to think you were going to stand me up, kitty cat."

I don't have a response for that, mostly because I was contemplating sending an SOS text to one of my sisters so I could get out of this thing, but that would involve explaining who I was with and why I needed a rescue.

Varg doesn't step back as I slide my feet down to the asphalt of the parking lot. He leaves one large hand draped over the edge of my door frame, the other flat against my roof. He's caging me in, and I'm reminded—not for the first time—that this man is more than a foot taller than me. He towers even over my vehicle.

Once I'm done noticing the height of the Arctic's captain, I can't help but notice just how close our bodies are to one another. Close enough that he can feel every one of my inhalations against the gray cotton of his shirt. Close enough that I can see the little white threads that make the color "heathered." Close enough that when I tip my head back to meet his eyes, the hazel of his irises breaks down into the obvious burst of amber brown that bleeds out into an almost gray blue.

His mouth is full, lips pink and curved. I watch as they part and he sucks in air. Every part of this man is hard and chiseled, honed by hours on the ice and in the gym. I know enough from my friend Sadie in the trainers' department that the players typically have between eight and fifteen percent body fat, and there's no way Victor Varg doesn't sit at the lower end of that range. Staring at his mouth, I'm pretty sure that at least one of those percentages is in his lips. I wonder if they'd be soft against mine while the rest of him isn't. I wonder why I'm wondering anything about the mouth that calls me Kitty Cat and about that wide grin he shares with everybody. I wonder why I care at all.

I pull my gaze from his mouth and up to his eyes again. His pupils are wide and dark and his irises are hazy. I can feel the warm puff of air as he breathes over me. His face is shadowed tipped down to mine. It feels intimate holding this connection. Not a single part of us is touching, but I swear I can feel his hands as if they were sliding along my ribs, cupping the bones of my hips. I break eye contact and slip my gaze over his forehead to his furrowed blonde brows. He's frowning. Why is he frowning? If Varg is known for anything, it's his lack of frowning.

This man has to lean so far down to see me I must be causing him neck pain. He must be uncomfortable. He must...

My tongue swipes over my lips before I realize I've done it and I frown, too. What am I doing? Standing in a parking lot with Victor Varg. Letting my brain take me to inappropriate places. Inappropriate because we work together. Inappropriate because he gets under my skin like a nasty rash and I want to scratch him out. Inappropriate because we don't like each other. Except, I can't remember why we don't get along. It has something to do with his frowning. Or lack of frowning. And there must be something on my face because Vic's eyes dart back and forth over my features. Then he straightens up to his unnecessary height and steps back.

"Shall we head inside?" he asks, turning away to look out over the empty parking lot. He moves toward the door and I instinctively reach out, my hand settling on his forearm.

"Wait."

His warm forearm. I swear I feel his muscles twitch under my touch. He stops but doesn't face me.

"What is the plan for..." I swallow, "inside?"

This time he turns. He's not frowning anymore, but his face is blank, a far cry from the jokester I'm used to. I shiver in a sudden breeze and he sways as if to step closer, but catches himself.

"We're just going to go play with some puppies, get some footage, and try to get them adopted."

Right. Puppies. I knew it would be something like that when he asked me to meet him at Quarry Creek Shelter, and it's a brilliant idea. The shelter is struggling. They have too many mouths and not enough space, and after what our smoothie videos did for Magic Mangoes, it's obvious we can do a lot of good for this place too. That's not even considering the draw of an attractive man holding a squirmy pup.

And Victor Varg is, objectively speaking, attractive. Even with the slight bend in his nose from that high stick against Tampa last season.

Infuriating.

"You aren't exactly dressed for this, kitty cat. Scared the puppies will cover you in hair?"

I must stay quiet too long, or there's something showing on my face because even I can tell the question was meant to be funny, teasing, but it doesn't last. "Hey."

My hand drops from his forearm as he steps into my body again. This time it's his hand that comes up to cup my elbow. I can feel the heat of his skin through the silk of my blouse. He's right. I'm dressed to stay behind a camera, not to get up-close and personal with anything with fur. Blue silk shirt, tailored black pants, and red-soled heels.

"I'm..." my gaze skates away from his. "I'm not that comfortable with animals."

I brace for the inevitable. I've heard it all before. *How could you not like animals? Only sociopaths don't like animals. Who doesn't think kittens and bunnies and puppies are adorable?* But it doesn't come.

"We can go somewhere else."

And we both know that we can't. We had to get permission to film here. Permission to post and tag the shelter. Everyone knows the reach Varg can get for the cause. The organization knows the appeal of fluffy little paws and puppy dog eyes.

Varg looks over my shoulder for a moment, running his free hand through his hair. It's longer now than it was at the start of the season. I know he pushes the strands back before putting on his helmet so they don't fall into his eyes. In another few weeks, it will curl up under the bottom of his helmet when he plays.

"It's a school day, so I can't ask Quinn or Jen until after three, but Erik might be free. I can ask him to come film. Or—"

I shake my head to clear my thoughts, but also because... no. I knew this was the plan. I agreed to this. I can't back out now. That's unprofessional and ridiculous and those are two things I *refuse* to be in front of anyone, but especially Victor Varg—team captain, Arctic golden boy, and a man who could completely derail my career. Again.

"I'm fine," I say and I regret the bite in my voice when he drops his grip on my arm. Snapping at him isn't very professional or controlled. I can admit that it was kind of him to offer me an out, even if it grated against my nerves.

Evidently the "thank you" I tack on to soften my tone works, because there's Varg's grin curving up the corners of his mouth.

"It's okay to be scared, kitty cat. I won't say anything. Wouldn't want to bust your tough-girl rep."

It takes superhuman effort not to roll my eyes. It's not a rep. It wasn't a conscious choice. It was a survival mechanism. I don't have the luxury of looking soft, or unsure, or vulnerable. I'm a woman fighting for a spot in a man's world. Marketing might be a career heading towards a more even split over gender, but it isn't there yet and the world of professional sports teams is even further away.

I'm already facing an uphill battle to prove I deserve a spot at the table, and while my height and hair color shouldn't matter, I'm not naïve enough to believe they don't. Maybe if I were average height, or brunette, my male counterparts would take me more seriously. Instead, I feel like a child at the grown-ups' table. I have to be twice as calm and collected. Twice as prepared with twice the results. No weaknesses, no distractions.

"I'm not scared," my voice cracks and I pinch my brows together, hoping he didn't notice. Of course he did. Hockey is more than just speed and agility. It's more than strength and guts. The good players, the best ones, know how to read people—their teammates, their opponents—to stay one step ahead of the puck. Varg certainly does. I can see it in the way his gaze moves over my face.

"I didn't have pets growing up." I square my shoulders, because I'll give him this tiny piece and then we're going to go inside and get the footage we came for. "There wasn't anyone to take care of them, so we didn't have any. But I'm not scared."

I step around the massive hockey player and head for the front of the building. I suck air in through my mouth and let it push my ribs out as I hold my breath to the count of three. I let it out atom by atom. Keep my heart rate low and everything will be okay. It'll be an hour—tops.

"I didn't have a pet growing up either," Victor Varg says

as he catches up to me easily and matches me stride for stride. He grabs the door handle before I can and ushers me into the quiet lobby. I was expecting to be bowled over with sound and smells, but this isn't terrible. "Between two hockey players and a figure skater on a single mother's salary, there wasn't a lot left over for animals. Not to mention we basically lived at the rink. And when we got older..." He scrubs a hand over his face.

When he got older, he was drafted.

I know he joined the juniors at sixteen and left home to live with a host family. Even if his mom had gotten a dog then, he wouldn't have been home to enjoy it. I open my mouth to say something, anything, but an older woman scrambles around the counter, her jaw open in wonder as she stares at my companion, and I force a smile so I don't roll my eyes. Victor Varg is just another guy. It's not like he single-handedly cured cancer or saved orphans from a burning building. He's just good with a stick and is easy on the eyes.

The woman shakes Vic's hand, pumping her arm up and down like it might detach from the socket, and I tune her out as she talks about a litter of puppies that will be up for adoption in the coming week. They'll all get homes, of course, but they also have the highest marketing appeal. I try to slow my pulse as I think of Vic cuddling small golden pups against the wide expanse of his chest. Puppies crawling over his stretched-out legs, pushing their noses against the edges of his ears. It's not really helping at all, but at least my heart isn't pounding out of fear now. It's racing for an entirely different reason, and if I think about it for too long, that might actually be worse.

"You good with puppies, kitty cat?" Vic's eyes are warm on me. I can't see the woman at all behind his overlarge frame. How much damage can puppies do? I nod once. "Lead the way," he tells the shelter volunteer, and then we're following her down a dim hallway and she's ushering us into a small room with peeling vinyl tiles and white paneled walls. I take out my camera and open my tripod, aiming it at one of the blank walls. I'm determined to be ready when the dogs come in. The less I wait to do, the faster we'll be in and out.

The puppies are cute. I knew they would be, but I wasn't expecting Marjorie—the volunteer—handing seven of them over the top of a wooden baby gate and letting them run loose around us. Vic sinks to his haunches, and I try not to stare at the bulge of his quadriceps. The little yellow fluffs swarm at him. They look tiny against the bulk of his muscles, scrambling over the curve of his biceps, pressing little paws against the width of his chest until he sits back hard on his ass.

I watch him play for long minutes; the puppies letting out little whimpers and mewls that tug even at my own heartstrings. Vic is talking to the camera, telling our future viewers when the puppies will be available for adoption and about the shelter's mission and needs. His words occasionally cut off as he presses his face to the side of a puppy determined to climb him like a tree. I'm fully disassociating from the moment, trying to reorganize my mind until I'm not consumed with the way our chests bumped into each other out in the parking lot, not drowning under the way the little paws pull at his clothes revealing strips of tan skin. How is he so tan? Doesn't he spend twenty-three hours a day under the rink's angry fluorescent lights?

"Hold on guys, I'm needed for a rescue."

The words break through my haze, and I frown. Vic is extricating himself from a mess of wagging bodies and he's staring at me. I cast around the room, trying to make sense of where this is going, when I notice the pup heading straight for me. His pink tongue flops out, little black spots in the center, and his fluff is so voluminous that he looks like a little sphere rolling in my direction. I can see the hint of small white teeth, sharp ones, before Vic scoops him up and cradles him against his body.

Me.

He was coming to rescue me.

"You okay, kitty cat?" Vic says, staring down into my face as his hands stroke through the golden fur. I can feel the heat spread up my neck to my cheeks and I pull in air through my nose to stop that right now.

"It's just a puppy," I say, and I know he can hear the catch in my voice when he smiles. It's not his normal ear-to-ear grin. This one is soft at the edges, full lips closed over his teeth, a shadow of a dimple in one of his cheeks.

"It is." He agrees. "A smart one too. Saw a pretty girl and made a break for her."

It's like a tornado whips through my brain, my thoughts scattered into fragments.

"Want to hold him?" Vic offers, and the puppy twists his head back to lick a kiss against the underside of the captain's jaw. And suddenly yes, I do. I want to hold the puppy and let it lick a stripe along my skin too. I want to brush my fingers over Vic's as he passes the dog over. Which means I absolutely shouldn't say yes.

"Yes," I nod my head too, as though I didn't just tell myself I would not do this.

Vic's eyes meet mine and that secret smile stays right where it is as he steps into my body and waits.

We're almost as close as we were by the car, but now there's a dog between us, and I'm so aware of Victor Varg's height and muscles and mouth that I'm not even paying attention to the puppy. The tornado is still howling in my mind, whipping my thoughts around and around as I try to find purchase.

"You need to take him," Vic says, and I shiver at the way his voice scrapes over my nerves. I hear the click of his throat as he swallows. "Hold your hands out. Like he's a baby. Then pull his body into your chest."

I'm grateful for the directions and my arms move to follow them without my conscious choice. Then there's a small weight passed over. A weight that squirms and whimpers and twists and I stop breathing as the puppy twists to face me, pressing his little head against my throat.

"When my sister was three, she got bit by our neighbor's dog Twinkles," I say as the puppy huffs air into my skin. I shut my eyes to block out the memory of Joey's scream. "He got her in the face. There was blood everywhere, and Mrs. Truett started yelling at us, and I didn't know what to do. That was the only dog I'd ever met. It wasn't even that big. Mrs. Truett lived across the hall and she was supposed to watch us after school."

"That must have been very scary," Vic says, and I get the sense he really means it. Maybe it's the small furrow between his blonde brows, or the way he seems to sway even closer to me. "It's hard seeing our siblings hurt. Did she need stitches?"

I think of the small silver scar over Joey's upper lip, of Mrs. Truett putting me, Joey, Max, Maddie, Palmer, and Hayley into the hall and closing the door as I pressed my shirt to Joey's mouth. I remember sending Hayley and Palmer to knock on doors until someone could call for help. Talking the EMTs into letting all six of us ride in the ambulance since I didn't have keys to our apartment. I walked to the hardware store the next day and made a copy of the apartment key, and we stopped staying with Mrs. Truett.

"She ended up with six. Another neighbor called an ambulance."

Mom had been pissed when she had to come get us all from the hospital. Even angrier when the ambulance bill came.

"A neighbor." Vic frowns. "Your parents met you there?"

I shake my head. "I told you, there was no one to take care of a dog. They could barely take care of my siblings. I handled it. I always did."

There's silence for a heartbeat and then strong hands slide over my elbows and up my arms. They squeeze my shoulders and slip up my neck before Vic cups my cheeks and tilts my face up to his.

"How old were you, Kitty Cat?" I watch his throat bob. "How old were you when you started taking care of everyone?"

"They split when I was twelve," I say. "Joey was only two, Hayley, the second oldest, she was seven. It was... messy. My dad had a new family, my mother fell apart, and I took over after that."

The puppy sighs and licks at my skin and it breaks whatever spell is settling over us like a heavy winter coat.

"So I'm not scared," I lie right to his face, "I'm just a little nervous around all the teeth."

Vic smiles at me like he can see right through me.

Maybe he can.

"I could tell you that you should have never had to grow up that fast, but we both know it won't change anything." He's still cupping my cheeks, the puppy pressed between our bodies. "Sometimes life is cruel and unfair. Sometimes it throws us curveballs we aren't ready for. You don't have to justify anything you do to protect yourself. You've earned the right to keep you and yours safe."

He drops his hands from my skin and steps back, putting a microscopic amount of space between us.

"My brother and his fiancée have two cats, Loki and Tesseract. They're pretty cool. I always thought maybe I'd get a cat at some point, but I'm away all the time and I can't ask my mom to look after a pet for me. If you want, we can get Marjorie to show us some kittens."

He's giving me an out. A way to protect myself without

having to admit I need to. He's right that I have the right to protect me and mine. I know it, but maybe Vic's also wrong. Maybe I'm wrong too, because I'm here holding a puppy and everything is fine. Self-preservation would have denied me this moment. The cuddles, the dog, the man putting my needs first. Maybe....

Maybe.

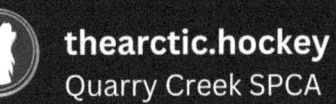

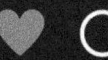

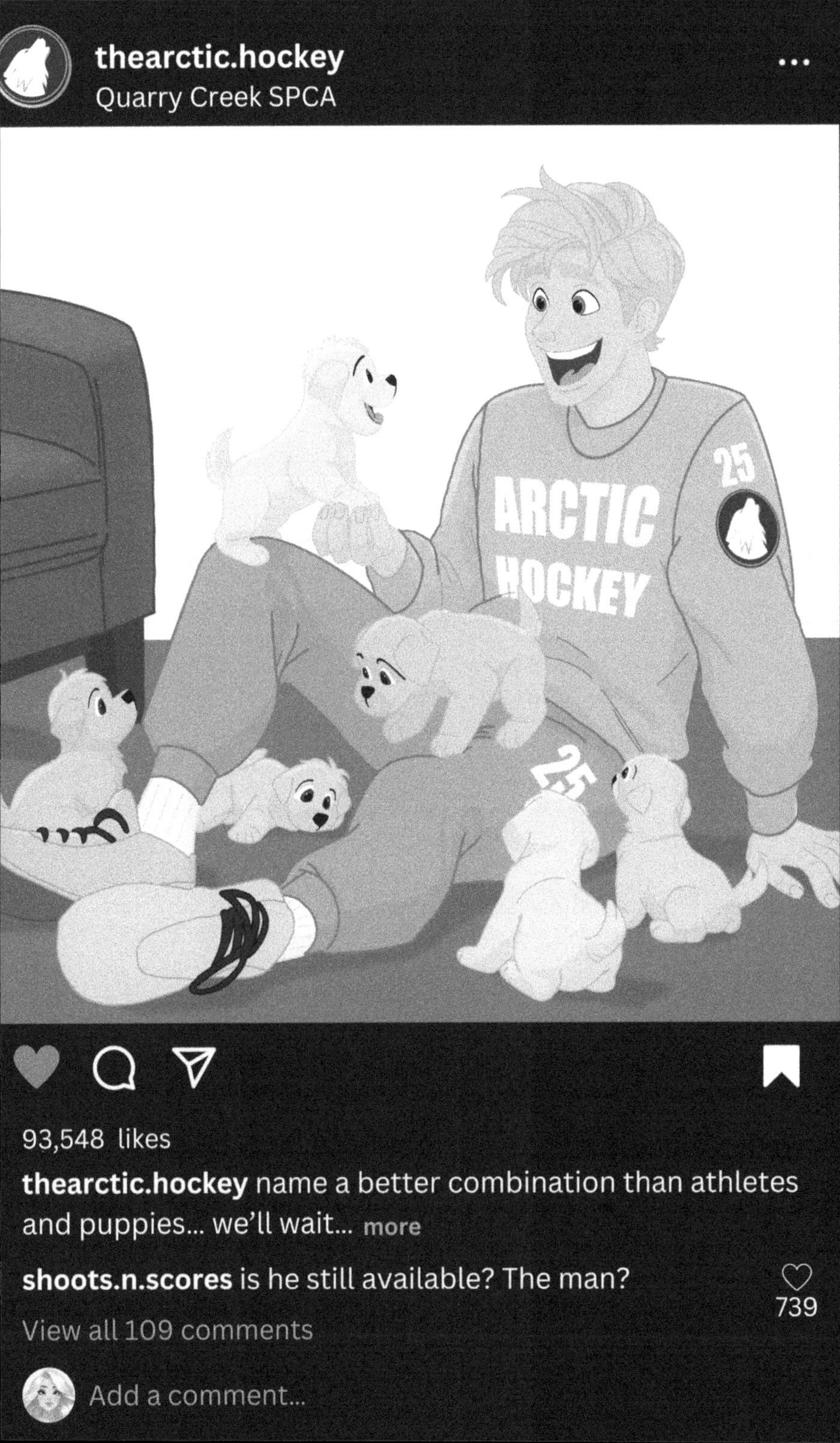
thearctic.hockey
Quarry Creek SPCA
ARCTIC
HOCKEY
25
25
93,548 likes
thearctic.hockey name a better combination than athletes and puppies... we'll wait... more
shoots.n.scores is he still available? The man?
739
View all 109 comments
Add a comment...

"YOUR GIRLFRIEND STOPPING BY TONIGHT?"

I can't see the rookie with my towel blocking my eyes, but I'd know Spaeglin's voice anywhere. The kid has a habit of belting out pop songs at full volume during after-skate showers. He's tone deaf, but what he lacks in musicality he makes up for in enthusiasm.

The locker room is almost empty. Most of the team has already hit the showers, stored their equipment, and left for the night. There's only a handful of us left. The players who had to see the trainers—Ólaffson—or talk with the press; me, Robbie, Spaeglin. A few others are here too. Pelletier always waits for Spags since they share a house, but the general buzz has died down. Even with our win tonight. We've played several games back-to-back and most of the guys are currently jonesing for their bed and heating pads. Sexy, I know.

I take longer to process the question because I'm not currently dating anyone. It's been ages since I've even engaged in some extra cardio with a partner. As a rule, I try not to mess around during the season. I used to. It's hard to find a wide-eyed rookie who doesn't spend a little time gorging on the money and attention that comes with an NHL contract. I had my fair share of a few wild years before the lure of extra sleep outweighed the desire for random hookups. Popping a handful of ibuprofen every morning can only do so much when your knees and back are pissed after holding a naked woman up against the slick tile in the shower.

Most guys fall into some form of long-term relationship, but I've avoided those too. I can't imagine someone being willing to put up with my travel schedule. I'm pretty sure about as much care goes into planning the league's away schedule as goes into mail routes. A lot of time and energy for something that ultimately is as chaotic as it is possible to be. A few of my teammates don't even live in Quarry Creek. They come here for the season and travel back home after the playoffs.

"No way. Varg is dating Elsa?"

That question comes from Pelletier, and I glare at the left winger.

"Elsa?" Spaeglin again.

"Watch it." I feel the words grate against my vocal cords and I turn back to my cubby before I say something I shouldn't. It's never bothered me before, the way the team sees the little marketing genius, but today the nickname and the insinuation scrapes against my skin like sandpaper.

"Yeah," Pelletier's voice sounds muffled as he pulls on

his undershirt. "She's got that white blonde hair, and she's an ice queen."

"Is this because she rejected you?" Spaeglin asks and there's a roar of laughter as the remaining guys throw wads of balled up tape at Beau. I have the urge to throw something harder. The game puck is sitting in my cubby. Right there. Within reach.

"Nah, she was colder than the rink before that. Why'd you think I took my shot?"

My knuckles ache, the skin turning bone white as I curl them into fists.

"'Cause you don't mind freezing your nuts off?"

There's a whistle of a towel and a slap as it connects with skin, then Spaeglin yelps and the room dissolves into another roar of laughter. I tune them all out, scrubbing the towel down my face. This one is a little worn. It catches on my stubble and the rasp echoes in my ears.

This conversation isn't something I want any part of. I don't know if Tristan will be down tonight after the game. She usually gets the footage she needs before we hit the ice, but she has been known to badger us into submission after we're put back together. She and I have nothing on our schedule for today, but she still has her regular content to push out. What we do, the videos we're working on, are a side project. She still has stuff for the whole team.

So I don't want a part of this. I don't know if she's coming down—although my gut instinct is no, she'd have shown up by now—not that it matters even a bit. I worked with her yesterday. We'll film again in the next few days. It doesn't bother me to see her pointing her camera at any of my teammates. It doesn't bother me when she rolls her eyes at them and raises that one eyebrow. I get the same glare when I smile at her. And sometimes, I get the tiny curve at the corner of her mouth, as if she can't help herself. That curve is better.

And maybe if I've tried to make those micro smiles happen? Well, it's just fun to see her riled up. I enjoy seeing her break through the cool exterior and show the fire roaring underneath. That's why I don't like this nickname, or the way the guys see her. That's why I'm not laughing it off and joining in. Not a single one of them understands that she isn't as cool and removed as she tries so hard to be. She's fire on the inside. She's an inferno kept under such tight lock and key that she's sizzling at the seams. They don't know her at all.

Not like I know—

"They aren't d-d... they aren't d-da... they aren't together," Ólaffson says, breaking me out of my thoughts. He's sitting on one of the long wooden benches, tossing a puck back and forth between his hands. "Just working."

"Right, working," the rookie says, thrusting his hips as if we all missed the sarcasm dripping from his pretty boy mouth. He's going to be toast after our free skate tomorrow. I'm going to have him bag skating until he can't move another inch. Maybe until he pukes.

"Be fucking respectful," Robbie says and for a moment, I remember what it was like growing up with him. Strapping on roller blades with my brother and my best friend and playing until the streetlights came on and mom stood on the front step calling us back inside for dinner. Even then, as a kid, I never believed that someday we'd strap on the same pads and colors and hit the ice together. Hoped, of course, what kid hasn't? But dreams are just that. Dreams. I remember getting the notice that all three of us —Robbie, me, and Erik—were going to play in the junior league. Erik and I had just turned sixteen, Robbie one year older.

I remember him sitting in the hospital waiting room with me as I fought back tears. There was enough crying all around me and I couldn't afford to add to it. I remember a shoulder pressed to mine, a knee leaving a solid weight against my thigh as we waited for the doctor to tell us the unthinkable about Erik.

The way he contacted the league for me with a hand-written note to see if I could pretty please with sugar on top play for a team closer to home. Close enough to visit my brother as he went through chemo and surgery and still lost his leg. So I wouldn't have to choose between my dream on the ice and leaving my mother alone. Anna was in college by then. If I'd gone to play in another state, packed up and moved in with a host family the way so many players do, she'd have been all by herself, drowning under the weight of her fear.

Our eyes meet for a sliver of a second and I watch his shoulders rise and fall as he sucks in a huge breath. And suddenly I'm not thinking about IV bags, and metal legs, and lost hair. I'm not thinking about red-rimmed eyes and shaky breaths as my mother and twin try to pretend every-thing is fine. I'm thinking about the girl who lived two houses down. The one Robbie left behind when he flew to

Wisconsin and donned the blue, gray, and white of the USHL team there. The two had been inseparable when Erik and I met them. She's a high-fashion model now, taking the world by storm while Robbie pretends he doesn't keep a google alert for her name almost two decades later. I remember finding him on our back deck, staring out into the yard, wet trails drying on his cheeks after he had broken the news to her that he was leaving.

There's a certain kinship that comes with navigating heartbreak with someone. A way of reading each other that gets etched into your bones when you know someone so well you can read them without words. I used to know my brother like that. I'm trying like hell to get back there now. It's been a year since he moved to Quarry Creek and while our telepathy hasn't been re-established yet, despite what most people seem to believe about identical twins, it's getting a lot better.

The conversation around us shifts to more mundane topics. The younger guys are excited about our first match up with Vegas this month. We're flying out to meet them on their turf, and while normally we all prefer to play at home, there's something magical about going to Vegas. Too bad the young ones don't know we rarely have time to do anything more than play, sleep, and come home.

"Is she?" Robbie asks as I pull my shirt over my head. When I don't answer, he adds, "your girlfriend?"

I shake my head, ignoring the swoop in my gut.

"You know she isn't." I keep my voice low so we don't attract any more attention. They're currently discussing the rules of Blackjack and from the little I hear, I am going to have to keep a close eye on the guys if we spend any time near a casino. Everyone knows you're supposed to split aces and eights when the dealer hands them to you as your first pair of cards. Well, anyone who beats the house.

"Everyone thinks you are," he says as he pulls his shirt on, too.

I send him my standard grin and shrug my shoulders.

"That's because hockey players are big gossips." It's true. The locker room trades in stories and secrets as currency. "We've been spending extra time together for this series the guys upstairs want."

"It's not that," Robbie says, and he smirks at me in a way that only reminds me of Tristan. I roll my eyes. "You watch all your videos, right?"

I mean to. Tristan sends them to me, but honestly I keep forgetting. Her goal is to make me marketable and make the team look good. I trust that she's not putting something offensive or embarrassing up. So no, I haven't watched our most recent video at the animal shelter. I followed up and found out that all the puppies have found homes, but I haven't watched the footage myself. I was there in person, after all.

Robbie pulls his phone out of his cubby and hits a few buttons before handing me the device. I watch myself on the screen, buried in puppies. And then I see the moment that the fluffy rascal makes a break for Tristan. She's cut all the conversation about her family, and mine—that's no surprise—but it is a surprise that she left herself in the shot. I see myself handing her the puppy. I see the corner of her mouth twitch in that tiny smile, and I see the way my eyes never leave her face as I tower over her. The heat there is unmistakable.

There are thousands of likes on the video and an impressive number of comments. Robbie leans over me and opens them so I can scan through the words. An overwhelming majority are asking if we're together, speculating about our size difference, lamenting that I'm off the market. My cheeks heat. I'm not off the market. We're partners in this project. Nothing more. She practically spits when she sees me.

Except when you had her pressed up against her car. The voice in my head reminds me. *She definitely wasn't spitting then.*

"I heard he was coked out of his mind," someone says in the locker room and Robbie and I swivel our heads in unison. There isn't any press in the room right now, but these kinds of conversations aren't anything the big brass would want us to be having on team property.

"Safe to say he's not coming back even after he's released." Someone else adds.

Haine. They're talking about Haine.

"Wasn't he caught with a stripper?" Spaeglin is a part of the conversation now too, which means the news must have broken wide open. I knew working with Tristan had something to do with Haine's accident, but I didn't know the details. She was cagey about them, and I didn't press. I didn't want to.

"I heard she was a pro," this sentence is accompanied by wiggling eyebrows and that means it's time to shut this down before it bleeds out of this room.

"Hey," I say and as a unit the guys turn to stare at me. "This conversation ends now."

"So it's true then? Haine really got drugged out and crashed his car into a building while cheating on his wife?" Spaeglin asks me, and his blue eyes glitter with the promise of something forbidden and juicy. Sometimes it's easy to forget that he's just a kid, while other times it's so obvious I want to pat him on the head and give him a glass of warm milk before bedtime.

"If that happened, the news would be bad for the entire team," I say. "The Arctic prides itself on philanthropy and our family-friendly atmosphere. Our fans want that from us."

"Shouldn't they just want us to win games?" Pelletier asks and I hear Robbie snort.

"They want to feel comfortable letting their *kids* watch us win games," I say. "We aren't talking about this. Not here, not outside of the rink, not anywhere but in the home office with a member of legal present."

Spaeglin raises his hand.

"If anyone asks about Haine, your response is, 'no comment'. Understand?"

"Yes cap," the guys say, and this time it's Ólaffson's hand that is in the air.

"W-what can we do to-to-to help?"

"Don't fuck up," Robbie says and the guys snicker as though he's not one hundred percent serious.

"This is why I've been working with Tristan," I say. "We're trying to really push the family-friendly, community-helper angle for the team before any news can break."

"Tristan?" Spaeglin repeats the name like he's never heard it before.

"Elsa," Pelletier says and I grind my back teeth together.

"It's working," Gage says, "plus you've gotten several thousand more followers."

I have noticed the steady uptick in notifications and I've been fielding calls from my agent about new products interested in working together. Magic Mangos has been making money hand over fist. I've been signing more autographs than ever. Just the other day, someone stopped me at the car wash. Neither of us had anything to sign or sign with so he got a drive through napkin with my signature scrawled on it in black eyeliner he'd found next to the cash register.

"I want more followers," Spaeglin says. "Can you ask El—Tristan if she could use me?"

"I want in too." Pelletier.

"Me three." Gage.

"I can't make any promises," I tell them. "But I'll let her know."

Doors slam as the guys leave, and I try to focus on buttoning my slacks and tucking in my shirt. Game day dress code always sounds like a good idea until you have to do up buttons on a dress shirt after three periods and almost twenty minutes on shift. Everything hurts after that kind of workout, and while I enjoy the fuck out of a win, the appeal doesn't distract from the aches and pains anymore.

"Be careful," Robbie says as I slam my locker closed

and shoulder my bag. And I want to pretend he's telling me to watch my muscles, or lift with my legs, but I know he means with her.

"I already told you she isn't my girlfriend." I tell my best friend and teammate. "There's nothing to 'be careful' about. We're working together for the good of the organization and that's it. There's nothing going on between us."

The words taste funny in my mouth. A metallic tang like when I split my lip on a high stick or bit the inside of my cheek during a nasty trip. Robbie stares at me. Big arms crossed over an even bigger chest and dark brows pinched together until they almost touch. It's the same look I've seen him give the younger players when he finds them in the hotel hallway at three am. The look that says, "No matter what words come out of your mouth, we both know they are complete lies."

"We aren't dating," I say again because we aren't. She barely tolerates me. I'm trying to change that perception because that's what I do. I make friends and soothe nerves. I smile and say 'yes' and put things back together. I put my comfort and needs on the back burner just like I started doing at sixteen. It's easier to be the person helping, to be the person taking action, than to risk being the person no one remembers. So that's all that's happening between me and Tristan. She needed help, and I was willing to provide it.

The small smiles I like to coax out of her? At one point in our past time working together, I clearly let her down. I did something that made her sure I was someone she couldn't count on. Wanting to change her perception of me is human nature, not personal. Wanting to rile her up until she strikes out with her claws and steam pours out her ears? Well, maybe I don't like seeing her encased in ice. I know Tristan is simmering under that cool shell. Helping her melt it down... well that's just human nature too. Right?

"There's nothing between us," I'm protesting too much, right? I can't stop repeating myself. Can't stop denying, denying, denying. I don't even know who I'm trying to convince at this point.

"You just want there to be." Robbie claps a hand on my back and words clang through my brain.

I just want there to be.

I just want.

9
TRISTAN

I THINK I read once that a fear of authority is a common trait of my generation. I don't remember the reason why; I wasn't all that invested in the article. It was in a magazine Hayley left lying around my bathroom. I'm only five years older than she is so I'm pretty sure we're in the same generation, even though she—and the others—like to pretend I'm ancient.

It used to bother me when I was younger and didn't understand what they weren't saying. Now I do and sometimes it makes me even more sad to think that they tease me like an adult because I'm the one who always showed up. I'm the one who raised them. I stopped being their sister at twelve, when dad moved out and mom checked out. Although in reality it was probably even earlier than that. Maybe when Hayley was born.

I wouldn't call what I have a fear. I'm not afraid of Chris or Bob or any of the supervisors at work. I just always think I'm in trouble when they call last-minute one-on-one meetings. I read the email or listen to the voicemail asking for a sit-down first thing in the morning, and for an embarrassing moment I forget the increase in ticket sales and Varg merch purchases. I forget the growth rate for the team and Varg's personal social media accounts. I forget Shelly has been playing nicely and refusing to talk to the press even as details of Haine's "incident" leak out. I forget all of that and start beefing up my resume. Just in case.

Then I shake myself off, pick a power outfit for the next morning, touch up my manicure, and set my alarm an hour earlier so I can work on some deep breathing before heading into the office. The hour earlier helps. I get about five minutes on my walking pad—not that I ever do much more than that—slick every single hair back into a twist that looks professional and no-nonsense, and make a full breakfast complete with an oat milk chai latte—all the caffeine, none of the coffee taste—that I then leave on my kitchen counter.

I smooth my hands down the front of my slacks, not to wipe the sweat off, just to ensure that I'm as put together as possible, then I raise my fist and knock on the heavy wooden door.

"Come in." Mr. Seever's voice doesn't sound any specific type of way, but my heart still does a tiny roll in my chest, and I tamp it down.

Fuck that. I'm kicking ass on Operation Distract Quarry Creek. I've only thought about killing Victor Varg once... a day. Which is an improvement over before when I thought about it once an hour. He's not as insufferable as I had assumed. Not restful, either, but tolerable. In small doses. When he keeps his mouth closed. Literally. His grin sets me off more than anything else. No one has that much to smile about. It's a fake, or a forgery, one or the other. Either way, it's not real.

The door swings open on its own, and for a moment I wonder if Mr. Seever has a butler or an assistant whose job it is to let people into his office. Then I hear the small whirring sound as I step onto the plush carpet and realize he has it on an electric mechanism of some sort so he can stay seated behind his massive wooden desk, the Quarry Creek downtown framed through the giant window at his back. It's intimidating, and I try to tamp down the indignant anger that is ruffling my nerves.

"Ah, Ms. Grant! Come in, come in."

I swear every sentence out of Mr. Seever's mouth sounds like it ends in a question mark. This time he almost seems surprised to see me, like he didn't send the email that mandated my attendance this morning. Come to think of it, his assistant probably did that.

"Mr. Seever." I nod my head and smile as if I'm not wondering if I'm about to be out of a job.

"Have a seat, young lady," he says, and I feel like I'm back in kindergarten. He gestures to the large armchair in front of his desk. It might be the comfiest piece of furniture I've ever rested my ass on, which makes sense given how much I know the team is worth and how much the big cattle rancher from Texas offered him for the team. "I thought it was time we have a small check in about Victor Varg."

Just the name sends my nerves into a tailspin. Why does he want to talk about Varg? It makes sense he wants to touch base about the videos we've been making, but he didn't say he wanted to talk about the accounts or the fan increase or even the increase in sales. He wants to talk about his star player. His captain. I take a steadying breath and remind myself that I have nothing to worry about. I am exceeding expectations and there can be no complaints except for maybe…

"Are you having an affair with him?"

Except, apparently, for that.

Without warning, I'm back in that shelter parking lot. Vic's big body pressing me up against my car door. I'm holding out my arms as he passes over a squirming puppy. I'm in the locker room and he's standing there shirtless, skin gleaming under the harsh lights. I'm leaning forward to wrap my lips around the straw he just took a drink from…

I can feel the heat spreading over my neck and climbing up toward my cheeks. I may have been "blessed"—as so many people like to tell me—with my pale skin, hair and eyes, but uncontrollable blushing is its own kind of hell when you're the one person everyone expects to take charge of every situation. Blushing amaryllis red kind of destroys my competent bad ass image.

Blushing also leaves me looking like I'm guilty of the very thing my Bob just asked me about.

I'm not sleeping with Victor Varg.

"I wouldn't ask such an uncomfortable question, my

dear, but given the current situation, I felt a direct approach would be best."

I'm not sure what situation he means and if I wasn't already caught off-guard, this would make things so much worse. I can't tell if he means the incident with Curtis Haine, although I'm not sure how a consensual relationship between myself and Vic would be anything like plowing one's car into the side of a business with a brick of cocaine on the backseat and a sex worker in the passenger seat.

Not that Vic and I are in a relationship, but if we were, it would be two hundred and eighty-three percent consensual.

We aren't, though.

We wouldn't be.

Noticing his objective level of attractiveness changes nothing. His attentiveness to detail and willingness to put in hard work changes nothing.

"There have been some whispers..."

And fuck it all, the team owner is still talking. While I've been *not* daydreaming about the captain of his team.

"We're not together," I say, ready to shut down the rest of this conversation, and another wave of red-hot anger pulses through me. Here I am again, getting 'talked to' by the people who hold my career and professional future in their hands. Whether or not they're true, the rumors—and this meeting—will sit like a black smudge on my permanent record. I've only ever had a dressing down from my boss once. And that was Varg's fault, too.

I don't even realize I've clenched my hands into fists

until the sting of my nails cutting into my skin registers in my brain.

Mr. Seever studies me, dark eyes boring into mine. I force myself to keep his gaze like this is some kind of lie detector test. As if a blink will betray the fact that I might have had a dream about strong hands slipping up the length of my thighs last night. And okay, the dream wasn't necessarily about Varg—it's not like I saw his face or anything identifying—but in my fantasy his hand spanned the entire distance from the inside of my knees to the soft fold where my thighs meet my hips. I know I'm small, but few men are *that* big. If it helps, I woke up angry with myself, and not just because Mads and Max let themselves into my apartment to raid my cereal stash before my alarm went off, leaving me short a happy ending.

"As you're well aware," the team owner says, "The Arctic Organization has a pretty extensive non-fraternization policy." Not that it stopped Beau Pelletier from asking me out when he first joined the roster. "But I'm not a man interested in standing in the way of true love. If you and Mr. Varg have genuine feelings for each other, then that's something I'd be willing to look the other way for, but I don't need to tell you we are all under extra scrutiny. The team cannot afford another scandal on top of..." he trails off, but I know what he means. "You are a fantastic employee, Ms. Grant, but we both know the team cannot afford to lose Victor Varg for the foreseeable future."

"I understand, Sir." It takes effort to not let my voice shake. "Victor Varg and I are filming videos for the team's social media accounts. There is nothing more than a working relationship between us." *We aren't even friends.* I don't add the last part. It seems unlikely that it will help convince the man in front of me I'm a consummate professional. That we're having this conversation proves he doesn't think I am.

I don't want to whine, anyway. I want to rage. I want to tip my head back and scream until the floor-to-ceiling windows behind Bob's desk shatter into a million pieces. I want the papers to fly off the desk and spiral through the room like an F-5 tornado tearing across the Great Plains. Just once, I want things to go my way. I want the world to be goddamn fair for five fucking minutes.

You're a fantastic employee, but...

You're a hard worker, but...

You've done everything we asked of you, but...

You're a good kid, but...

But...

But...

But...

It's never enough. Nothing I do is ever good enough. No matter how much time and effort I put into a task, there's always someone else ready and able to do it better. No matter how perfectly I slick back my hair, no matter how carefully I apply my makeup, no matter how much I practice and center myself so I can ooze responsibility and control, there's always someone else older, taller. Someone with a penis willing to come and take it all away.

Mr. Higgins, the department of child and family services worker who tried to step in and send my siblings to different foster homes despite the years that I'd been holding everything together. Dr. Agarwal, the one who stitched up Joey's dog bite, asking pointed questions about where our parents were. Ms. Jones, the third-grade teacher who went toe-to-toe with me about whether I could attend parent-teacher conferences for the twins. Or sign permissions slips. Despite being a month away from my eighteenth birthday. Chris, my boss, setting me up on this project and then making decisions without consulting me. Mr. Seever, making sure I know that no matter how well I do my job, I'll lose to the superstar captain every single time.

Victor Varg, smiling without a care in the world and getting everything handed to him, while some of us have to carve out every crumb that comes our way.

My dad, for starting a new family before he could have the decency to quit his old one. For leaving us alone in a too-small apartment without enough money coming in, and a mother who hadn't worked since I was born.

My mom, for choosing to let her self-worth be determined by a cheating louse, and ignoring the children she birthed once he was gone. Letting her oldest daughter hold them all together with stubbornness and willpower.

Mr. Seever is still studying me and I force a smile.

"You don't have to worry about us." I'm looking up through my eyelashes, trying to project competent but sweet and innocent too. "You can trust that we both have the team's best interests at heart."

"I don't doubt that," Bob agrees. "I'm sorry to start your day off on such a dreary note, Ms. Grant. Hopefully, we can put all this fraternization stuff behind us."

I shake his hand and thank him for his time because it's what I'm supposed to do. I leave the office on autopilot, barely restraining the urge to reach into my bag for my cell and pull up the team accounts. The minute the latch catches on the door behind me, I'm scrolling my way to our most recent video so quickly that I almost lose my grip on my phone.

Rumors.

Bob Seever, the owner of the Arctic franchise, said there'd been rumors. I need to know if the rumors are internal—the team gossiping around the locker room—or external—fans and followers seeing something that isn't there. My approach to handling each will need to be different. I'm not in any of the videos, just a word or two, a few seconds of me holding a puppy in the last one we posted. Almost all of them are just Varg. Solo.

My guess is that it's the guys pulling his chain even when they know there's nothing there, and the gossip slinking through the team and the coaching staff until it hit the big office. But I need to be sure.

I don't bother watching the footage, although Vic's voice is still chatting away as I pull up the comments. I don't have to scroll very far before I see the first insinuation that we're a couple.

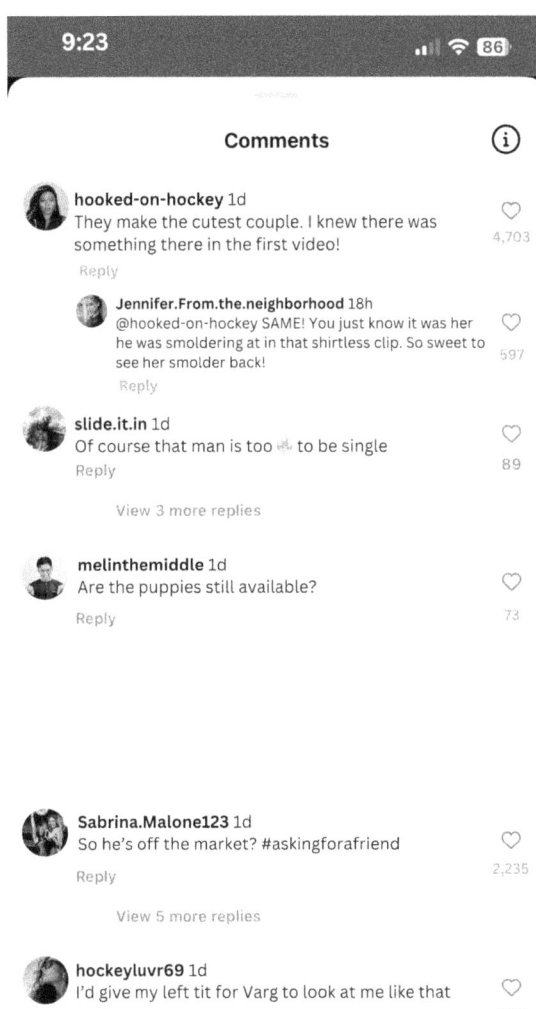

9:23

Comments ⓘ

hooked-on-hockey 1d
They make the cutest couple. I knew there was something there in the first video!
Reply ♡ 4,703

Jennifer.From.the.neighborhood 18h
@hooked-on-hockey SAME! You just know it was her he was smoldering at in that shirtless clip. So sweet to see her smolder back!
Reply ♡ 597

slide.it.in 1d
Of course that man is too 🏒 to be single
Reply ♡ 89

View 3 more replies

melinthemiddle 1d
Are the puppies still available?
Reply ♡ 73

Sabrina.Malone123 1d
So he's off the market? #askingforafriend
Reply ♡ 2,235

View 5 more replies

hockeyluvr69 1d
I'd give my left tit for Varg to look at me like that
Reply ♡ 980

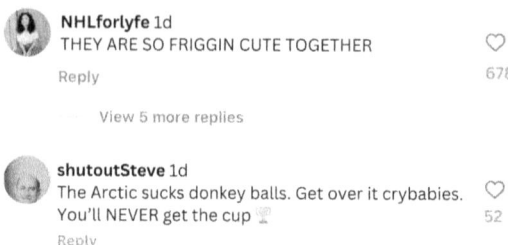

NHLforlyfe 1d
THEY ARE SO FRIGGIN CUTE TOGETHER ♡
Reply 678

View 5 more replies

shutoutSteve 1d
The Arctic sucks donkey balls. Get over it crybabies. ♡
You'll NEVER get the cup 🏆 52
Reply

I roll my eyes at the last one. Trolls will troll no matter what, and I've seen enough to confirm that the talk isn't just from the team. I'll need to tackle this publicly. I'm just unsure if I can go the route of setting Varg up on a few public dates, or if I need him to put out a statement. I open the video again and see the comment count has gone up again. And it's the tiny detail I missed the first time around, missed because I didn't pry further than the initial thread, that has me squaring my shoulders and sucking in a fortifying breath.

Victor Varg has liked every. Single. Comment.

And now I have to murder him.

"THERE'S A WOMAN HERE FOR YOU," my mother vibrates in the kitchen as she passes along the information.

Maria Varg does not look old enough to have three children in their thirties, but I can't argue with the year on my birth certificate. We all have the same dark blonde hair and hazel eyes, although Anna has curls like nobody's business. Erik and I get waves when things get a little long, but nothing like the Shirley Temple corkscrews that our older sister beats into submission. Although the way my mother wiggles her eyebrows as she grins at me makes me wonder if she's still a middle schooler instead of nearing sixty. I'm a grown adult with a bank account and a job. It's possible I could want some privacy.

There was a time in my childhood—when my brother first got sick—when I would have given up almost anything to have her take an interest in my life, to chat about any girls that had caught my eye, ask how my grades were doing. I don't blame her. Having a kid who needs multiple rounds of chemo and numerous surgeries, all while facing the loss of his dream, can't be easy for anyone. Let alone a single mother. Anna was already in college and had a fancy internship no one wanted to ruin for her. Erik had enough on his plate with the cancer, so it was just me and mom.

I learned quickly to smile and tell her I was fine. Fine is relative. I didn't have cancer, and I had made it to the juniors, the USHL. I was absolutely fine. Just somewhat invisible.

Now sometimes it feels like she's been trying to make up for those years of distance. She pries like it's an Olympic sport and she's taking home the gold come hell or high water.

"She's pretty." Mom's brows wiggle again, and I can see the questions behind her irises. She's like a pressure cooker, ready to pop.

"I know. All my women are pretty." I slide the juice carton back into the fridge and eye the Tupperware with today's date on it. Pasta. It's always pasta before games. Different shapes, different sauces, different veggies. Still pasta.

There's a smack to the back of my head and I grin, closing the fridge.

"I only meant that I see all women as beautiful in their own unique ways." I press a kiss to my mother's temple. "Don't worry, mom. I'm not a giant, superficial asshole. Just a little one." I wink at her and she rolls her eyes right back.

"You're too charming for your own good," she says. "So who is she?"

I have no idea who's at my door. I'm not expecting anyone and the only women who drop by unannounced are women my mother loves. Quinn, my brother's fiancée, and her best friend Jen. Quinn rarely comes over without Erik. They're pretty much super-glued to each other, and I usually meet somewhere away from the house so that my mother doesn't get any ideas like the one she's clearly having now. About marching us down the aisle and drowning us in rose petals. My mother means well, but she gets a little overzealous at the idea of her babies finding their true loves.

"Well, seeing as she's out there and I'm in here, I'm not sure who she might be."

I have a guess, though, because 1) she has to be someone from the team or team office if she has my address—I learned the hard way to keep it unlisted—and 2) she clearly knew the right things to say to get into my house and past my mother. Any obvious slip up, and my mom would have had the police escort her from the front gate.

My brain trips over itself, scrolling through a million images of the woman I *wish* was in my front entry, but I know better than to assume. My best guess is Sadie, the dark-haired, darker-eyed assistant trainer. My balance was off at practice yesterday and she's probably here to follow up with some exercises to ensure there's nothing serious.

Sadie is the most junior trainer and we all know she's the one sent to hunt us down if it requires a drive. If she's here in an official capacity and has showed up in her Arctic gear, mom would let her in, even without an explanation. And Sadie's sweet. Cute in a quiet, tutor-the-football-captain kind of way. She just isn't the woman I want to be in my entryway, and not because the trainers are secretly sadists.

"Don't keep her waiting. It's rude," my mother says, "I raised you better than that." She nudges me toward the door.

My mother is tall, but not nearly as tall as me and Erik, so I make a show of standing my ground as she pushes harder.

"I'm going," I tell her. "Don't forget eavesdropping is rude, too."

"I would never." The mock outrage is accompanied by a wink. Eavesdropping might not be my mother's style, but she'd definitely just waltz into the room and stare at us like a sideshow attraction. She wouldn't even pretend to be looking for something or clean. She'd just watch us, probably with a snack. Not popcorn or pretzels either, probably cantaloupe wrapped in prosciutto or Brie baked in puff pastry. She's a classy lady.

I make my way down the hallway and let out a sigh. This house really is too big for just me and my mother, but I wasn't thinking much about property size when I bought it. I was more concerned with having a place before preseason training started. Maroni's wife is a realtor, and she showed me three basically identical houses—ones that looked remarkably like her own home—in the same neighborhood as several of the other Arctic players.

Maybe when I put in an offer and got a home inspection and signed the closing paperwork, I was imagining having my whole family gathered around my dining room table for thanksgiving dinner. Or Christmas. Or, more likely, a Fourth of July barbecue, considering we're usually playing games during the holiday season.

Not that mom or I cook, but Anna is passable in the kitchen and her wife is a goddess with baked goods. Erik can handle making sandwiches, but Quinn is a fantastic chef. I thought of the house as aspirational. A place where our fractured family could come back to each other. We're getting closer every day, even if we're not quite there yet.

The curve of the grand staircase comes into view, and standing under the giant abstract light fixture is a woman staring daggers in my direction.

"Hello kitty cat," I lean my shoulder against the door frame and cross my arms over my chest. "Follow me all the way home?"

Did I say daggers? The look she sends me is a flamethrower or a bazooka, ready to separate my skin from my bones and reduce me to ash. I grin wider.

"I'm not complaining. I always knew the cat distribution system worked in mysterious ways."

"You insufferable, egotistical, pig-headed—" frothing. She's frothing with rage as she mirrors my pose, crossing her arms over her chest, too. It plumps her tits nicely but, ever the gentleman, I keep my eyes up and on hers.

"Now, now," I almost let out the laugh that's bubbling up in my chest "It's rude to call me names in my own house. What if my mother heard you call her precious boy all those vile things?"

My mother would probably laugh her ass off. She'd ask

why I deserved it and, while I enjoy pissing off Tristan Grant—enjoy seeing her eyes flash like hazard flares and her cheeks flush with rage—I'm not sure what I did this time. Or what I ever did to make her react like I just dragged my sock-covered feet across a few hundred feet of carpet before giving her one hell of a static shock.

"Your mother?" Apparently, that got through to her. She frowns, lips twisting sideways as if she's chewing on the tender inside of her cheek. Not that I'm staring at her mouth.

"The woman who let you in," I say, and Tristan looks away.

"That was your mother?"

I nod. "She lives with me."

A very unladylike snort. "Isn't that what neck-bearded losers say when they still live in the basement?" A hand comes up to cover her mouth. "Ohmygawd forget I said that. It was incredibly rude."

I drag a hand up my throat and scratch at the stubble I haven't shaved today. It rasps under my touch and when Tristan meets my eyes again, I grin wider.

"You might have me on the neck beard," I say, "but my big boy room isn't in the basement. It's on the second floor. Wanna see it?"

"No." Her glare is scalding hot, but the blush is still there and her throat bobs as she swallows.

I push off the wall to step closer and I watch her shoulders come up around her ears. This woman is so tense she could turn coal into diamonds with her bare hands. It's half the reason I fight with her. No one should be this wound up. Not without good reason.

I could give her a reason. A toe-curling, sheet-gripping, name-gasping reason.

No, I couldn't. Not without risking bodily harm. My kitty cat has claws, and she'd happily sharpen them on my spleen. Good thing I like the risk.

"All you have to do is ask," I say. "It's okay to give into your overwhelming attraction to me. I can't help my animal magnetism."

Tristan mutters something under her breath that I can't quite make out, but the flashing eyes are exactly what I was going for. It makes sense; I suppose. I play at an elite level of a brutal sport. Of course I enjoy playing with fire and risking dismemberment. I'm in some form of pain almost every hour of every day. Some part of me has to enjoy that at least a bit.

I know I'm a sick puppy when I lean into her personal space to say, "I won't tell anyone, kitty cat."

She snarls this time. An actual growl of sound paired with a curl of her red-painted lips. Heat floods my body, a familiar weight settling low in my abdomen. It would be easy to lean forward and cover her mouth with mine. I want to. If for no other reason than to feel her fire against my skin. I wonder if she'd bite, draw blood, prick me with her nails, or if she'd melt into the wall of my chest.

As it turns out, her nails *are* sharp, but instead of pressing into the muscles over my shoulders or tracing the length of my back, she has one finger shoved into my sternum as she practically hisses her response.

"You. Absolute. Bastard." A poke punctuates each word. "You're so full of shit your eyes are brown."

Actually my eyes are Hazel. I open my mouth to tell her so because apparently I lack any form of self-preservation with this woman.

"Don't even start," she hisses. "I *know* they're Hazel. It's an expression."

Seeing this woman spitting mad is doing things to me. I'm torn between shifting my hips so she can't see what things I mean, and wondering if that will draw her attention down. Am I ashamed of being attracted to her? No, not at all. Am I aware that despite all my teasing, despite her flushed cheeks and blown pupils, despite the way her breath catches at my flirting, she has slammed every single door closed as I cracked it open? Yes. Very. The tent in my pants takes our interactions from casual flirtation to the very edge of a line that I refuse to cross without explicit permission.

I decide to go for a distraction as I tug the hem of my shirt out to obscure her view. "It's okay kitty cat. I know you can't help but stare into my eyes every chance you get. Obviously you know they're hazel."

I open my eyes wide and tip my head down so our gazes can lock into place. I'm sure I look like Quinn's students when she makes them draw self-portraits, trying to see their eye color in the hand mirrors she gives them. The fury is still there in Tristan's eyes. It's scorching in its intensity, but her pupils expand and contract and I swear there's a small amount of amusement trying to break through. I will myself not to reach for the threads and tug until she unravels. I had adjusted without being caught. That was the only goal. Now it's time to let her say her piece. She came here for a reason.

"Victor."

It's supposed to be a warning, but the way she breathes my name into the inches between us has my dick twitching and my heart hammering against the cage of my ribs. It sounds like an invitation, and I want to accept.

It's not though.

I step back and run a hand through my hair before opting for my regularly-scheduled, easygoing grin.

"What do you need, Tristan?" *How can I help?*

There's a pause, as if she doesn't understand my words. She stands in my Italian marble foyer, under a chandelier someone probably spent a gazillion dollars on, and outshines all of it, her chest heaving as she sucks in air. I'd give her just about anything in my power. All she has to do is ask.

"What brings you to my humble home?"

The snort is a good sign. At least my words are getting through. This home is ostentatious as hell and very in-your-face about it. Maybe after this season I'll put it on the market. Having my mother live with me is a great idea when our away schedule is so intense that I'm barely home enough to understand how to work my full entertainment system, but the team also has people for that. Pet sitters, house sitters, plant sitters. They hooked me up with my chef and housekeeper and landscapers. I could downsize to a two-bedroom apartment that I could put together the way *I* want.

"I had a last-minute meeting with Bob Seever," she says and the heat pours out of me so fast it's hard to breathe. Last-minute meetings are reserved for emergencies. For players packing their bags, being sent to the minors, being benched. The videos are doing well. Everyone thinks so. Does Bob not agree? Does he blame her? Is she in trouble? Are we done? I'm spiraling.

"I can talk to him," I say, the words coming out with little conscious thought. "I'll set the record straight."

Bob has always liked me, and I know he likes the points I put up for the Arctic night after night. There's a reason I have a C on my jersey. It isn't just because I play well. The guys look up to me. Management respects me. I can fix this, whatever it is.

"You've done enough." There's venom in her voice and I frown, lost.

I have done everything she and Chris have asked of me. I've filmed, posted, and interacted. I've made myself friendly and available to fans. Approachable. Isn't that the brief? What could have gone so wrong that she had a meeting with the big cheese? So wrong that she stormed the gates at my front door? Because as much as I didn't *want* to plaster myself all over social media, I'd be lying if I said I wanted out. That has significantly more to do with Tristan than anything else. If I thought I could extend our time together beyond the videos, then maybe I'd be fine with calling it quits, but I know she won't give me the time of day otherwise.

"Everyone thinks we're fucking," she hisses the words and I barely hold in my laugh. That's the problem? That's nothing. "You've been helping that little rumor along quite nicely."

This time I freeze. I have? I think back to the videos. To the first one where I walked fans through our pads and dressing for a game. How I couldn't help but preen at the rich flush that bled across her pale skin. To watching her cheeks hollow as she sucked on the same glass I'd rolled over my tongue as we made smoothies at Magic Mangoes. To the memory of her cradling a soft yellow puppy as her pink lips drew my gaze like a magnet. To the erection that is still clinging to life as she stares daggers at me in my foyer.

If she's mad that my attraction has been obvious, she's a little late to the game. It's been there in each meeting. My teammates know she's the quickest way to get a rise out of me. My family, Quinn, and Jen have all made comments about our chemistry. The comment section on each of our videos just assumes we're together. This cannot have been news to anyone with even half of a functioning brain. And Tristan Grant is dangerously smart.

"You basically told them we are."

I shake my head because no; I haven't. I would *never* do that to her. To any woman. To any *person*. There's nothing wrong with a healthy sex life, but I would never lie about my conquests. I don't need to, despite going almost a year between sexual partners. In fact, I've done the opposite and vehemently shut down the rumors among my teammates.

"I haven't," I say and it's Tristan closing the space

between us this time, and of course my cock sits up to say hello. Dumb fucker. "I wouldn't!"

"You've liked every single comment that assumes we're together!" The huddling whisper is gone, her volume rising to fill the vaulted ceilings. "Everyone and their cat knows what that means."

Did I? Do they? I shake my head again.

"You told me to interact with the comments to boost the post. So that more people see it. To build a sense of community with the team's followers."

Long fingers press into the skin across her forehead. She's rubbing just above her eyebrows, hard enough to turn the tips of her fingers milk white. Okay, maybe I can see what she's saying, but I swear I was only following directions. I thought some part of her knew she was playing up our chemistry when she left herself in our most recent video.

"I told the guys we aren't dating and aren't sleeping together," I offer, but she's not upset about that. I sent a message I didn't mean to send, but I still did it. "I'm sorry Tristan. I never meant for it to be misunderstood."

The fight seems to deflate out of her as her shoulders drop and her chin hits her chest.

"I told Bob there's nothing there, and I think he took my word for it. I'll draft a statement for you and we can think about putting it out just so everyone is clear. I think that's the best option. It might even have the effect of bringing in other followers who want to see for themselves. This could work."

She isn't talking to me anymore, running through her

own options. Her eyes meet mine and she offers me a small smile. "you can remind the guys that there's nothing between us, too. That'll help. Or we can set you up on a date with someone."

"No," I say, stomach turning at the idea of a blind date set up for me by the woman who has captured my interest. No thank you.

Tristan waves her hand as if my opinion here doesn't matter. "Right, you don't really date during the season. Okay. A statement about our utter lack of anything should be sufficient."

For a moment, I'm caught on the idea that she's noticed that I don't date. That maybe she keeps track of my female friends. I'm conveniently ignoring the part where she was going to set me up with someone.

"I'll put out a statement that we aren't fucking."

"That we aren't *anything*," she stresses.

"That we aren't dating."

Her blue eyes narrow, cutting through me like shards of glass, and I stare resolutely back. I can't put out a statement that isn't true. There's *something* between us. Chemistry, attraction, magnetic pull. Whether or not we act on it, it's still there, growing between us like a little weed. Taking every resource to grow bigger and stronger.

"There's a no fraternization policy." Tristan wets her lips with her tongue, and I shouldn't be following the movement, but I can't stop myself. "Mr. Seever was all too willing to remind me you're irreplaceable, but I'm not."

Fuck Bob Seever.

"I don't want to be a social media coordinator my

whole life. I thought this project would be my chance to show the organization that I can take on a bigger marketing role, but that can't happen if I lose my job because they think we're fraternizing."

"They can't punish you for me," I say, but even as the words leave my mouth, I know I'm wrong. Just because it isn't right doesn't mean it won't happen. I have a multi-million-dollar, multi-year contract. Tristan would be significantly easier to replace in terms of cost. Job proficiency wouldn't even come into play. I'm good at my job too.

"They have before," she says, the words so quiet I almost think I imagine them.

"I'll fix it," I tell her and it's a promise—an oath—because I created this mess and I will be the one who puts it right. I will not be another burden to this woman. To anyone. "Let me fix it. I promise I will."

She pushes up onto her toes, her hand pressing against the thud of my heart, and then her lips feather across my cheek. I cup her elbows on instinct and almost turn my head, wanting to draw her mouth to mine, but I can't. Not after everything she just told me. The door is firmly shut now, locked and dead-bolted, and I have instructions to stay away. There might as well be laser security criss-crossing the threshold, just in case. Her thumb wipes the spot she just kissed, but it's too late. I think I'll feel that one platonic press forever. I hope I do.

"Thank you, Vic."

I don't notice her leaving. I don't hear the snick of the lock catching on my heavy front door. I don't move a muscle until my mom pokes her head back into the foyer and asks what I'm doing. Then my whole body jolts like I've stuck my finger in a light socket and, for a moment, I want to tuck my head into my mother's shoulder and cry like a kid. Robbie was wrong. I don't just want Tristan Grant. I think I might have actual feelings for her. And there's nothing I can ever do about that.

WE STOP short of drafting an actual statement. Despite my telling him it wasn't necessary, Vic paid a visit to Bob Seever and said something to assure him we were on the up-and-up. I have no idea what he said—Vic would not to tell me on his own, and I refuse to show how much it bothers me he didn't by asking outright—but he's assured me that everything is fine.

I also don't know what he said to his teammates, but in the last week we've had some additional players tag along to our filming. If their smiles are a little extra wide, if they spend a little extra time glancing from me to Vic... well, boys are dumb. What did I expect?

The comments haven't stopped, but Vic responds to as many as he can instead of liking their posts. Is he flat out denying there's anything between us? Not really, but he draws the focus time and time again back to the video itself. He talks about the community programs, tells fans he hopes to catch them at the next home game, makes comments about how if he *were* in a relationship, he'd want it kept private. Either way, I'm not concerned about being ousted from my job.

To be fair, I wasn't all that worried by the time I left Varg's house. My elevated heart rate? In his fancy-as-fuck foyer? That was because of rage. Not the way his biceps popped as he crossed his arms, or the way the strong cords in his neck moved as he swallowed. And okay, fine, the heat in his hazel eyes.

We film some partner drills with Robbie Oakes. He glowers more than he speaks, but the appeal is there and the videos double most of our other engagements, not including the puppy video. The guys are competitive, something I knew from spending even a little time with the team, but Oakes and Varg take it to another level. When Vic tells the camera they started working on one-timers—taking shots right off the pass—as kids, I know we have winning footage.

They start simple, tight to the net and emphasizing the sweeping motion of their sticks. They offer pointers for the shooter—hands out and away from the body for leverage, proper alignment with knees over toes, a snap of the hips for power as they send the puck into the back of the net. Then they back up, covering more and more distance with each slapshot. The filming devolves when the guys take turns rushing each other after each pass. I know there's contact in hockey, but they devolve into wrestling moves I *know* are not league-sanctioned.

"It makes us move faster. Both to pass and shoot," Vic

tells the camera. "Not a lot of time to think on the ice. It needs to be instinct, muscle memory."

"The not thinking is why you're leading in goals. Not sure it's a fair competition when your brain doesn't work right to begin with," Robbie quips and then their gloves are on the ground as they grapple, but both are smiling.

Ólaffson films with us twice, something I wasn't expecting from the shy Icelander. He takes us through some goalie drills with Vic explaining each move for him, and then he walks us through his goalie gear. He's quiet enough that I have to get in close as he talks about his pads and blocker and glove. It's not his accent, hitting every letter of each word before rolling hard into the R sounds, it's the pauses he takes as he tries to work with his stutter that are so endearing. Our female followers think so too, and for one blissful week the focus is on the sweet, shy, hulk of a man who stands alone between the pipes on game day.

I feel a burst of pride as he talks about the artwork on his helmet. It's painted to look like a gyrfalcon, the national bird of his home and a fierce predator from the high arctic. There's pink on his cheeks as he explains that his little sister designed it for him, and I know the poor man will have to beat prospective dates off with his hockey stick for the foreseeable future.

Chris didn't want me to work with Ragnar for this series. He didn't think the guy could carry content. I had my doubts, too. I was wrong. Goes to show they shouldn't underestimate either of us.

I also can't help the warmth that spreads through my

body when I remember it was Vic who advocated for the goalie's chance to film. It was Vic who put in extra time helping Rags practice what he wanted to say and to find alternatives for the words that tripped him up, and it was Vic who stood right next to me with a smile to rival my own as we pointed the camera toward the Nordic mountain.

Spaeglin takes us to a local bowling alley, one owned by the same family for almost fifty years. It's candlepin bowling, played with a small ball and ten skinny pins that look like candlesticks. Each player gets three turns instead of two, and I lose track of the rules myself, but Spaeglin and Varg play frame after frame before taking on the ancient bubble hockey machine. The two argue about who gets to be team USA until Vic pulls rank and whoops the rookie into submission with his plastic team.

Spaeglin is the only one who sidles up to me and asks if I'm dating the captain, although he doesn't use the word dating. An icy stare—combined with a thump to the back of the head from Varg—is enough to have him offering me a sheepish grin and a shrug of his over-wide shoulders.

I'm not concerned. Especially not after Chris calls me into his office and tells me I'm heading on the road with the team. Management wants to show that the men can still be good, wholesome, upstanding citizens, even when in Las Vegas. I never travel with the team, and I'm not sure I want to this time, but I do feel confident that they'd never send me if they thought I was fucking their star player.

Unless it's a long con to give me the boot... but they wouldn't have to go through the motions of getting me a hotel room and a seat on the chartered plane. Bob would have just sent me packing that day in his office.

At least that's what I tell my siblings when I break the news to them. I'll be gone for just about 48 hours.

Palmer, Mads, and Hayley are incensed that I'm leaving them with less than a day's notice. They want my phone GPS on to track my whereabouts, texts when I board and land, and get to the game, and the hotel and dear god don't get kidnapped and trafficked like some dateline special. When I point out that I'll be surrounded by twenty-some professional athletes, not including coaching staff, and it's doubtful anyone will get anywhere near me even in Sin City, Joey tells me that if I come home married, she'll disown me. I try not to laugh so hard that I fall off my couch.

If I'm not supposed to *fraternize* with a player, I definitely can't marry one.

Not that I'm going to.

"I'm going to do my job, get some footage, eat the food the team provides, and go to bed. I won't be socializing, let alone wedding anyone," I tell my siblings as they perch on any surface they can find in my apartment.

Max nods as he opens one of my granola bars and takes a huge bite. "Yeah, you don't want them to think you're there to babysit them." When five sets of female eyes narrow in his direction, he adds, "You don't want to become *persona non grata*. You'll never get them to work with you again."

"I'm sorry," his twin rolls her eyes, "did I miss the day

you joined the NHL? I wasn't aware they drafted baseball boys."

Max is talented enough to go pro—I think—and I purse my lips, wondering if I need to intervene. But as his twin it's Madison's job to keep him humble and grounded. Also, I think she might be defending me.

"Superstition is superstition," Max says around another mouthful. "Better hope they don't lose."

Palmer smacks him with one of my sequined throw pillows, something I know like a vengeful bitch.

"I've been working with these guys for a while now. I doubt they'll even notice I'm there," I say, full of confidence and zero fucks to give.

But four hours later, when I get to the private airstrip, it turns out I was actually full of delusion. My bravado leaks out of me like I was punched full of little holes because my baby brother was right. It turns out that hockey players are superstitious and joining them on this trip is just different enough from the status quo that it has most of the guys on edge.

It doesn't matter that it's already dark, and that the team won't be landing in Las Vegas until almost midnight, players are expected to represent the team whenever they travel. That means I am too. I appreciate the armor of my suit and heels as I face down two dozen men watching me with wide eyes. I don't mind when they fear me. It gets results, but I'm overwhelmed with the realization that this five-hour plane ride is just the start of what might be a very uncomfortable trip. It's one thing to be the hardened bitch, unwilling to let them toe the line for a few hours at a time. It's another to expect them to maintain their good behavior for a full two days.

Heads pitch toward each other and the soft murmur of hushed conversation reaches my ears as I calculate how many hours it will be until I can lock myself into my hotel room. We aren't staying on the strip, but the team has rooms for the players, coaching staff, and trainers. I glance to my right to see if Sadie is on the plane. I'd welcome another female and a familiar face, but it's just our two primary trainers, both already tucked into tablets wearing noise-cancelling headphones.

"Listen up." Head Coach Noris' voice cuts into the conversation. "We have a guest joining us on this vacation." There's a rumble of laughter. "She's here to do a job just like we are. I expect no funny business. We focus on Vegas. We don't let them bait us. We don't give them the power play. We protect Rags and we put the biscuit in the damn basket. Understood?"

There's a chorus of "yes sirs" as Noris takes his seat at the front of the plane.

"Sit anywhere sweetheart and pay no attention to my boys," he tells me and then he and his assistant coach pull out a team laptop and turn their attention to it. I've been dismissed.

There's an empty row between the coaches and support staff and all the players. I push my suitcase in front of me, trying not to notice that most of the players are watching my every move like I'm a rabid chihuahua with an injured paw.

I make it to the empty seats and turn my attention to

my luggage so I can store it in the overhead compartment, but a pair of large, tanned hands cover mine on the handle.

"Welcome aboard, kitty cat," the low voice says near my ear. "Glad to have you with us."

I can't stop the snort that leaves my nose and my eyes snap to Vic's. Not a single one of these guys seems happy to have me, and I can't imagine Victor Varg is any different.

"Don't mind the team." His breath fans over my neck as he leans down to lift the case. I turn to face him as he slams the overhead door and I'm nose to nose with the silk tie and crisp white shirt he has paired with his charcoal gray suit. Literally. If I move even a millimeter, I'll be touching him.

I chance a glance at the rest of the players, all watching us

"I think they'd throw me out at thirty-thousand feet if given half the chance."

"Nah," his grin is blinding up close. Perfect shiny teeth all in a row. He must be religious about wearing a mouth guard. Or he has a fantastic dentist who does some mean work with implants. "They just don't know you like I do."

He steps out into the aisle and winks before moving toward the back of the plane and his seat next to Oakes.

"N-nice to see you again Ms. T-t-t... Ms. Grant." Ragnar Ólaffson says from the row behind me, and I give him a small smile and a wave of my fingers before I take my seat.

As the cabin lights dim and the plane taxis to the runway, it occurs to me I might be glad Victor Varg is here too.

thearctic.hockey
The Stand, Quarry Creek

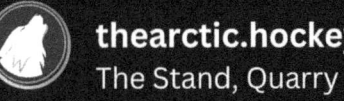

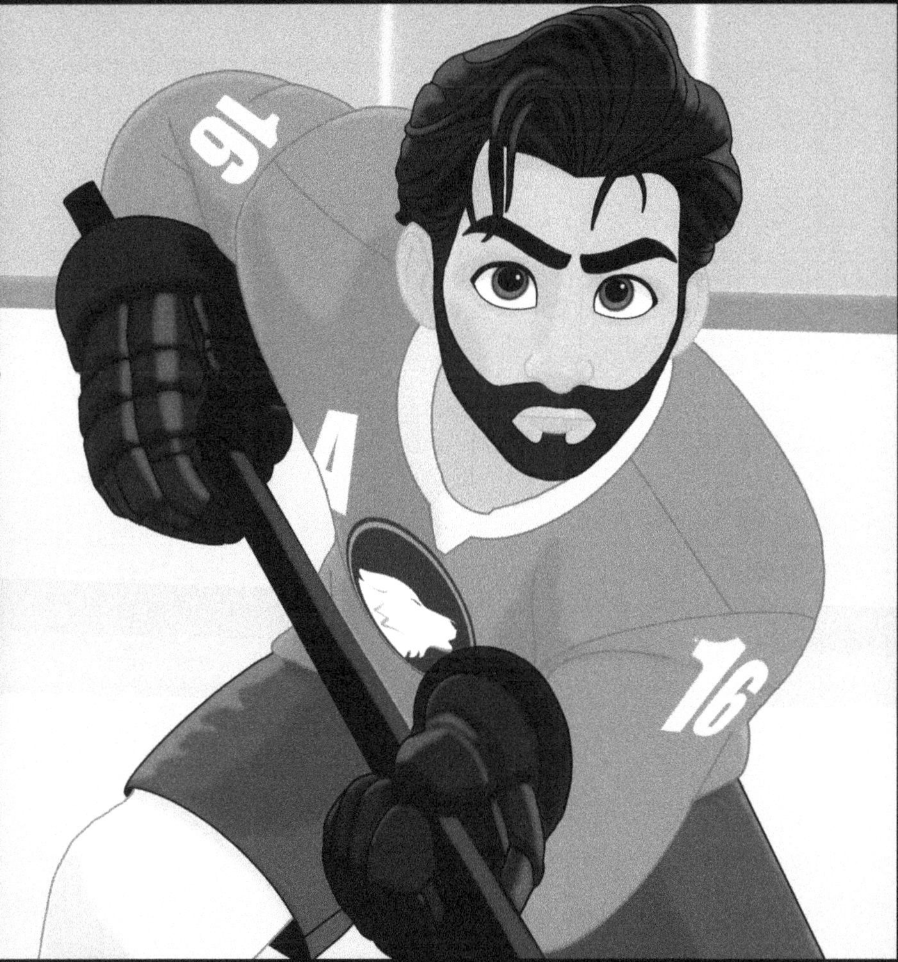

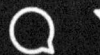

97,220 likes

thearctic.hockey did you know our captain and assistant captain go way back? They started together as mites at age seven. No wonder they seem telepathic on the ice... more

Numba1Fan Let's be honest. Now they're even cuter!!! 26.5k

View all 1,044 comments

Add a comment...

IT'S A PACKED CROWD, not that we expected any different. Vegas has sold out every home game since their inaugural season and just because casinos and local businesses buy up many of those seats, that doesn't change the press of bodies lining the glass and the electric feel in the arena. Vegas isn't the loudest place we play, not by a long shot—that honor goes to Carolina—but between the light show and crush of fans, there is something intense about being here. A pounding rhythm inside the cavity of my chest as the clock counts down until the end of warmups.

Robbie keeps trying to catch my eye as we skate loops in our zone, sending shots at Rags so he can get a feel for the puck. I'm ready to take shots, to practice my approach and my follow through, trying to slip past the wall that is Ólaffson's chest. I'm just feeling off tonight and my head isn't in the right spot. Maybe a goal, even just for practice, will set it right.

There's a reason most guys are superstitious heading

into a game. A reason they went still and quiet when the blond head stepped onto the plane, not even having to duck the way a good number of us do. There's a worry that any change will upset the flow. A pretty woman among two-dozen testosterone-flooded males is a distraction. I know Robbie thinks Tristan is the reason my head's in the rafters. He's been trying to pin me down to talk about it since she stared up at me with big blue eyes as I almost dropped her suitcase.

Ironic that the man who barely strings two sentences together can't seem to stop trying to talk to me about our social media manager. Or, more accurately, about the influence she has on my thoughts and feelings. I'm not even trying to deny the fascination—or the feelings—but they don't matter here. Robbie can try to pep-talk me all he wants. There's no move to make on Tristan Grant. No move that doesn't leave her worse off than where we started. No move that doesn't harm her.

It doesn't matter that I can't stop looking for her in the sea of dark jerseys, despite knowing I won't find her. It doesn't matter that I crowded her in the aisle of a chartered plane despite telling myself I was going to give her space. She pursed those red-painted lips, tiny strain lines furrowing at the corners as every guy on the plane went silent staring at her, and I knew beyond any doubt that she felt alone and unwelcome. I also knew she was enough of a professional to find her seat, do her job, and then go home, all while feeling uncomfortable and out-of-place.

Acknowledging her meant the other guys relaxed. Meant she could get her game footage done with a minimum of hair-pulling and threats. And it wasn't just for her, either. Acknowledging and welcoming the pretty kitty cat onto our plane helped put the guys at ease, too. My job as team captain isn't to be the best player on the ice. It isn't to score the most goals or to put up the most assists. It isn't to make the headlines or rake in the highest sponsorships. My job is to keep the team together as a cohesive unit. To lead by example. To set the tone of each game and practice and appearance.

It's something I'm practiced at. Pushing down any stray worry or discomfort in order to make things easier for the people around me. It's a skill that always came naturally, but one I also honed to a razor-sharp edge during Erik's diagnosis and treatment.

Be scared on your own time, Varg. Your twin is the one fighting for his life.

Hold it together, buddy. You have Robbie and his girl, Vera, and the other guys on the team. Your mom has no one but you. Be the one she can count on, not another person she has to take care of.

I saw something once about glass children, kids born into families where a sibling has a chronic condition or disability. How they're often overlooked or their needs aren't met because their sibling takes up the time and attention. I looked into it after a girlfriend called me one during the argument that ended our relationship.

"What do you even *want*, Vic?" she'd yelled at me. "Do you even know? Or are you so busy trying to balance everyone else that you don't go after the best thing to ever happen to you?"

She meant herself. Our relationship. Two of my team-mates had proposed. Another was having a baby. She wanted a ring and a promise and thought I was too afraid to take what I wanted—aka kick my mother out of my house and move her in. She thought I needed to be goosed in the right direction.

She was wrong.

But after she blamed it on my horoscope—"you aren't a Libra? Cancer maybe?"—she decided it was because of my brother. Because I hadn't had my needs met enough as a child. A child whose twin developed bone cancer in his left tibia.

The research, while valid in its own right, didn't fit me or Erik or our situation at all. First, my brother wasn't diagnosed until sixteen. That means over a decade and a half of a childhood where I had everything I needed, no matter how hard my mom worked to make it happen. Second, when Erik *was* diagnosed, I wasn't ignored or forgotten about—no matter how unintentional it is for most of those families—because *I'm* the one who made the choice to be as easygoing as possible. It wasn't my leg and my future. It wasn't my child. I didn't need to add my complaints to the pile of shit our life became overnight.

I kept playing.

I got drafted.

I could do whatever was necessary to ease the way for other people. Why not?

The relationship ended that day. Not even because I walked away from her—I wasn't invested enough to care one way or the other—but because she was fed up with me. So I went back to my regular life of ibuprofen with a side of caffeine, pasta by the pound, endorsements that only asked me to strip to the waist for the occasional photo shoot. Easy peasy fresh-squeezed lemonade.

So yeah, if Robbie is trying to corner me to make me admit once again that I want Tristan Grant splayed across my sheets as I make her moan, but also that I want her smiling and tucked into my couch as I bring her a mug of hot tea and a warm blanket while we watch British baking shows... well, it doesn't matter much now does it. Because even though I could still try to install the woman on my couch even if she was out of a job—and I could supply her with anything she might need—Tristan is not the woman who'd say thank you and smile around her first sip of chai. Nope. If I impede her professional career, she'll castrate me with my skate blades on her way to fuck right out of my life forever.

"Vic," Robbie says as I glide past him, the clock now flashing down the last minute of the warmup, "You can't ignore me forever."

"I'm not ignoring you," I say, as if I haven't skated in the opposite direction almost every other time he's tried to pin me down today. Or locked myself in my single room at the Park MGM after morning skate under the guise of taking a nap instead of going to eat a mountain of carbs with him. I ate those alone on my king-sized bed thanks to room service. Something I'm sure I'll hear about later when the GM wants to know why I skipped team lunch.

"I'm not going to mention Tristan," he says and I lift my hand to give him the finger—something no one else will recognize since my gloves get in the way, but I know he reads my message loud and clear. "I was just going to tell you to look at the bin."

I know better than to fall for whatever he's doing, but my eyes are moving toward the penalty box before I can stop them, and there—I'm not sure how I missed her in the first place—is my kitty cat.

Between her white blonde hair and her light blue sweater, she glows like a radioactive dial on one of the World War Two watches the radium girls died for—Quinn was in charge of movie night the other month—and my mouth goes dry around my mouth guard.

"She's here?" Pelletier asks, skating over, eyes locked on my social media manager who still hasn't noticed that we're all three staring. Four, Spaeglin is on his way over, too.

Tristan almost never comes to games, and if she does, she sits in the box with the families. There are plenty of people collecting footage for her to use, and her primary focus is drumming up excitement. I've never seen her in the stands before, and I don't know how she got a prime seat at the last minute for an away game. I'm just grateful she did.

I skate toward the net and snag Rag's water bottle from the top, squirting a healthy stream of water into my parched throat. It's fine that she's here. It's good. Right? She's probably working.

"Cap," Spaeglin calls to me, "What is... she doing here?"

The pause tells me he almost called her Elsa. And I

would have high-sticked him myself if he had. Off the ice, of course. Where no one would see. It's apparently also my job to teach the infants on my team some manners. Later, if she asks, I'll tell her it was a move calculated to put my teammates at ease. It's not entirely a lie. There's a tremor weaving through Jack's voice and his blue eyes are wide as he stares out into the crowd. The kid is about as superstitious as they come. It won't be the real reason, but I'll go to my grave pretending Spags' nerves are why I skate over to the penalty box, my steps loose and unhurried, even as the clock counts down the last minute.

She doesn't look up until I tap the glass right in front of her face, and then I almost forget why I skated over because I've never seen her this casual before. Even when we film, she's in office clothes. Slacks, blouses, dresses. Her makeup flawless and her heels both tall and expensive. But here she is in front of me, blonde hair pulled back into a ponytail, wisps escaping to frame the pale, smooth skin of her cheeks. Her nose is pink from the cold. She's not in a jersey, but her sweater is Arctic blue and she's paired it with simple black leggings. Her feet are in those fuzzy brown boots again, and I don't think she's even wearing makeup.

She's fucking stunning.

"Hey," I call to her over the roar of the crowd. The fans on either side of her are watching us, mouths open in shock. It's not unheard of for players to interact with fans, but it's ballsy in someone else's arena. I doubt they recognize her as a member of our organization. She isn't in team gear. For all they know, she's one of them and I've skated over with my cockiest grin. So of course I follow it up with a pickup line.

"Come here often?"

Her brows furrow as she frowns at me and then glances side to side like I'm not Vic and she's not Tristan and as if there's anyone else I could be talking to.

"No," she says. I can't hear her, not over the crowd, but I can read the word on her lips as a hint of what might be a smile tries to break through. Her head shakes side to side and some more hair slips out around her face. If I wasn't seconds away from the buzzer and the national anthem, seconds away from—for all intents and purposes—a work event, I'd have a real problem on my hands. Popping a stiffy in front of twenty-thousand people should be the stuff of nightmares, but seeing her like this... casual, softer, almost like someone took their thumb and smudged out her hard edges... well it's almost enough to overcome decades of self-preservation. Almost.

A puck slides toward my skate and I lean down to scoop it into my glove. From the corner of my eye I see Robbie with his skates pointed my direction and his chin dropped to the center of his chest in a nod. I toss the puck, letting it flip and fall into the center of my black glove. Then, with the grin I know drives her crazy, I flip it up and over the solid glass that separates us.

Her eyes are wide as the guy behind her catches it and —with my pointed look spurring him on—reaches around her right shoulder to drop it into her lap. I can't read the expression in her gaze. There's a chance she's plotting my death with a creative use of the Zamboni and a pair of extra skate laces because I know what this looks like. I know it looks like a check in the "fraternization" column, but that's not why I just put her front and center, all eyes glued to the two of us.

I did it because when we win this game—not if, when —I will have made her the team's good luck charm. No more staring on the plane, no more worried whispers as she approaches the guys to film her segments. I will have made her belong, and the guys will follow her off the edge of the earth every time she travels with us.

She clutches the rubber disc in her hands, looking from it to me and back again. The timer hits zero, the buzzer goes, and warm-ups are over. I give her a wink and skate backward toward the bench, my feet curving apart and back together like I learned to do when Erik and I first started skating. She holds my gaze until she's far enough away that I can't make out the hint of a smile that curves her lips or the faint blush painting her cheeks.

I don't hear much of Coach's pre-game speech. I go through the motions as I fix a corner of tape that's pulling up on the handle of my stick. I give the guys the standard give-em-hell battle call that I do before all our games, but the words come on autopilot as Robbie grunts his agreement. We slap the shoulder pads of each of the guys as they file out into the tunnels again. And still it feels like my body is driving itself, like my mind is a million miles away, wrapped up in pink skin and glittering eyes. Robbie and I bump fists before his name is announced. I don't hear mine, but I count out fifteen seconds before I skate out.

I take my spot next to Robbie at center ice, slapping my

right hand across the front of my chest and turning toward the cameras along with Vegas starting line. He bumps his shoulder into mine. I bump back and when the opening lines of the national anthem echo in the arena; he leans into me, turning his head to whisper.

"I guess I was wrong."

I play his words over and over in my head, wondering where the change of heart came from. He's been so sure of my interest, of my attraction, and despite my many protests—I had little choice after Tristan asked me to put the rumors to bed—Robbie has pushed forward with his goal of making me face what he thinks I'm ignoring. Skating over to Tristan, flipping the puck over the glass, it doesn't matter how I justify my actions. That should have done anything *but* convince my best friend he's wrong.

The song ends and Robbie takes his fist and thumps it twice over his heart before pointing at the camera, something he does before every game he's ever played, starting when we were kids. The ref moves into position. The announcer says something unintelligible over the loudspeaker. I need to get my head back into the game, and fast.

It's going to take a miracle to manage it at all when Robbie meets my eyes and says, "You don't want that woman, Vic. It's more than that. You need her."

And now I also need to win for her.

I skate to the edge of the circle and look past Robbie and Ahlstrom to the blonde head sitting along the glass. She's focused on the ice now, and my nerves buzz with excitement. *Look at me*, I think. *Pay attention to me. Watch what I can do. For you.*

At the ref's command, Robbie puts his stick blade down on the ice. Vegas' center follows. I watch as the puck drops and Robbie lifts the other man's stick as he goes for it, sweeping it back. And then I don't have time to think about Tristan at all as we push towards Vegas' goalie, but I still swear I feel her eyes on me the entirety of my fifty-second shift.

IT ISN'T JUST A WIN, it's a blowout. I don't realize how hard my heart is pounding, how my adrenaline is flooding my veins, until I'm back at the hotel. I love hockey—I work for the team, after all—but there's something about watching the boys live that gets every nerve ending in my body vibrating like a nine on the Richter scale.

The seat was an impulse buy thanks to plane Wi-Fi. I'd been interested in how many tickets were still available, which led me down the second-hand rabbit hole. A single seat on the glass was too good to pass up. Especially at the listed price; still more than I want to think about, but less than I expected. It was probably available because most people don't go to games solo. I clicked buy before I could talk myself out of it and figured I'd eat the cost if I joined the press box or stayed at the hotel. Since travel isn't part of my contract, I got a nice bonus check from the team for making this trip. I put together all the video footage I'd need on the plane and during morning practice.

I also owe Hayley a chocolate croissant for sneaking comfortable clothes into my suitcase. I wasn't sure which would be worse: a business suit at the game, or my fuzzy cow pajamas. It might not have been Arctic gear, but the sweater and leggings were better—*"just in case you want to do something NOT work related"*—the note said when I pulled them out at and put them on. I can't even be frustrated that she went into my suitcase.

Now I'm standing in the hotel lobby, debating whether I want to order a late-night snack in my room or head to the bar for a quick drink, when I spot a familiar face. It shouldn't surprise me to see the players here when we share the same hotel. I'd assumed they'd either go out and celebrate or hit their mattresses since we have an early flight home. I had pegged Jack for the former category, sure he'd go find a pretty girl to snow with his puppy dog grin and blue eyes, yet here he is in the hotel lobby, waving at me. Nary a model in sight.

He's showered, hair still damp in the overhead lights, and he's underdressed by Vegas standards in a t-shirt and a pair of jeans, a baseball hat turned backward on his head. For a moment, I wonder if I can pretend not to see him standing there, but his wave gets bigger. He's calling something across the room, and he reminds me so much of my baby brother I don't have the heart to turn away.

Also, I'm *not* here to babysit these guys, but I know the team wants good, wholesome press. I could go nudge him toward a quiet night in. I'm not above wrangling him into a late-night bite with me to keep him out of trouble. We do *not* need a Roxanne repeat. Thank you. It took a monumental effort to rehab the kid's image after the model sent his unsolicited dick pics to numerous gossip sites.

"Hey lucky charm!" He gives up on the wave to cup his hands around his mouth. "Over here!"

He bounces toward me like a toddler who got into a bag of sugar. I try to put on my stern face, but it's been a long day and even I'm riding the high of the win.

"Lucky charm?" I ask when he's close enough for normal conversation.

"Are you coming out to celebrate with us?"

It hadn't occurred to me to spend time with the guys. I'm working. We have an early flight, and the tension was palpable when I boarded the charter plane to get here. I'll go to my grave before I'll admit it to him, but Max was right. There was a distrustful hush to the team when the change in plans became apparent. No matter how much I tell myself I'm not here to be their friend, I'm not here to gamble and play, there's still a dull ache that comes with feeling unwanted. Unwelcome.

It's the same way I felt at twelve when the other kids got wind of the fact that my dad had left. I don't mean the few vicious remarks about how I wasn't good enough for him to stay, or about how I drove my father away—pre-teen girls can be terrible humans. It was how friends pulled back, especially after I took over running the house. Invitations dwindled. Conversations hushed when I walked into a room. There was a wall that went up between me and my classmates. It hurt less when I stopped hoping for things to be different. It hurt less to focus my energy and time on Hayley, Palmer, Madison, Max, and Joey.

The same is true with the guys. Putting on my game face during work differs from feeling out of place and unwelcome during play.

"You have to," Jack says before I can give him any kind of answer. "Did you see the numbers Cap put up today? His best game of the season. He's never been so hot!"

Were the Arctic the dominant presence on the ice today? Yes. Was number twenty-five a huge contributing factor? Yes. Two goals and two assists are phenomenal, but that's not because of me. Vic leads the team in goals *and* assists. He's in the top five for both in the league, too. I have yet to see him miss a shootout goal. He dominates on the power play and routinely walks away a star player of the game—more often than not, first star. None of that is on me.

"Didn't you have a goal tonight, too?" I ask the nineteen-year-old and he grins, shaking gold hair out of his eyes.

"I did. Thank you for noticing." He pulls up the leg of his pants to show me a pair of turquoise socks covered in tiny citrus fruits. "But that's because of my lucky socks, not my girl sitting on the glass."

I've been in the locker room. My brother plays collegiate level baseball. I don't want to be anywhere near any item of clothing that played an entire game, soaking up sweat. It's automatic for me to step back to avoid the smell. I take an extra moment to realize I'm supposed to correct him about being Vic's girl. By the time I do, the chance is gone and Jack's grin is even wider. It's the same look Max gives me when he bests our sisters at anything.

"I'm not—" I try anyway, and the kid bulldozes straight through me.

"Cap was looking for you all warmup. I wasn't sure having a girl with us was a good idea. No offense. But if you keep his game like that, I'll get you a fucking jersey and we can ask to put you on the roster. Four fucking points. He was a fucking masterpiece."

"Language, Spags," a deep voice says and the rookie blushes scarlet, dropping his eyes to the ground with a mumbled "sorry, Cap," and I don't need to turn to know who's standing next to me.

I didn't need to hear his voice either, to know that Victor Varg is the one blocking out all the light. He towers over his teammate too, and I know Jack Spaeglin is at least an inch over six feet tall. It's not the size or the eclipse he creates that tips me off. It's a tingling that starts low in my spine and creeps up to fizz at the back of my skull, like my whole body has fallen asleep and now is just starting to wake up. A pins and needles awareness that leaves me breathless.

"Victor," I say with a nod, refusing to turn my head and look at the man. If just standing here is giving me heart palpitations, then goodness knows I shouldn't make any eye contact.

"Kitty cat," the man says, and I close my eyes as I try to calm my racing everything.

There is no reason for me to be reacting this way to Victor Varg. Sure, the man is attractive. Yes, I have eyes, but that's not a reason to feel like the temperature in this damn hotel has cranked up fifty degrees. Isn't it a thing that hotel rooms are supposed to have air conditioners that don't shut off? It must be the travel, and the time difference. God, these guys just played an intense hockey game after a red-eye flight and a three-hour time change. How are any of them awake right now? It must be adrenaline. They haven't crashed yet.

It must be the fact that it feels like it's past two in the morning that has me realizing that Jack Spaeglin walked away without me even noticing. Leaving me alone with his captain.

"Don't worry, he doesn't play in the lime socks. Just wears them to and from the rink," Vic says, and I almost don't remember the lucky sock comment and the recoil I experienced trying to get away from them.

"That's a relief," I say. "You didn't have to scare him off."

"I didn't," there's something in Vic's voice, a laugh maybe, and I make a production about looking around the lobby.

"He's not here, is he?"

Vic shrugs, his collared shirt pulls tight over his chest, and I swear I didn't mean to look, but now I can't help it. The top buttons are undone and there's the hollow of his throat and the cords of his neck, all wrapped up in tanned skin. And yes, okay, Victor Varg is one of the most attractive men I've ever encountered in real life. And yes, I know if circumstances were different, I'd let him yank me up so I could wrap my legs around his trim waist. I doubt we'd even need a wall. He could keep me there with just the strength in his arms.

But things aren't different. We still work together. I'd still be out of a job.

He's still the man who almost cost me that job last season.

"He did what he was supposed to do," Vic says and when I raise one eyebrow at him, he grins. "Come out with us tonight."

I'm shaking my head even as I feel my resolve waver.

"Come out with us."

"It's a bad idea."

It really is. The last thing the guys want is me hanging over their head like a nanny cam. Not that I'd tattle back to headquarters, but they don't know that. The last thing I need is more one-on-one time with this man standing next to me. Admitting that I want him is dangerous enough. Especially when I'm not stupid. I know he wants me, too. Of the two of us, I'm pretty sure I'm the one who will need to keep the lines clearly drawn. I trust Vic will respect my boundaries, but I need to set them. That I know.

"It's a great idea." He's closer now, the voice almost a murmur. Our height difference is the only thing that keeps him from pressing the words to my temple, my ear, my neck. There's a fine tremor that runs through my limbs at the thought, and I step away. I need to get some space. I need to climb him like a mother-fucking tree. Something. Anything.

"Victor."

"Tristan."

It feels like I've had the wind knocked out of me. Like the time I tried to coax seven-year-old Joey down the big slide at the park and she kamikazied off the top of the structure, pinning my seventeen-year-old body on the damp wood chips at the local playground. She'd laughed and run off like I wasn't lying there like a flattened pancake.

"The boys want to celebrate with their good luck charm."

"The *boys* don't even want me here," I correct.

"They're dummies, but even they know a good thing when they see it." I don't think we're talking about the team anymore.

"You promised." I remind him. In his foyer, he told me he'd take care of the rumors. This is not taking care of anything.

He hums something noncommittal, and I wonder how many people are watching us right now. The man who just handed the home team their asses, and a girl half his size who won't even look at him. I'm braver than this, meeting every single challenge head on. This isn't fear. This is self-preservation.

"You promised there was nothing going on between us."

"No," he says, "I promised I would fix the rumors."

"And then you singled me out in front of a packed arena."

He's closer now, a hand resting on the small of my back. His fingers span my entire waist as my eyes slip closed. I can feel the warmth of his palm through my sweater, heating my skin better than any fireplace ever has. I could step forward out of his touch, but I don't. I lean into it.

"And then I won," he says. This time, I feel his breath across my temple. He had to lean down for that. My resolve is hanging on by a frayed thread. Forget going out. He knows my job is on the line, but what happens in Vegas stays in Vegas, right? We could grab the nearest elevator and head to my room. I could have him just this once and no one would ever need to know.

"You belong to the team now," Vic says.

What am I doing? What am I thinking?

"Come out with us. Celebrate with us."

I can't lose my head here. I can't. I knew I'd have to be the one to hold firm.

"You're going to go rub your win in the city's face?"

I turn my head and my nose almost bumps his chin. There's a faint stubble there. I can see the tiny gold hairs growing in and I want to rub against him. Feel the rasp and the sting and the heat against my skin. In my bones.

"It's our duty as professional athletes." I can feel his lips move. I need to step back. "Come with us."

"Victor."

How many times have I said his name? I'm not even sure what I want to follow it up with.

Pin me to my mattress.

Make me forget this is a bad idea.

Be strong for both of us.

We can't do this.

"I know," he says, and this time his mouth brushes my

temple and I try not to shiver. "I feel it too, but I promise you can trust me. I won't put you or your job in jeopardy."

My laugh sounds suspiciously like a sob. I know I'm being ridiculous. I know my grudge is stupid and overblown, and I have nothing to worry about. There's no way he knew the trouble I got in when he refused to let me interview him and his twin. There's no way he ignored my calls, knowing that I was almost fired for not bringing them in. No way he knew that the reason I was the one to ask was because Chris assumed Vic would never say no to me. None of that is his fault. I *know* that.

I know that.

For the first time.

"This is a bad idea," I say, but even Vic can hear the difference in the words. I'm going to say yes.

"I'll take care of you, Tristan. Let your guard down. Come and have some fun."

I meet his eyes this time. Blues and greys and browns swirling with warmth and heat and something that looks a lot like affection.

"Just let me go change my clothes," I say beyond grateful that it wasn't just Hayley who snuck outfits into my suitcase, although maybe I should withhold thanks until I see the dress Palmer sent. Her taste runs short. And dipped in glitter.

"I'll wait here for you," Vic says and if it wouldn't send all sorts of mixed messages, I would kiss him for already holding my boundaries and not offering to come up with me. His fingers flex on my back, sliding around to cup and squeeze my hip before he drops it down to his side, shoving those long fingers into the front pocket of his jeans. My mouth goes drier than the Mojave. "Go fast, Tristan. I can't show up at the club without the team's good luck charm."

"Am I the team's?" I can't help but ask, "Or yours?"

A shudder runs through his big body and his pupils swallow his irises. My lips part as I suck in air.

"Don't ask me questions I'm not allowed to answer, kitty cat."

It takes all my self-control to walk to the elevators as if my panties aren't ruined. I feel his eyes on me the entire time.

**thearctic.hockey**
The Stand, Quarry Creek

64,981 likes

thearctic.hockey goalies often decorate their helmets with symbols close to their hearts. We got to see Ólaffson's up close and personal... **more**

goaliegurrrl I could eat him up.

11.2k

View all 732 comments

 Add a comment...

I'M EITHER the dumbest man alive or a genius. I don't have the blood in my brain to figure it out right now, and I'm not sure when I will. The same can be said for the guys because we apparently brought the team's social media manager to a strip club. I would lean towards idiots, except for the fact that she seems to be enjoying herself.

The Velvet is as if a strip club and a burlesque club had a baby. It has girls in fancy lingerie and smartly placed handheld accessories, but it also has private rooms and two smaller stages with poles. It's not like any of the other places I've been to in my time. And I know, I know, that makes me sound seedy and creepy and like I'm a first-rate predator, but it's hard to find any pro-athlete who hasn't been to at least a few. The team travels in groups, and not many places are open after the game ends.

At the start of my career, it was a good way to blow off steam. Contrary to popular belief, most kids getting drafted at eighteen don't have a lot of sex or dating experience. There's no time for either when every spare moment goes toward conditioning, skill practice, proper nutrition, and rest. Playing in the juniors may seem glamorous, but most players are living with host families and their goal is to be drafted into the pros.

It's after the contracts are signed, after the photos are taken, after training camp and preseason, that the rookies relax. Most of us head into the adult world with no concept of what to do with hundreds of thousands of dollars a year or the constant attention of the fans. A lot of kids let a little too loose, myself included. But the shine and appeal of all-night parties wears off.

Now I only go out to these kinds of places because I'm the captain and *someone* has to keep an eye on the team. As much as we'd love to say that losing Haine was no big deal —our record would indicate as much—the team has had to bust their asses. Haine left a hole behind when he totaled his car and his life. I'm not about to do that again because someone did something stupid when all he needed was a babysitter.

I'll admit that I should have done my due diligence before inviting Tristan to come with us. If I'd planned ahead, we could have seen a show—with clothes—or grabbed a drink, but my brain has been glitching since I saw her seated in the stands at the game. Time speeds forward until my head starts to spin and then it slows to a crawl. I blinked and was scoring a goal. Blinked again and the final buzzer sounded. A third time and there she was, standing across the lobby from me being chatted up by Spags.

"You're doing a great job keeping things friendly," Robbie says, falling onto the velvet seat next to me with all the grace of a demoed building going down. I tip my head back to keep Tristan in my line of sight as I look at my best friend. "I'm just saying. Kudos for not humping her like a caveman."

It takes effort to shrug my shoulders as if I don't care.

I do.

"I don't think the boys have seen a single dancer. They're just falling all over themselves to play with our shiny new friend." Robbie's trying to goad me into a response. I *know* he's trying to get me up and out of my seat. To claim my kitty cat as mine and mine alone, but I can't. It's not as simple as he thinks it is.

She looks stunning. I can't blame the guys for being starry-eyed, little hearts beating away in the centers of their pupils. I don't know what I expected her to change into, but it wasn't this tiny white scrap that reminds me of a nightgown. The fabric shines in the low lights, flowing over her skin like water as it drapes low enough to show the dimples over her ass. There are two slender ties across her narrow back. That's all that holds the entire thing together. If I snagged just one finger in the loop of that top bow, the entire thing would slip off her. I'm trying not to think about that too much.

"She's having a good time," I say instead because it's true. Her red-painted smile shows off the straight white gleam of her teeth. I've seen her throw her head back to laugh at something one of the guys has said no less than six times since we walked in the door, my palm *not* at the small of her back. If I get my hands on her bare skin, I'm not sure I'll be able to remember to keep things just friendly.

"It was a good idea inviting her to join us." Is Robbie still talking? I thought the man barely knew how. "Maybe they'll send her on the road with us again."

And maybe that's an awful idea. Maybe I stood in the hotel lobby and willed myself not to follow her to the bank of elevators. To not follow her up to her room and lean against her doorframe as she picked out the outfit meant to torture me. Maybe I thought about how she'd get down to her panties—I'd bet money that they matched her bra —and I'd press up against her, backing her to her King-sized bed and taking her down to the plush comforter in the span of a single heartbeat. Maybe I thought about pushing her thighs wide and looping them over my fore-arms as I ground against her until we both forgot we were supposed to go anywhere.

What happens in Vegas might stay in Vegas, but the way I want her won't stay neatly packaged on the road. I'll damn us both. Tristan, because her job is on the line. Me, because I'm not sure I want to hit the ice every day in my baby blues without her nearby.

Fuck.

"She's looked over here no less than once a minute." Robbie leans forward, dropping his elbows onto his knees. "Man up, Varg. Stop letting life happen around you and take what you want."

It's a flash of white-hot rage that fuels my response.

"What, like you did?"

I regret the words the minute they're said, but I can't take them back. They're horrible, but true. Robbie Oakes might be my best friend. I may have known him since we were missing teeth and dreaming of stepping onto the ice in our first NHL games, but he doesn't have a leg to stand on giving me advice like this. It's like a slideshow of images sliding across my brain. Robbie sitting on the back porch, holding the hand of the girl next door. Him sliding an arm around her shoulder anytime she was close enough to touch. Him tipping her chin up and pressing their mouths together under the old oak tree in his parents' backyard.

"How is Vera, anyway?" I hear the words and they aren't me. They're mean, vicious, meant to wound, and I hate the way they taste in my mouth. "Didn't I read an article about her in Vanity Fair?" An article about Vera Novak and her new boyfriend, an underwear model from Italy.

I'm a fucking dick. I might wish I hadn't said it, but I'm still pissed when Robbie doesn't even flinch.

"So learn from my mistake," he says.

I shake my head. "It's not that simple."

"It never is."

Beau Pelletier leans down and whispers something in her ear and I wait for her to pin him with her fuck-off stare, but she smiles up at him instead. I swear someone shoved all my internal organs into a food processor and hit pulse. I can hear my heartbeat thrumming in my ears, blocking out all the sound in the room as my focus narrows to where he's slid a hand against her waist.

His fingertips are touching her skin. I can't breathe. I can't move. I'm going to kill the kid. I'm going to—

"Hey," a strong hand grips the back of my neck, squeezing as I suck in air. "She stepped away from him. Breathe Vic."

Can't he see I'm fucking trying?

I have to get out of here. I have to go away. Far away.

But I can't. Someone else might stand too close to her. Someone else might try to touch her. Someone else might...

"If I make a move, she'll lose her job," I say, and the hand falls from my neck as Robbie blows out a breath. "No fraternizing or something like that."

"Fuck." Yup, fuck is right. "I thought you were just being a chickenshit."

I'm aware of that.

"Nope."

I should have just told him this earlier, except telling him this is admitting he's right and I didn't want to do that. I can feel him re-grouping next to me, changing tactics. He's always been right. Bastard. Robbie can be a real dick with the I-told-you-so's, but I'm madder at myself. Admitting the hurdles means I'm thinking about them. About how to get around them. Which means I'm fucked any way I look at it.

"So you can't fuck her." Robbie says, and I swear I want him to go back to being fucking mute.

"We can't *fraternize*." I hate that word. The policy should say what it means. We can't date? Got it. Can't have sex? Got it. Can't spend time together? It's her job to spend time with me right now. To spend time here with the guys. Can she not be friends with us? Associate with us? Wouldn't that make her job impossible? And yes. I might have borrowed a dictionary from Jen and looked the damn word up. Just to be sure.

Robbie runs his hand across his mouth, dark brows furrowed.

"That gets in the way a bit," he says, like there's a work-around. There isn't. "So you can either go spend the time you have together, or you can go back to your room and get some distance. Either way, sitting here and moping isn't working."

Across the club, Pelletier leans in close to her again and I'm on my feet before I mean to be.

"I'm not moping," I lie. "And I'm not leaving her here with a bunch of horn dogs."

Dogs she's better at controlling than I could ever be, but whatever.

"Dude, she does not need you to protect her from the team." Robbie is shaking his head as he tries to hold back a laugh. "She just needs you to listen to her and be there. So go do that."

Right.

Go do... that.

Maybe I should just go.

But then Pelletier's fingers start playing with the straps on Tristan's dress and all thoughts melt from my brain. It's like an out-of-body experience, the way I move through the small crowd inside The Velvet until I'm standing right in front of one Tristan Grant. Red pinpricks are bleeding through my field of vision as I look down at her white-blonde hair, shining pink in the warm red light of the club.

"Go get me a drink, Pelé." My eyes add, *or I will make your life hell,* but I know better than to say that out loud.

The winger meets my gaze over Tristan's head, and I stare him down until he looks away.

"Sure thing Cap," he says. His hand taking its sweet-ass-time dropping from my kitty cat's waist. I don't look away until he's across the room at the shining wooden bar. Then I glance down.

I expect Tristan to be scowling up at me, a statement about macho male posturing ready on her lips, but she isn't. Her head is tipped back, blue eyes heavy as she stares up at me. Her lips are parted and I watch as they curl into a smile. I'm not sure what to make of the look she is giving me, but heat pools in my belly as my balls draw up tight.

"Hi," she says, slipping into a full grin. She looks younger like this. Softer. Warm and sweet and fuck, I should not have walked over here.

"Hi," I say back with my own smile. "Having a good time?"

"I am! But wanna know a secret?" She curls her fingers to beckon me forward and I lean closer. I couldn't stop myself if I tried. "It's better now that you're here." She's laughs. "I wasn't supposed to tell you that."

"I've been here the whole time," I tell her, lifting my own hand to the small of her back. My thumb is just grazing the warm indentation of her spine and I swear I can feel the nerves shiver under my touch. I need to get my skin off her. Now.

"No," she shakes her head and more blonde escapes her ponytail. It would be so easy to slip my hand up her back to tangle in her hair. "You were sitting in the corner being grumpy."

"I'm not grumpy now." I don't tangle, but my hand slides up to tug at the strands. Tristan's head tips back, baring the long line of her throat. I want to drag my teeth along the tendons.

"No," her eyes flutter shut as the music shifts and the crowd seems to melt away. No one here is paying attention to us. One reason the team comes here, to The Velvet, is their strict no photos policy. I could just.... No one would even see....

"Here Cap." Pelletier is holding out a neon pink drink swirling and glittery in the dim light. "Enjoy."

"Ooh" Tristan uses a hand on my shoulder to boost herself up even higher to look in the glass. "What is *that*?"

"*That* is a pink bikini," Pelletier smirks. "Cap's drink of choice."

It's not, but I'm game to try it. Or I would if I was drinking. Sending Pelé to the bar had nothing to do with alcohol and everything to do with his proximity to my... Tristan.

"You don't drink during the season," she says, a little furrow between her blonde brows. I want to smooth a finger over it.

Pelletier grins at me. I can see every one of his teeth. Including the fake front one.

"That's not why he asked for it," he says, leaning in like it's some big conspiracy theory. He's opening his mouth, probably to tell her I was scaring him off, pulling rank, peeing on her like a dog, when she cuts him off.

"Can I have it?"

I can't help the way my hand slips around her waist again, pulling her into the heat of my body. I stare at my teammate and the man stares back. All the teasing gone from his expression. As much as I wanted him away from my kitty cat, I know he wouldn't have done anything to this drink. Still, I'm having a hard time reminding my nervous system that she's safe. She's okay. Beau Pelletier is a horrendous flirt. He isn't great with boundaries, but he would never *drug* someone. Never *hurt* anyone off the ice.

Pelletier's dark eyes are wide as he shakes his head back and forth. The movement is slight, just a small tip side to side, and he follows it up with, "I watched them make it, Cap. I would never..."

Tristan takes the glass from his hand and wraps her lips around the narrow black straw.

"There's coconut in this," she tells me with a sweet smile, and my fingers flex against the slippery fabric of her dress. Her voice drops to a whisper. "It's delicious."

And something hits me like a freight train.

The tension locking down my muscles isn't jealousy, it's worry. I'm not worried about my teammates. I'm not worried any of them is going to put a move on her or that she'll let them. I'm worried because Tristan is not acting like her normal self. She's loose, relaxed, smiling. Her walls are down. And I want to take credit for it, but it's not that at all.

She's drunk.

It's not surprising, given her size. I knew she was cagey about coming here with us. Nervous. I know she ordered a drink when we got here, but I guess I didn't know she'd be such a lightweight. Not that I blame her for taking the edge off. My chest puffs with pride. I think it shows her trust in me. In the team. She knows we'll take care of her. We won't let anything happen to her. Ever.

I don't need to protect her from the guys on the team.

I just need to be here. To keep an eye on her. To know she's okay.

I can do that.

Pelletier turns back to the stage, leaving us with a semblance of privacy. The woman dancing wiggles her fingers from behind a large, feathered fan. She's holding it over her front until all that's visible is long legs and a head of dark curls. She sashays into the wings as guys around us holler and whistle. I keep my eyes on the empty platform as Tristan leans her weight against me and sips more of the frothy pink drink. She's right about the coconut. I can smell the Malibu from here. My arm slips more fully around her waist. She isn't sloppy, but I've got her, anyway.

"I can dance like that," she says, and I'm startled enough to tighten my forearm before I make myself relax. She pats the back of my hand, blowing any hope I had that my reaction went unnoticed.

"Like that?" My voice is hoarser than I anticipated.

"There was a movie that came out years ago, the one with Cher in it? I taught myself some of the dances because it looked fun. I never got to take actual dance class as a kid, but I think I would have liked it."

"I bet you're a great dancer," I say, trying not to imagine her naked except for a bedazzled thong and pasties, playing peekaboo from behind a large feathered fan. She's pressed too tight against me to not notice the state of my dick. My self-control is excellent, but even I can't stop myself from getting a fucking erection.

"Wanna see?" She asks, pushing her now empty glass into my free hand.

Yes. More than anything. But I don't want anyone else to.

Then again, she's not naked.

"Do you want a chance to dance on the stage?"

"Yes," she nods her head, "No. Yes." Strong white teeth bite into her plump lip. "There are a lot of people here."

Not really, but I can change that.

"We can shut the place down," I tell her. I can cover the cost on my own, but I'm sure the guys would chip in if I asked.

"You can do that?"

She twists in my arms until we're chest to chest and I try to pull in air. I'm a professional athlete and I can't catch my breath at the look in her eyes. It's easier to suck in oxygen after missing a shift change during an icing call than when she looks at me with utter faith and trust.

"One empty club, coming right up."

I look over her head to catch Robbie's eyes and beckon him over. He knows the promoter here and this shouldn't take much more than a check to cover the night's losses and a few minutes to clear out the other patrons.

"When Chris told me he wanted clean, wholesome

content, I don't think he thought I'd be performing at a burlesque club. Thank you, Vic, for doing this for me."

As Robbie strides toward us, I wonder if she knows I'd do just about anything for her. Including keeping my hands to myself.

HEAT.

Is that my heart or the bass line?

Vic's hands dragging across my skin, goosebumps rising as he leaves my whole body tingling.

A firm tug on my hair. My pussy clenching on absolutely nothing.

Swiveling my hips under the spotlight as I feel my arousal wet on my thighs.

A calloused hand sliding against my palm. Knuckles just big enough to leave my fingers aching as we interlock.

Cool air as we step outside. Grinding against the firm line of his back, seeking some kind of friction, as he hoists me up. My legs aren't working when I try to walk, but we're still moving down the sidewalk. My heels dangle from his fingertips.

The smell of roses. Petals baby soft as I rub my cheek against them.

A weight on my hand.

Gold glimmering in the light.

Soft lips sipping at mine. The pressure firm. I shiver. Soft enough for me to sink into him and never come back up. My tongue wants to join the fun.

A hard wall against my back as I breathe in through my nose. A muscular arm banded under me as my legs twine around a slim waist. A groan pouring into my mouth as I suck his tongue.

Something hard pressed right between my thighs.

Rock my hips. No thoughts. Another groan.

A bruising grip on my hip as he pants over my face.

My name breathed over my lips. Hazel eyes shuttered, dark blonde lashes making half-moon shadows on tanned cheeks.

A hand slipping between my legs and finding my clit.

Circling, circling, circling, then a pinch and I'm coming.

Coming and coming and coming.

And then...

I THINK I've made a horrible mistake.

But I can't bring myself to regret a single second.

I DIDN'T CLOSE the curtains before falling asleep, and the sun has decided my eyes are the perfect place to focus their brightness. Something I did *not* intend to sign up for. I squeeze them even tighter, but instead of blissful black on the back of my eyelids, I'm seeing the haze of orange. My mouth is painfully dry, making it hard to swallow, and my head and limbs feel heavy; sorer than I expected. I have no idea what time it is, although the sun is a hint that my scheduled wake-up call didn't come as planned.

I should roll over and check the clock, but I'm too warm and comfortable to care right now. Lack of light-blocking curtains and wake-up call mishaps aside, this hotel has quality mattresses. The blanket must be weighted too, sitting low on my back, cocooning me in three-hundred-and-sixty-degree heat. My head doesn't feel great, but the rest of me does. Which is a win, considering I have very little memory of last night after meeting Vic in the lobby.

Nerves about the evening with the guys may have had me indulging in an edible as I pulled on the cream satin dress. I'd already felt loose, lips tingling, as we walked the short distance to the club. My eyelids were heavy by the time we stepped inside, and that's where the memories end. I'm not a frequent user, but Palmer suggested bringing one just in case being on the road was more taxing than I anticipated. She also supplied the gummy, which explains why it hit me harder than normal.

My sister is a rebel. I try to ignore the fact that she knows way more about THC and alcohol than a newly twenty-one-year-old should.

There's a vague memory of stepping up on a spotlit stage, but I must have imagined that. Or maybe dreamed it. I rarely dream when high, but maybe this time was an exception.

I burrow deeper into my bed. My phone isn't screaming yet, so either it's dead, or I still have time to catch the bus. Either way, it can wait an extra minute or two. Just another snooze before I have to get up and face the real world and the hot-as-sin hockey captain that I'm trying not to jump on like a trampoline.

I rub my cheek against my pillow and the blanket tightens around my back.

That can't be right.

Blankets don't tighten.

There's an arm wrapped low around my waist. Now that I know it's there, I can also feel the hand cupping the curve of my ass, fingers dipped into the warm juncture between my thighs. Those fingers flex and my stomach swoops as my lips part. I should be horrified. There's a strange arm and hand becoming intimately acquainted with my panties. I shouldn't feel the tightening in my abdomen or the tingles in my belly. One of my legs is bent at the knee and I shouldn't be considering widening my thighs and canting my hips so those fingers can brush my pussy again.

I open my eyes. My face is pressed against a firm pectoral, a dusting of light gold hair cushioning my cheek. The large fingers flex again, sliding against my center, and I can feel the unmistakable bulge of a hard cock pressed to the soft skin of my stomach. I don't think he's awake yet. The movements seem more involuntary than teasing, and I need to sneak out before that changes. I need to extricate myself from the tangle of limbs and find my clothes and leave because this definitely counts as fraternizing. But if I leave now I can pretend it never happened. And if those movements *become* purposeful, I don't think I'll be able to walk away. I don't think I'll want to.

It makes sense that I'm being blinded through curtains I didn't forget to shut. I closed them when I changed my clothes and left them closed. Thank you very much. It makes sense that my wake-up call didn't go off. Because this isn't my room. Those aren't my curtains. This isn't my phone with my scheduled reminder. And now I also understand why I haven't panicked over the prospect of being naked with a stranger.

The man I'm starfished on top of is not a stranger. He's Victor Varg.

And I know this, not because I looked at his face—my

gaze is still fixed on one flat, pink nipple—but because the molten awareness I always get around this man is racing through my veins at an alarming clip.

This is a colossal fuck-up. The megalodon of fuck-ups. I heard all the warnings and still took it as a green light to jump into bed with the man I can't have. Fuck.

I lift my head and try to look around the room. I need to get out of here now. My sister's dress is lying in a crumpled heap on the floor. I can't see my heels anywhere, but once I'm upright, I hope they'll be obvious. Shoes are the least of my problems if I can't escape the bungee cords Vic has for arms. I've been focusing on the one cupping my ass, the one with the fingers rubbing me insane. His other arm tightens across my back, palm curved around my shoulder, holding me firm against his chest. Any other time, any other man, and this would be one of the most romantic ways to wake up. Today it's a nightmare.

I wiggle. The tiniest shift left to right, trying to slide out from under the arm, and everything under me tenses. I freeze, waiting for him to relax. His hips punch up once, twice, a slow grind that has my eyes fluttering closed as I bite my lip to hold in a gasp.

Time to go.

Or maybe not. If we've already come this far. What if I stayed? It's not like this could get worse. I might as well....

No.

I need to leave now. We can pretend this was a fever dream, that I did not wake up draped over this man, bare breasts pressed to his skin. I shift again and he groans, deep in his throat. A sound that settles in my core. Then his arms tighten, and he rolls us, tucking his face against the top of my head. If he pins me under him, I will not be responsible for my own actions. I'll take it as a sign the universe is saying "stay here, fuck him again," but he keeps us on our sides and the hand cupping my shoulder loosens and drops to the mattress.

It's easier to get free now and I should be thrilled, but there's a tiny part of me that's disappointed. I wanted the option taken out of my hands. I wanted to not have to be the one to think through consequences and make tough choices. I've been doing that since I was twelve. For once, can't someone else be in charge?

I back myself to the edge of the mattress, pushing a pillow at Vic. He wraps his arms around it. Once my feet are on the floor, I see my shoes. They're half under the bed. Like I kicked them off or dropped them. My panties are... still on my body.

They're damp with sweat and other things, and suctioned to my skin, but I'm pretty sure this means we didn't have full-on sex. My inner muscles ache, but not the well-used kind of throb. This is the hungry, needy pulse that tells me I've been keyed up and held on the edge for too long.

I suppose I should feel better about that. If this ever comes back around to Bob, it won't be a lie when I say we haven't had sex. I'm ninety percent confident.

A glance at the clock spurs me into action. My wake-up call should have come and gone over an hour ago. We're due in the lobby to catch the bus to the airport in just under thirty minutes, and I still have to find my phone and get my things from my room. I need to make a dash for it and cross my fingers that none of the other players will catch me making my escape.

Phone, phone, phone.

There.

It's on the nightstand next to the bed, plugged into—what I can only assume—is Vic's charger. He either plugged it in for me or forwent his own charging so I could have mine. I almost tear up, which is a ridiculous overreaction, and has me grabbing my things and my bag from the floor with enough speed to make a sprinter proud. Did he know my sisters would have sent in the cavalry if I were unreachable? I mean helicopters, the FBI, the coast guard, mounted police, private eyes, the whole nine yards. Max is more levelheaded and wouldn't take part, but he'd also have no luck convincing them not to panic. A glance at the screen tells me I've already missed twelve calls and forty-five texts.

There's a muffled sound from Vic and I hit the floor and crawl my way to the door. I have my eyes screwed shut like I'm a child. If I can't see him, he can't see me. I have to stand up to get the door open, and I chance a look behind me to see the expanse of Vic's broad back glowing in the light from the window. It's unfair how attractive he is. He shifts, the sheet tugging lower, and I yank the door open before bolting into the hallway.

I don't run into any other Arctic players on the way back to my room. It's a minor miracle, and I know I'll pay for it later. It's not that I think they'll assume I was with Vic —although they will—but seeing any of them during my walk of shame is the epitome of unprofessional. My entire night was the epitome of unprofessional. It was just a string of poor decisions that I have no excuse for. I should have turned Jack and Vic down on their invite out. I shouldn't have gone back to my room to change into this dress, no matter how gorgeous it is, because I only put it on to get a certain captain's reaction. I shouldn't have indulged in a gummy—although, to be fair, I didn't expect how hard it would hit me. I expected it to ease my nerves, not send me to the stratosphere.

I throw my stuff into my suitcase as I yank on my travel clothes and double check the bathroom counter for any extra toiletries that escaped my first grab. I yank my hair back into the French twist I could do in my sleep and check my face in the mirror. I look like a raccoon that got stuck in a commercial sized dumpster and made it my new home. I scrub the dark smudges from under my eyes and that'll have to do for today. I can almost hear the Madison lecture about proper skincare—as if I didn't teach her everything she knows—but my vote is for caffeine over moisturizer. I'll apologize to my T-zone with a mask once we get back to Quarry Creek.

One last glance around the room I barely used, and I let the door slam shut behind me as I wheel my suitcase down to the lobby. I take the elevator ride to double check my messages. Not surprisingly, they're all from the family group chat.

HAYLEY:

Has anyone heard from Tristan?

PALMER:

Not since last night when she found the dress I slipped into her bag.

MADS:

Oooooh, which dress?

PALMER:

The white one you ordered from that online boutique.

MADS:

The one that didn't cover my ass?

JOEY:

Ass or tits. You had to pick one. Lol. That thing was microscopic.

PALMER:

Like Tristan!

HAYLEY:

I liked that one!

MADS:

Me too, that's why I held onto it.

JOEY:

Now Tristan can hold on to it.

TRISTAN! SEND US A PICTURE IF YOU HAVE ONE!

HAYLEY:

I thought they had to catch the bus at eight. No one's heard from her?

JOEY:

Maybe she's sleeping in. She could use the vacation.

PALMER:

Hopefully, she got laid.

MADS:

By who? One of the players? Ew.

PALMER:

I mean, they're not *my* thing, but they're decent looking. Right?

HAYLEY:

She spends a lot of time with the captain.

MADS:

I stand corrected. He's gorg.

JOEY:

So maybe she's not texting because he's balls deep right now.

PALMER:

There is something to be said for morning sex.

MAX:

I am begging you to please take me off this group chat. For the love of fucking god.

HAYLEY:

Sorry, Maxie

MADS:

Stop whining, bitch.

JOEY:

Do all athletes smell, Max? Or just you?

MAX:

Are all little sisters the worst? Or just you?

HAYLEY:

Max!

MADS:

What is wrong with you? Didn't anyone teach you manners?

MAX:

SHE STARTED IT!

PALMER:

She's going to soak your jock in hot sauce again.

MAX:

One brother. I couldn't have had just one brother...

MADS:

Lucky you.

I slide my phone away, a headache already brewing. I'm staring at the entrance to the closed steakhouse and wondering if I'll have better luck sourcing a latte at the French restaurant across the way, when a big hand thrusts a white and green cup under my nose.

"Thank you," I say and lift the cup to my mouth without even asking what's in it. Chai tea with a splash of vanilla, and I'm pretty sure I taste oat milk.

"It's on the other side of the convention center." Robbie gives me a look I'm starting to understand is his version of a smile.

I take another sip, risking the third-degree burns to my tongue. "And you knew my go-to order?"

The bus will be here any minute, and already the lobby

is crammed with exhausted-looking hockey players. They're still dressed to the nines, and clearly they've been given travel instructions because, despite the plush seating areas, not a single one of them is even leaning against a wall. I stop myself from looking for tanned skin and hazel eyes.

"No," Robbie says as I take another sip of what is *definitely* my preferred drink. "Vic knows yours go-to order, and I just picked it up since he's running late." The center's eyes sparkle down at me and I know why the women online fall all over themselves for him, glower or no glower. "You wouldn't know anything about that now. Would you?"

Tricky motherfucker.

I glare up at him, but the guy doesn't seem to care at all.

"How fast did you run out on him this morning?" This time his words are hushed as behind us, coach Noris claps his hands and announces the bus.

"I'm not judging," Oakes is quick to add, "I just need to know if you and Vic talked before you bolted."

I glower harder. The only thing stopping me from ripping this man a new asshole is the fact that he handed me liquid caffeine. If he doesn't shut up—and soon—the entire team will know where I spent the night. And since the players gossip more than a bunch of grannies at a bridge club, management will know before we even board our flight.

"Excuse me?"

"We have about two seconds before we need to get on that bus, and Vic needs you to be cool about something."

Since when is Robbie Oakes this talkative? Since when am I the one who freaks out about things? I'm the cool-headed voice of reason. I'm the trustworthy one. The one brought in to clean up other people's messes. I lift my hand, one finger raised to ask Oakes to wait a moment, hold on, let me gather my thoughts, and something catches my eye.

Something gold and polished to a shine.

Something circling the ring finger on my left hand.

Something that looks an awful lot like…

"Holy fuck balls," Jack Spaeglin's sounds like he's both a million miles away, and also bellowing into my ear with a megaphone. "Lucky Charm got fucking married."

EVER BEEN STUCK in a situation so terrible that time seems to stop? Grind down to a halt until seconds stretch like decades? Ever contemplated murder? I might take the rookie out at the knees.

I'm feet from Tristan when Spags' words break through the crowd and her eyes drop to look at her hand. It reminds me of the cartoons Erik and I used to watch as kids. The way her eyes go wide as she stares down at the gold band wrapped around her ring finger. I promised myself I wouldn't take it personally when she freaked out —I knew she would—but seeing the panic is still a gut punch.

There was no faking sleep while she shimmied her way out from under my arms and bolted to the door. I wasn't pretending in order to avoid a conflict. This conversation needs to happen, but I meant to wake up before her. Or maybe not fall asleep at all. I brought her to my room and not her own, because my intention was to have an honest discussion before we got on the bus. When I rolled over and found my room empty, I sent her drink order down and asked Robbie to head her off until I could get my ass downstairs. Someone needed to put the night before in order for her. I can do that.

To be fair, asked is putting it mildly.

I begged my best friend. With less than zero shame.

"I'm not buying you Plan B, asshole. It's not my fault you thought with your dick instead of making smart choices," He'd growled into the phone when I dialed him for the third time in as many minutes while I stood in my hotel room with one leg shoved into my dress pants, but that wasn't what I needed.

I needed someone to slow her down before she jumped on the bus or set the world on fire. Starting with my nuts.

"What the fuck did you do?" Robbie asked, with all the resignation of a sullen teen being given a list of chores for Saturday morning.

The answer is not as much as I wanted to do.

I shove my left hand in my pocket, feeling the cool smooth weight of the ring I'd dropped in there, as Robbie meets my eyes.

I tried, he shrugs. *Not my fault Spags is an idiot.*

"I didn't think you'd do it." Spaeglin is still fucking talking and I swear there's a twitch in the corner of Tristan's eye. I can't tell if she's gone catatonic or if she's about to explode outward like a supernova, engulfing the rookie in a white-hot flame. Not sure I wouldn't shove him right into her path. Several of the guys are pushing closer, wanting to get an eye on the simple band looped around her finger. They all want to see for themselves and get close enough to hear what she has to say about it.

"Was Elvis there?" One defender asks as he dekes his way around Jack to look at Tristan's hand up close.

Yes. He was.

"Who's Mr. Lucky Charm?" Pelletier asks. "Or Mrs.? We don't judge."

Both Beau and Jack flick their eyes to me and then back to our shell-shocked social media manager. My fingers loop around my own ring, squeezing until I'm sure there's a perfect round indent in my palm.

Tristan's hand is still up, floating in the air as she unfurls her fingers to stare at the piece of jewelry. Her face is so carefully blank that I just know her brain is moving a million miles an hour, trying to sort out the night before. I'll admit, I wasn't sure how much she'd remember, but I didn't think she'd be blindsided quite like this. I assumed she'd have seen the ring while getting dressed, sneaking out, grabbing her luggage. At any point in time before now. I wonder if there are even snippets of potential memories, like a movie trailer of our night together.

"It's obviously V—" Spaeglin cuts himself off at the murder on my face. "someone very lucky," he finishes, but it's too late. The only person who hasn't turned to stare at me is Tristan herself. She's still looking at the ring as if she believes that if she stares at it long enough this will all turn out to have been a nightmare and she'll wake up.

My stomach twists, painful and sharp. I should have grabbed something to eat before rushing down here.

Except if I had, I would have thrown it up by now. I knew she wouldn't be happy about this. I knew it was a colossal mistake, but it still sucks to see her shut down over the prospect of marrying me. The look on her face, the absolute shock and horror, well it's enough to crush any guy's ego under the pointy-toed shoes she loves to wear.

"Hey Spags." Tyler Gage pokes the rookie in the shoulder. "Didn't we see her and Cap buying rings at that wedding chapel?"

Spaeglin gives the defenseman a look that has Gage swallowing down his smile.

Fuck. I'd forgotten that. I'd also forgotten they're both too young to drink and while that doesn't stop most players, especially on the road, I was pretty sure tweedle-dee-one and tweedle-dee-two were both sober when they saw us last night. A responsible choice I'd praise both for on any other morning. This time I wish they'd been drunk enough to not know their teammates from a herd of elephants.

"What were you guys doing at a wedding chapel?" Pelletier elbows Spags in the ribs, oblivious to the preternatural calm that has descended over the group.

"We're madly in love and saw our chance," Gage says as the tips of Pelé's ears turn pink.

"He wanted to see Elvis." Spags says, "And I wanted to offer my services—"

"Yeah, you did." The statement drips with innuendo as some of the team laughs.

Of course, I've lost every ounce of control and this is now a spectacle. Someone is probably filming the descent into madness. We're going to end up on TMZ. At least Noris, and the rest of the coaching staff, have stepped out to locate the bus and aren't witnessing this unfolding horror.

"Hey." Spags turns to find the source of the heckling. "I offered my services as a witness to true love. It's not my fault you—"

"Enough." Robbie's voice cuts through the chatter like a hot knife through butter. "Get your things and get on the bus. Everyone. Now."

The guys move in degrees, grabbing an overnight bag, sliding into new conversations, filing towards the hotel entrance. I can see the charter bus sitting in front of the revolving glass. Robbie leans in as he grabs his duffle, mine, and reaches out a hand for Tristan's suitcase. She doesn't even notice as he wheels it to his side. I'm not sure she's moved at all.

"I can buy you guys about two minutes here," he tells me, "But you know how coach is about leaving on time, and we're already behind schedule."

I nod. I'll take whatever time I can grab, and then I'll follow my pretty kitty cat right onto the bus, plant myself in the seat next to her, and we can talk this out.

"About last night. What I said about Vera..." I meet his gaze. "I'm sorry. It was uncalled for."

Robbie shakes his head. "It's fine. I poked an open wound. Don't waste your time worrying about me."

He's halfway to the door, following the stream of players, before I look back at Tristan. She'd dropped her hand now, her fingers curled into a fist as though she's trying to keep the ring on. Or maybe mangle her own fingers. I turn so my body can fully face her, use my size to block out the image of the bus and the team.

"Hey," it's not what I meant to start off with, and the way she flinches makes my heart clench in my chest. That can't be a good sign. Maybe I need to schedule a check-up with my physician.

"Tristan," I start over. "It's not as bad as it looks." Although my statement was more honest before the team descended on us like vultures. "Actually—"

"Not. As. Bad. As. It. Looks." A hollow laugh as she turns her body to face me. My nerves are singing at both her acknowledgment and the proximity. Buzzing, like the time I heard someone play Greensleeves on the edges of thick, crystal water goblets. "Waking up in Vegas with surprise jewelry. Not as bad as it looks? On a work trip? The entire team knows. I'm going to lose my job. But you're right, it's not as bad as it looks. At least I woke up with my panties still on."

Heat burns through me so fast it's like a wildfire spinning out of control. Hurt and shame at the jab, combined with a dose of arousal at the memory of how she ended up in just underwear. How I did.

"Wait a minute," I say. My hand reaches for her, without my conscious thought. I pull it back.

I have about a minute left to fix this. And I can. It wasn't supposed to play out this way, but I can spare her at least a little torment. I just have to figure out how to get her to hear my words.

"No." Tristan's face is cloudy. "God, I've been so fucking

stupid. I thought I could trust... I thought for one night I could let someone else..." she shakes her head again and turns away, lifting her almost-forgotten cup to her lips. Her hand is shaking and I want to wrap her in my arms, tug her into my chest, hold her tea for her, buy her a million gallons more, anything. "I made a stupid mistake last night. I knew better than to take an edible on a work trip, but I was nervous and let that sway my decisions."

Her throat bobs as she swallows, and I'm so focused on the pale skin of her slim neck that I almost miss what she's saying. When I do, shame grips both my shoulders and shakes me until my teeth rattle. A gummy. I knew. I knew something was different with her last night. I suspected when she met me in the lobby. Knew it when I barged in on her and Beau's conversation. I let her drink that pink cocktail. I bought her another later. I told myself she was drunk, but I was there to protect her and fuck... I failed.

I'm not a stranger to marijuana. It's off-limits during the season thanks to random drug testing. And pot's a downer. Great for nerves or performance anxiety on the ice, but not the best choice for athletes trying to improve their game. That doesn't mean a lot of players don't indulge in the off-season. Doesn't mean I haven't.

Marijuana isn't the taboo subject it once was, not with so many states legalizing its use. My family was introduced to the plant before public opinion shifted. Turns out cannabis can be super helpful for chemo patients, especially when fighting nausea. That doesn't mean being high was ever on my radar for Tristan last night, and it should have been. The friendly chatter, the easy smiles, the hooded eyes. There I'd stood, thinking it was me. Thinking she was finally comfortable with me. And then I let her add alcohol on top of it. I didn't protect her at all.

Is it possible to die of shame? Because I think I might. My organs feel heavy, squeezed into a space not big enough to hold them. Not embarrassment. That's different. Shame that seeps into my bones, whispering against the edge of my ear, "You were supposed to keep her safe. You didn't."

"I'm going to lose my job here and there's no one I can blame but myself. I knew better than to let my guard down. I'm smarter than this. How could I be so stupid?"

Tears shimmer across her irises and my arms ache to reach for her again.

"You aren't stupid." I reach for her anyway, brain be damned, but she steps away, putting a foot between us. "We need to have a chat, Tristan.

We have maybe thirty seconds left and there's something we need to discuss before we get on the bus. Something about last night. Something that could change everything. I just need a minute of her time. Her undivided attention.

"Talk. Right." Another humorless laugh. "No. I don't think so. Here's what's going to happen. You are going to give me some space to figure all this the fuck out before we land back home. I'll set up a meeting with Mr. Seever and beg to keep my job. You will not look at me, talk to me, or draw attention to the fact that we have matching wedding bands. Got it?"

We could also take the bands off, but I don't say that.

"I can do that." As long as I only have to leave her alone for the flight. I don't think I can manage beyond that. "But you should know—"

"Goddammit." She paces a few steps away and then marches back to poke one razor sharp nail into the divot between my pecs. My kitty cat has sharpened her claws. "I need space, Vic. Please. I already messed up once this weekend. Let's try to get back to Quarry Creek without any more incidents. Do you think you can do that?"

It feels wrong to push her right now. Wrong to keep trying to give her the words she doesn't want to hear. Maybe it can wait. I can give her today—the bus ride, the flight home—and then we can talk about how to face this head on. Together.

I open my mouth, close it. Open it again. Close it once more as she glares in my direction.

"C-captain?" Ólaffson is standing just inside the revolving door, looking a little like an injured baby deer surrounded by hungry wolves. He might be insane—the way all goalies are—but he still has some amount of self-preservation. I know what he's going to say before he says it. We're out of time. "Coach s-sent me to g-g... to remind you we're leaving."

"Thank you, Ragnar," Tristan smiles and even though it's not meant for me, I swear the lights in here shine brighter and my heart skips a beat. "We're on our way."

She pushes past me, still clutching her chai tea. For once, there's no red lip print around the plastic top. She didn't stop and put her armor on this morning. Ólaffson steps out of her way, hinging like he's bowing to a queen.

He is. And I can't help but swallow down my grin as I see her board the charter bus, all with a shiny gold band still hugging her ring finger.

"Congratulations," the goalie says and I think he's the first person to seem anything other than shocked. "I'm h-h-hap...glad you have each other."

I run a hand through my hair and head for the bus, too. Coach is probably having a litter right now, waiting for us. Sometimes being captain and the lead goal scorer has perks. He'd never even consider leaving me behind. Well... he might consider it, but he wouldn't do it. As I climb the three steps leading past the driver, I have to duck my head to avoid seeking my kitty cat.

She's frothing mad now, and I'll give her some space to cool off, but that's as far as I'm willing to go. I'm happy to have her too. And I intend to keep her.

Claws and rules be damned.

thearctic.hockey
Las Vegas, Nevada

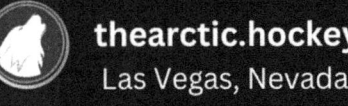

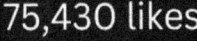

75,430 likes

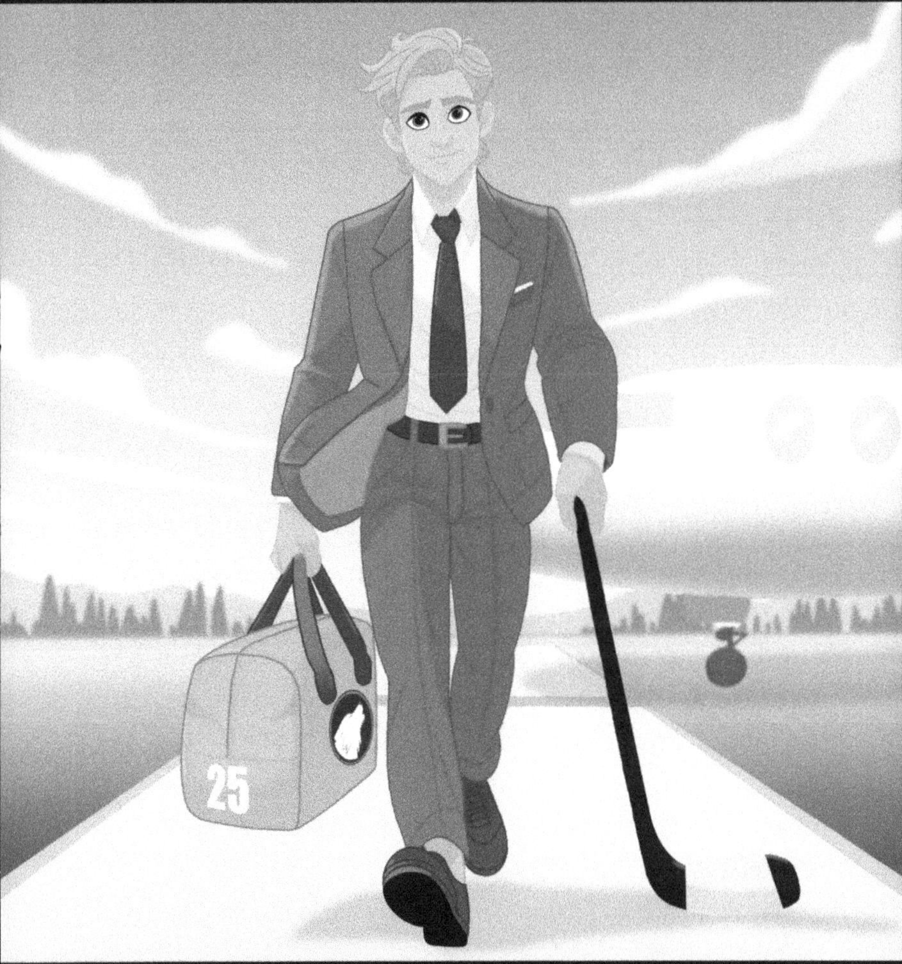

thearctic.hockey come on the road with us as our Arctic boys take on Vegas during our first head to head of the season... more

SaraiJune I volunteer to get drunk and marry one. 5k

View all 632 comments

Add a comment...

VIC MAKES it a lot longer than I thought he would. I was sure the minute we hit out cruising altitude, he would slide into the seat next to me and force a conversation I'm not sure I'm ready for. To be honest, I'm not sure I'll ever be ready for it, which isn't an option. Everyone heard Jack in the lobby. Anyone who wasn't a witness to the news had been filled in on all the details by the time we got to the private airstrip. It's like a perverse game of telephone. Each new telling adds more details.

Victor Varg and Tristan Grant were a little chummy at The Velvet.

Tristan Grant was a thawed-out version of herself.

They left together.

Victor and Tristan picked out simple gold bands at a local wedding chapel overseen by a pot-bellied Elvis wearing fake sideburns.

Victor couldn't stop smiling. Neither could Tristan.

Tristan had the best orgasm of her entire life. Waves of plea-

sure cresting again and again with the raging force of the actual
ocean.

Okay, so no one is saying the last part, just my fogged hint of memory. I can't tell what was real and what was a fantasy No one is saying anything about the wedding beyond the bands either, something I don't need explained since I can always look down at my fingers and see mine for myself. No one watched us say our "I do's." Small miracle. Or maybe Vic barred the door. That last thought shouldn't make me feel warm and fuzzy, but it does. I have to remind myself that I'm mad at him.

We've touched down in Quarry Creek and I'm collecting my suitcase when Victor Varg corners me. That sounds more ominous than it is. I wish I had an actual reason to be mad at him beyond our circumstances, but I am still trying to hold on to my fury with shaking fists.

Waking up plastered across the body of an attractive man, willing his hands to sink a little lower, press a little harder. That's not a reason to hate someone. Matching gold bands isn't a reason either. It takes two to tango and all that jazz. In fact, the only real reason I have to be angry seems less and less legitimate the more time we spend together, but I'm damn good at holding grudges. The idea of letting go of this one feels strange. Alien.

It's part of who we are. Vic and Tristan. Opponents. Enemies. Two people in permanent stasis. Terminally frustrated by one another.

And okay, maybe that's been fading, perhaps since that first day of filming in the locker room. Not just because of the man's ab muscles, or the V that disappears under his hockey pants. And maybe, just maybe, I like the way he grins at me when I'm trying to be tough. The way he leans in when he calls me kitty cat. Maybe I could admit to myself that the reason I'm determined not to give in to Victor Varg's charm is because it feels like letting him win this tug-of-war between us. Maybe I like the effort he puts in, and maybe giving in is the thing that would leave me vulnerable.

I know it's hard to believe, but I don't handle vulnerability well.

It's easier to pretend that Vic has me cornered, even if I know it's not true. He approaches quietly, hands empty and loose in front of him. Soft smile. The real one, with the single dimple, tipping the corners of his pink mouth. Not that I'm noticing.

"Hey Tris," he says, his voice gritty as if he just woke up. Daytime flight or not, most of the guys slept the entire trip. I wish I could say my eyes don't drop to the naked skin of his left ring finger. I wish I could say that something doesn't twist inside me at the knowledge that he isn't wearing his ring. I wish I wasn't self-conscious about still wearing mine. "Would now be a good time to have that talk?"

It's self-preservation that has me shaking my head like I'm a novelty bobble head. We gave one away for Vic just last month. Right after he broke the arena record for the fastest goal scored during a game. I brought one home for Madison since she says he's such a dreamboat. I'll give it to her, eventually.

"No, thank you."

If his voice is deeper, mine is at a decibel level only dogs can hear. I did not sleep on the flight. Instead, I turned over scenario after scenario, trying to find a way to keep my employment despite the warning I'd received not even a few weeks ago. One upside about chartering a plane is the faster security process. The downside is less time to find a solution to my—our—minor problem. I'd be grateful for a plan that would afford me even a thirty percent chance of success, but I'm not sure it's possible.

Vegas should have a grace period after you get married. Three days until the license is filed. Three days to call the chapel and beg Elvis to drive over that document with his baby pink Cadillac convertible. Tear it to shreds. Fertilize the rose bushes with it. Burn it into ash. Like a game of dress-up. No harm, no foul, no legal ties binding two people together.

Would you even call them? A tiny voice says from the back of my brain. A tiny voice that is clearly still stewing in THC and alcohol.

"I understand you're upset." Vic says, and those claws he says I have? I want to sharpen them on his face. I want to drag raised welts down the strong line of his back. I want him to feel as off-kilter, as at-risk, as I do. But he won't. "I think you'll feel a lot better if we talked about this."

Why?

Why can't men figure out that telling women how they'll feel or what they'll feel isn't just counterintuitive, it's a kamikaze mission? Tell me to calm down? I'm guaranteed a ten-level increase in rage. Tell me to do something?

Even if I was about to do it, I'd pack up and move to Siberia to get the point across that it's now off the table. Vic's a smart guy. He has a wife, a sister-in-law, an almost-sister-in-law, and a mother he's close to. How has he still not figured this out?

"The team cannot afford to lose Victor Varg for the foreseeable future." That's what Bob said in his office. I'd be out and Vic would be in. The man standing in front of me can't possibly understand that I'm a dead woman walking. I'm staring down the plank at the churning water below. I've turned over every possibility and not a single thing seems guaranteed to keep me employed.

Except...

Except there's something else Bob said. Something about true love. Something about scandal. Something about choosing Vic over me.

I look down at the ring on my hand. It glows in the fluorescent lights of the airport and my chest feels tight. I pull in a shaky breath and flip my palm over, feeling the weight of the gold. When I was twelve, right after dad moved out to be with his other family, I found his wedding ring in the back of a kitchen drawer. I wore it for a whole day, as if pushing it past my knuckle and curling my fingers to keep the too-big band in place, as if wearing that piece of him, would bring him back.

Spoiler alert. It didn't work, but I also remember how heavy that ring was. I couldn't forget it was there, changing my balance as I did homework and tried to put together dinner for Hayley, Palmer, Madison, Max, and Joey. I'd assumed the next time I wore a ring it would be the same.

Something I had to get used to. But I keep forgetting that it's there. Not forgetting that I'm married to the team captain, but forgetting that I haven't yet taken the damn thing off. And maybe I don't mind the idea of a physical tie to a guy like Victor Varg, so much as I mind feeling like I didn't get a choice.

Sorry, a coherent choice.

"Tristan. Please." He steps closer. I can smell the cedar and ice scent of him and the bands in my chest pull even tighter. "You should know we—"

No.

No!

I hold up a hand, still trying to chase the tendril of thought that hinted at an actual solution. Tied together. Bound in marriage. And I got it. The only thing that might work. The major problem... I'll need this man to play along. This man who is probably going to tell me he has a lawyer on standby and we can file for a quickie divorce.

"It's too late to undo this," I tell him. "The entire team knows, which means it's only a matter of time before someone else does, too." The next video we upload will probably lead to the story tumbling out. Someone knows someone who saw us walking into the chapel. Someone snagged a picture and uploaded it to Reddit or TMZ or BuzzFeed. Whoever was willing to buy the photos. My one chance here is to get ahead of the story. To twist the narrative the way I need it to turn.

Honestly, it feels a little skeevy even considering this plan. The kind of thing that happens in romance novels and not in real life, but here we are. All I can do is ask. Lay my cards out on the table and he can say no if he wants to. As much as I want to lay all the blame right at the toes of Vic Varg's Bauer skates, I can't. I'm the one who went out with them. I'm the one who got high first. I'm the one who added alcohol to the mix, and I'm the one who would have had to say "I do." I'm pretty sure fall-down-drunks aren't allowed to get married. I had to have been at least semi-coherent.

"Listen," I say to him and he snaps his mouth closed. Nice, Tristan. Don't be a bitch. You need his help. "I'm likely going to lose my job over this."

"I won't let that happen."

Furrowed brows, lip curled into an angry arch. Victor Varg looks pissed off, dangerous. He's looking at me the same way he looked at that Jersey player before dropping his gloves and throwing the first punch in his one and only fight this season. It shouldn't twist my insides up in anything but apprehension. I should be nervous being the focus of this massive man and yet... I go wet. My knees threatening to tumble like a precarious stack of Jenga blocks.

"We can—"

"We need to stay married." I cut him off again, before he can mention divorce or annulment or anything of the sort.

I'm not sure if I was expecting protests or agreement, but stunned silence was not on my bingo card for this interaction.

"The only leverage I have in any disciplinary meeting is the fact that we're now tied together. The team won't risk losing you, so I'm hoping that means they'll agree to keep me." Even after I macerated their rules.

"If they try to send you away..." He trails off on his own because we both know he can't promise what he's about to. The man has an inked contract. They will not let him out of it. Not for a nobody social media manager, someone they could replace by tomorrow. I'm banking on the fact that they'll want to keep him happy. "They can't just fire you."

They can.

"My job was to distract the world from the Haine scandal. I did that pretty well, sure, but now I'm their newest scandal."

He frowns deeper, steps closer. "You aren't a scandal, Tristan."

I choke on a little laugh. I've only ever been a scandal. My dad had another family and chose them over us before I even hit my teenage years. My mother couldn't cope without him and spent most of her time comatose on the couch. I had five younger siblings to take care of. We were nothing *but* the scandal of Quarry Creek. I was told, to my face, that I was a mistake. A joke. I learned to get mean to get through it. Even now at work, I'm constantly fighting for a modicum of the respect and trust that my male counterparts get without trying. And when I succeed... Well, I'm the one given what boils down to a sex talk from my boss.

"The team's golden boy. The captain. One of the leaders in the fucking league. He got drunk and married in

Vegas. To a nobody. On a whim." I'll be the butt of the joke for the rest of my life. What else is new?

"I didn't...we..." he runs a hand through the strands of blonde hair. They stick straight up because he's been worrying them constantly, or because he needs a shower. "You are not a nobody."

I need to schedule a CT scan or a full workup, before I lose my health insurance, because the urge I have to press up on my toes and yank this man's mouth down to mine is clearly the sign of a brain tumor or a personality disorder. What is wrong with me that his affable smile and easy-going attitude makes me spit, but the glower he's turning on me, looking like he wants to grip my shoulders and shake until my teeth rattle, is sending the blood racing through my veins and heating me from the inside out.

"I know," I soothe, "but to the world? To hockey fans? Compared to you?"

"Fuck the world."

I feel the shiver race across my skin even as my phone buzzes. I can't keep looking at him. I'm losing the thread of the conversation as he stares into my soul. As he sees me. This gorgeous, talented, kind, compassionate man. He's looking at me like I matter to him, and what I'm about to propose could get us all twisted and confused. It won't be as simple as not splitting up. We're going to need to pretend that this wasn't a mistake. Wasn't an inebriated accident. Pretend that it was inevitable.

This man could take down every wall I've built over the last fifteen years without even trying. And then when the time comes to let him go, I might crumble under the weight of everything they held back. What if I break the same way my mother did? Shattered into a million pieces and left to curl inward, blocking out the real world every single minute he's gone. I'm already too twisted up, too mired in confusion to keep my head on straight. Two minutes ago, I wanted this man to bleed. Now I want to find a private corner and climb him like a tree.

I pull out my phone for a distraction and there's an email from Bob's assistant confirming my meeting request.

"I'm meeting with Bob and the GM tomorrow morning. You should come with me."

"I will." He says. No hesitation. No question of timing. I know he has a day off, but the guys get together and work on drills. I guess, being captain, he can decide when they meet.

"Right now we're scheduled for nine, but I can ask for a specific time if you have a conflict."

"I'll be there." His words vibrate into the marrow of my bones. Did he step closer again?

I drop my eyes and tap out a quick reply, confirming I'll be there. We will be there.

"I think it's time for that talk now," Vic says. "Let me take you to dinner, Tristan."

I shake my head. I can't spend another minute in this man's presence. Not without losing the last grip on my sanity. I twist the ring on my finger and his eyes zero in on the movement. His hands flex, clenching and releasing, before he shoves them back into the front pockets of his slacks.

"We are—"

"There's nothing to discuss. We'll go in tomorrow and tell them we're married and that we won't be rushing into a divorce. Just let me handle Bob and smile and nod when needed. No big deal."

I'm a fucking liar.

"Tristan."

I press my shoulders back and look down at my blank phone screen.

"I have to go. My siblings are waiting for me. I'll meet you at the main office at nine."

He's not stupid. I'm running and he knows it.

"I'll pick you up at eight thirty. We can drive together."

Drive. Together. So we can talk about all of this even more? No, thank you.

"No need. I'll catch a ride over with Hayley." She's doing a clinical at the hospital across the street and we'll be taking my car, but if I tell him I'm dropping her off, he'd probably offer to do it for me. The considerate ass.

"Tristan."

I shut my eyes and suck in a breath.

"Dammit Victor. I'm trying to get some space. Can't you understand that? I need to be somewhere where you are not right now. Please. Please, just pretend you already picked up on that and let. Me. Go. We can talk all you want tomorrow after the meeting, okay?"

"This is what you want?"

I'm not sure what he's referring to, but yes. I want space. I want to pretend we're happily married. I want to survive this meeting with my boss. I want to keep my job. I want...

I nod and he blows a breath.

"Okay."

This time he steps back and I feel the cold knife through me as his expression shutters. No more glare, but no more smile, either. My eyes burn and my throat feels thick. The apology sits heavy on my tongue, but I swallow it down.

I tuck my phone away, take a deep breath and back away from the stoic player standing in front of me. Guilt chews through my stomach again. That man should never do anything but smile.

The private terminal has cleared out, just a man with a mop cart emptying the trash can on the other side of the space. That's my cue to leave, too. Walk away.

"You know what I regret?" I call out as I put my hand on the door and Vic's head snaps up to look at me. "That I finally had you in bed and I don't remember any of it."

For a moment, his mouth drops open in shock. Then the grin spreads and his dimples appear as he throws his head back and laughs.

And I leave before I can ask him to help me fill in the blanks with fresh memories.

I DON'T BROACH the subject of talking again. After everything else, Tristan's been vocal about needing space, so that's what I am trying to do. My intention is to snag her right before we walk into Bob's office. I'll buy her a tea, ask how she slept, and then give her a play-by-play of the night in Vegas, but everything changes in the morning.

It starts with my phone vibrating so hard it falls off my bedside table. When I wipe the sleep from my eyes and pick up the damn thing, I almost drop it again. I'm not unused to social media attention, but the little red flags on my phone seem to have given up the good fight. My phone looks like it has chicken pox with the number of dots all over my screen. I have twenty-five missed texts—I snort at the fact that it's the same number as my jersey—thirteen missed calls, uncountable numbers of social media notifications, and yeah, it's still vibrating in my hands.

Mom is standing in the hall, her own phone pressed to her ear.

"He's up now. Hold on." Her eyes dip down the length of my body and back up, before zeroing in on my left hand ruffling my hair. "I don't see it," she says into the phone. "I'll call you back."

"Erik?" I ask as she slides her cell into her pocket, and I'm on alert when she nods. My relationship with Erik has been tense since his cancer diagnosis at sixteen. He's finding his way back to us, or us to him, but he isn't one for random morning phone calls. "Everything okay with him? With Quinn's dad?" Sean Cooper is another cancer survivor. He's been in remission for a while now, but we all still worry. I'm not sure that ever stops.

"Yep. Sean's fine. Quinn's fine. Erik's good." Mom's eyes dip to my hand again. "A little birdie told us some interesting news."

Another call scrolls across the screen of my cell phone. My agent's number. I send him to voicemail. I'm already running late for the day, and my mom is more important than the guy sitting at his fancy desk out in Los Angeles.

I pause.

Except LA is three hours behind us. Which means it's —I check the clock—five in the morning his time. Not that I care. I'm running late to meet with Bob and Tristan. It's possible my priorities are a little out of whack. If my agent is calling me this early in the morning, it's not usually a good sign, but I refuse to be tardy to this meeting. I refuse to leave Tristan hanging.

Stay married. We have to...the words roll through my brain, echoing as they bounce off sluggish neurons. She asked me to meet her at the office. She asked me to stay married. I will give the woman anything she asks for. Except a divorce.

My phone rings again and I look at my mother. She smiles.

"Go on, you know he'll just keep calling and he's already cranky that he had to get up early."

She's not wrong, but I still roll my eyes as I swipe to accept the call.

"Varg," I say into the phone. I press it tight to my ear, but my mother inches closer, clearly interested in what Harv has to say and not willing to miss a single syllable.

"*Married. You got fucking married. At a dive in Vegas. And you didn't give me or Mindy the heads up to put out a press release. Fuck a damn waffle, Victor. We didn't even know you were dating. And then I see on the fucking news that you got married. To some random nobody. Because what, you couldn't think with your head—the big one, dumbfuck—for even a single night? Who even is this girl? What reason could you have for rushing this and being sloppy enough to get nailed by the paps? And giving the best head of your life isn't a rea—*"

"Enough." My mother's eyes go wide at the harsh tone of my voice. I'm not the one who yells at people. I'm not the one who gets mad. But I'm also fucking tired of the idea that people may think there's something wrong with me and Tristan. Beyond the fact that we work together and it's against organization policy. There is no universe where she is undeserving of me. None. No universe where she isn't enough. "Tristan is not random. And watch what you call her."

My mother is fucking grinning and doing some weird shimmy dance in the damn hallway.

"Tristan. As in Grant? The angry little thing that FUCKING WORKS FOR YOU?"

First, I do not know how Harvey Gunther got any information about what happened in Vegas. Did he say the news? Fuck. Second, Tristan does *not* work for me. She works for the same organization I do. We technically have the same boss. If anything, I work for her.

"We go almost thirteen seasons together without so much as a blip on TMZ's radar and then you turn around and pull this shit? There are clauses in your contract about not fucking the goddamn help! They could trade you for this. Did you know that?"

I hadn't really thought about it, mostly because I know they won't. I've been way more concerned about what will happen to Tristan.

"Bob wants the cup and we both know I'm the guy who's going to deliver it. I'm not going anywhere."

"And what about when they fire your little wife? Did you at least sign a fucking prenup? Do they do those in Vegas? Have you taken too many hits to the head? You live in a no-fault state. You'll owe that woman half of everything, Victor. HALF! Two rules. TWO! Wear a fucking condom. Sign a fucking prenup. I didn't think I had to spell out: Don't be a goddamn bastard fucker toaster strudel and marry your one-night-stand in Vegas."

I pinch the bridge of my nose, a headache already brewing. I've wasted too many precious minutes on this damn call, and if Harv doesn't stop insinuating I've made a colossal mistake I'm going to break things. Starting with the glass awards. The ones he keeps lined up in neat little rows on the shelf behind his massive desk. I bet they'd shatter into a million beautiful sharp pieces.

"I'm hanging up now, Harv. I have a meeting with Bob and the GM this morning. Kindly fuck right off. I'll call you if I need you, but right now, I don't. Neither does my wife."

I can't stop the little shiver that rocks through me at the last two words. I end the call and slide the still buzzing phone—Harvey looking a little desperate trying to call me back—into the pocket of my pajama pants.

"So it's true then?" My mom asks, hands over her mouth to hide her smile. "She's the one who came by that day. The one you've been filming with?"

The one you have it bad for? Goes unsaid, but we both know it's there.

"No," I tell her, tipping my head back to stare at the weird texture on my ceiling. I should hire someone to remove that.

"Victor," my mom glares at me. "I heard Harvey. I also heard Erik when he called and I've seen the photos on the social medias."

"Social media, mom, just social media."

Then her words really hit me.

I thought Tristan would be wrong. Stupid, I know. One thing I love about her is how good she is at her job and her job is to know how these things work. It seems so random sometimes, but she's perfected the hooks, the bait, and she knows exactly how to reel in the followers she's looking for.

Even so, I really thought I'd gotten the team under wraps. I'd talked to every single player. I'd asked them to keep the news to themselves. To let Tristan and I lead the discussion with the public the way we saw fit. They'd all agreed, and I thought that meant I'd have time to let her know we didn't have to say anything to anyone. That she can take her ring off and no one will be any wiser about what happened that night in that little white chapel.

Then mom's words hit again on the rebound.

Photos.

I don't even pull my phone back out, just hold out my hand for my mother's. She's already loaded up the article —although how this can be newsworthy with no comment from me or Tristan is a mystery—and I scroll past the text to find the photos. There's one of me carrying Tristan on my back down the Vegas strip, my hands high on her thighs to help hold down the short, silky skirt. Her eyes are closed, her face pressed into my neck, and I can still feel the warm, wet press of her lips to my bare skin. My head is turned to the side, like I'm watching her out of the corner of my eye.

There's a photo of the two of us walking into the chapel, her shoes back on her feet and my hand low on her back. She's smiling as I pull the door open. Again, my face dips down toward her. I'm smiling too. The last photo is…. Well, I like it the best, but it's also the most damning. I'm towering over her, her back pressed to the wall of the chapel. She's looking up at me, a dreamy smile painting her beautiful mouth. Her hands are resting on my chest, and the glint of gold on her ring finger practically shines out of the phone. The only thing even more noticeable is an identical glimmer on my left hand. The one pushing a lock of hair behind her ear. I look moments away from devouring her.

All my plans for the morning go up in a poof of smoke. The news has already broken. We're already a juicy piece of gossip. And if I don't get a move on, I'm going to leave her standing alone in front of the man who has already told her he'd fire her.

"I have to go." I shove the phone back at my mother and throw myself into my team warm-ups, dialing Tristan's number as I do.

She doesn't answer. Not the first time. Or the fifth. Or the twelfth. Not as I punch the call button on my steering wheel as I break multiple traffic laws to get to the head office on time. Not as I dial again while the elevator doors snick shut. Instead, I find her exactly at nine, looking whiter than fresh ice, as Bob Seever's heavy office door opens and we're ushered inside.

"Cutting it close?" She whispers under her breath and I let my hand come up to rest on her back. She's wearing a fitted blue dress and I can feel the rise of the zipper under my palm. It zips literally all the way up, from the small slit at the back of her thighs to the high neck tucked under a perfect twist of hair. How did she get into this thing by herself? Will she need help unzipping it later? I'll volunteer.

I lean down and let the words, "You have no idea, kitty cat," ghost over the shell of her ear. I feel her shiver under my hand and I grin. Stay married, she said. Make it look real, she said. I can give her that. Judging by the look on the team owner's face, it might be working.

"Let me do the talking?" She whispers back and I don't know if she's seen the pictures yet, seen the news, but I owe her this. She was right about what would happen. Even when I had doubts, she knew. It's time to let her take control and do what she does best. I nod.

Bob sits behind his enormous desk, downtown Quarry Creek framed in the full-length windows behind him. He doesn't make a move to stand when we approach, simply gestures to the two chairs facing him. He also doesn't smile, but he doesn't look frothing mad yet either.

"Victor, Tristan. I hear congratulations are in order."

It shouldn't surprise me he's heard the news. He probably has a google alert for the team. I know my agent does. Or someone in the organization is tasked with keeping tabs on our media coverage and would have called him first. Either way, I catch myself frowning at the way he addresses me first.

"Thank you, Mr. Seever." Tristan sits down in her leather chair and crosses her legs at the ankles. I plop down like it's the bench and I'm coming off a too-long shift in all my gear. Her voice gives nothing away, but the chance that she hasn't seen all the gossip is slim to nonexistent. I reach over and she slides her hand into mine, squeezing my fingers between hers.

"I'll admit," our boss says as he opens the top drawer of his desk, fiddling with something inside. "I was shocked to see the photos after our last chat, Ms. Grant. Or should I say Mrs. Varg? Will you need a name change form for HR?"

"A name change form?" She leaves a hanging pause between each word, like maybe she hasn't parsed his meaning yet. I suck on my lips, biting down with my teeth to stop the smile threatening to break across my face.

"I assumed this meeting was to inform the organization of your change in marital status and name."

"Yes," Tristan says, her fingers squeeze tighter, strangling mine. "So you're saying..."

"You're still employed," I finish for her, adding, "darling," on to the end to really sell this.

"But I thought..."

Watching my kitty cat be left speechless is more entertaining than a barn burner game seven of the Stanley Cup finals. Her eyes blink once, twice, and her perfect blonde brows dip together. White teeth worry her bottom lip and I'm torn between running my hand down her back and snapping a picture so I can see her adorable confusion whenever I need a pick-me-up.

"Ms. Grant, surely you can understand my position here," Bob's saying the right things, but even I can hear the condescension. I unwind my fingers from Tristan's so that I can cup her knee in my palm. Her arm winds through mine and I wonder if it was a conscious choice to sell our couplehood, or if she's seeking me out for some form of support and comfort that even *she* isn't aware of. "It's one thing to condone a torrid affair between you and one of our players. It's another thing to condone a marriage. I assume this is more than just poor decision-making while under the influence?"

Don't look at her, I tell myself. *It'll look like you're comparing stories which would be highly suspicious.*

"Mr. Seever." Tristan shifts in her chair and I let my thumb rub circles against the soft skin of her inner thigh. "Vic and I did not make this decision lightly. It may appear that way, especially after our last meeting, but..."

She's floundering. I can see it in the tense cords of her neck and the lines at the corner of her mouth.

"We knew about the policy." I break the silence. "So we were trying to keep our feelings under wraps. But I hit a wall, sir. I couldn't imagine another minute of my life when I couldn't call this woman mine. It's cliché, yes, but when Tristan told me she'd always imagined running off to Vegas and getting married by the Hillbilly Cat, well... I'd have done just about anything to give her what she wanted."

I don't even look at Bob. I'm too busy watching the rosy pink blush climb up the sides of Tristan's neck. I want to drag my tongue along the same path. I wonder if she remembers how much of what I said is completely true.

"Anyone with eyes can see what the two of you have, son." Bob smiles. "It would be very shortsighted of me to penalize you two for falling in love. Besides, it's nice for the team to have some positive press."

"Positive press?" Tristan shakes her head. "We hit the tabloids, sir. I... lied to you. You warned me. The last thing the team needs is a scandal."

"I see you haven't been reading the comments." Bob's

chuckle morphs into a cough and he lays a checkbook on the top of the gleaming desk. "Normally I'd agree with that idea, but in this case, you might want to take a look. I think you two might be just what my team needs right now."

I don't mean to stare down our owner as he pulls out a checkbook, filling in each line with a fountain pen that easily cost more than all my equipment combined. Well, the retail value of my gear. I can't remember the last time I had to pay for pads or skates or sticks. There's a lot more wrist flourishing than I expected, but I'm doing my best not to let my gaze drop to Tristan. He just said she was still employed, so I don't think he's writing a severance check.

"I'm guessing you scheduled this meeting so you could ask to keep your job. Is that correct?"

A tight nod from the woman next to me, and I slide my hand more firmly around her knee, feeling the heat of her skin crawl up my wrist and sink into my bones.

"I can tell you aren't often trusting of gifts, Ms. Grant, so I'll make you a deal." He recaps the pen and steeples his fingers. "You let the fans into your lives. Show them, first-hand, the story of your love and relationship, and I'll pretend we didn't have a chat or a clause about inter-organization fraternizing. Deal?"

He slides the check across the table to us and I see Tristan's eyes flare with surprise. It's a respectable number of zeros, even considering what my contract is worth.

"This is just a little wedding present. Contracts, and the team aside, I'm happy for you both."

Tristan is frozen, and for a moment I wonder where my take-no-prisoners girl went. The one who told me to follow her lead and let her do the talking. I fold and pocket the check for her with a "thank you, sir" thrown at Bob. He waves us off with instructions to enjoy our new marriage, and an apology that we won't get a honeymoon "until after playoffs, right, Varg?"

And then we're in the hallway, the door clicking shut behind us, and Tristan turns to me with a look of horror on her face.

"I'm so sorry," she whispers the words, her face stricken. "I thought it would be a lot more begging, but I didn't think we'd have to actually pretend..." She shakes her head, hair sliding free of the twist. "I'm sorry Vic."

I'm not sorry. Not about this, at least. I don't mind the idea of dating Tristan for real. Showing her we're as good for each other as everyone else seems to believe.

I am sorry about one thing. I was supposed to tell her before now, definitely before the meeting, but preferably on the morning we woke up in Sin City. There was a window of opportunity, a chance to get ahead of this part of the story. If Robbie had headed her off and she'd taken off the ring before anyone saw it. If we hadn't been spotted on our way to the chapel, or on our way out. If, if, if...

It doesn't matter now. We're in this. Partners stumbling along together, making the best of the hand we've been dealt. It's too late to turn back. The hockey-loving world has seen the photos. My agent has seen the photos. My mother thinks she has a new daughter-in-law. We've agreed to perform for the cameras. For the fans.

It won't change a single thing now if I tell her we aren't actually married.

BREAKING NEWS

Hockey Heartthrob Hitched

NHL Superstar **VICTOR VARG** was spotted last night in Sin City. After leading his team to a win against the hometown favorites, Varg was seen cuddling up to a mystery blonde. Sources close to the two said the captain shut down local club The Velvet to enjoy some alone time. And the two were later seen

WE DON'T DISCUSS IT, but Vic follows me back to my apartment. Hayley didn't keep the car, so I lead him down Main Street and through the two hanging yellow lights, wondering if I'll accidentally lose him. I'm not *trying* to, but I'm not doing a great job of keeping the convoy together. I'm glad we're going to sit down and talk about this, but I'm also grateful for the fifteen-minute reprieve in the car. I could have used a little extra traffic, or stoplights, or something.

He pulls into the empty spot behind me and I blame the difference in our stride for how he opens my car door for me while I'm still fighting my seatbelt. I remind myself I don't need his chivalry, even as my heart twists in my chest. He says nothing, just stands like a bodyguard behind me as I unlock my front door and let us into my tiny apartment.

I can't help but sneak a glance over my shoulder, wanting to see him take in my space. It's nothing like his sprawling mansion with marble and gold and crystal. My fiesta ware in my open cabinets. My purple couch looks like a dollhouse accessory compared to the hockey player standing in my open doorway. If he was in his skates, he'd have to duck under the doorjamb. I'm struck again by how big he is. I barely reach his sternum. It should be terrifying to be that close to a man who literally uses his body all day, every day, in the most brutally physical way possible. But it isn't.

He's staring down at me, a soft smile curving the softness of his lips. I feel that bubbling squirm just under my belly button and, for the first time in a long time, I don't force it down. Instead, I wet my lips and watch his eyes darken, pupils spreading to swallow the hazel. I drop my gaze so I can take a breath and see the white of his knuckles pushing up against his skin.

I'm suddenly very aware of how close we were in that Vegas hotel room. And how I don't have any memories of the fun parts.

"Hi," Vic says and I shake my head to reorient myself into reality. I'm about to say hi back when someone else does it for me.

"Hey man," Max says, and I whirl around to see my baby brother slurping my orange juice straight from the carton in my tiny kitchen.

"Who are you talking to?" Madison says, shutting my bedroom door behind her, one of my favorite sweaters clutched in her hands. "Oh, hi Tristan. Brother-in-law. Can I borrow this?"

Vic raises one hand to wave at them both.

"If you want it to come to the top of your ribcage, sure." I say to my five-foot nine baby sister.

"Perfect," she says just as Max says, "Come on Mads, we're leaving."

"No, we aren't." My sister's smile is pure evil. "We're going to grill Mr. Hockey Superstar on his intentions for his new wife." Her smile grows bigger. "You're aware you're basically like our daddy now, right?"

"W-what?" Vic is choking behind me, eyes wide.

"Madison Rose." I can feel my cheeks flaming, and I guess this is one way to break the previous tension. Now we're just marinating in embarrassment.

Her smile grows even wider. Why couldn't it have been any other sister here?

"Well, he knows you're basically our mommy, right?"

I'm wracking my brain, but I'm not sure if he does know that. He must have had some idea based on what I *have* told him, but I rarely share conversations about our childhood trauma.

"I had an idea," Vic's words rumble through me as his hand finds my lower back. I lean into the touch, feeling grounded even as I want to strangle my sister.

"Good job, Mads," Max says, putting the juice back in the fridge. "You just cockblocked them."

"What?" Later, I'll think it's cute that Vic and I spoke in perfect unison. Once I'm done also strangling my baby brother. It shouldn't surprise me he's adding to the discomfort. They're twins, after all.

"I doubt the newlyweds are that easily put off. Aren't they supposed to be in the honeymoon phase?" Madison says and slings my sweater over her shoulder. "Come on, Maxie, let's go so they can bang." Then she grips her twin by the wrist and drags him from the apartment. For a big guy, Max knows well enough to let the woman in his life lead him around.

"Bye," he calls out as they maneuver around us and the door closes on their grinning faces. "Have fun."

"Sorry," I say to Vic as silence descends on my apartment. "They're twins. They can't help but share a single brain cell. Apparently, neither decided to use it today."

"I get it," he says, "my twin, Erik, and I used to be the same."

It's like ice water over the top of my head at the mention of his brother Erik. The one who was smack dab in the middle of the last time I was in trouble because of this man. And yes, okay, we came out of this one unscathed—sort of—but it's another reminder that no matter how much I want to feel comfortable and safe with this man, I'm giving him too much credit. My brain is running away with the fantasy that he could take care of me the way I've always had to take care of everyone else.

I drop my purse onto my loveseat and step out of my heels. My ankles and the balls of my feet ache. I want to strip down to my pajamas, but I'm not ready to fully remove my armor, because that's what the makeup, the suits, the heels are. A suit of armor. An illusion. *I've got this*, they say. Even when I absolutely do not have anything remotely under control.

"I knew you and your siblings had a rough go of it, but I don't think I realized how much they count on you," Vic says, as if this is a regular conversation and not a decades-old wound

"It's normal to love your siblings even when they drive you crazy." I say the words as if it's that simple. As if I didn't give up every piece of me for years to make sure that they were taken care of. That they had some semblance of security.

"There's nothing normal about what you guys had to go through with your parents." He follows me into my space, leaving inches between us, and I stop myself from swaying into him.

"It's fine." I step away. I need something to do with my hands.

"It's not," he follows me again. Does the man not understand I'm retreating? Fleeing? "I know a little something about that. About loving your family through the worst of it and knowing no one else will ever quite get it."

It's instinct to want to scoff. To lash out. How could he and his twin possibly understand? I know they have a sister living out in the mountains with her wife. Happy and supportive, even from a distance. I've met their mother. She's wonderful. His mother lives with him, for fuck's sake. She comes to all his games. His brother met his fiancée at one. They were put up on the kiss cam over and over until they caved and the crowd went wild. Vic played like the devil was chasing him down the ice that night.

And then Vic hung me out to dry and I almost lost my job.

"Where'd you go?" He asks, and I'm not sure what he means because I haven't actually moved that far away from him. "I can see you shutting down. Don't do that. Talk to me, Kitty cat."

It's nothing, I want to say. *I'm being an idiot. I should be able to let this go.*

"Nowhere," I lie. "It's fine."

This time he bridges the space between us and cups my face in his wide palms, tipping my chin up until our eyes meet, like a kiss between souls. His pupils splay outward again and I think his fingers are trembling. Maybe that's me.

"You beautiful little liar." His lips almost brush mine. When did he lean down? My eyes flutter closed. "Tell me what's on your mind."

Where did my spine go? My resolve? Because I want to give this man anything he asks for right now. What's wrong with me? I was just mad. Wasn't I?

"It's nothing."

"Not to me." This time his mouth brushes mine and I chase the feeling as he pulls back. I'm sucking his air into my lungs and I barely know what we're talking about. "Please, Tristan. I feel like I did something wrong and now you're using it to shore up the walls you throw up between us." Another brush of his lips and I moan against his mouth. I've officially lost my place in this conversation.

"Let me fix it."

Fix what?

"Let me fix whatever it is I did to make you not trust me."

But I do trust you, I want to say. Even though I shouldn't. Not because he's not trustworthy, but because I have no reason to put myself into his hands and trust that he'll bring me out on the other side in one piece. Not when the last two times I did that he let me down. And I know that's not fair. I know I didn't tell him what I expected. He can't read minds. But sometimes I feel like he can. He should. No matter how wrong that is. He should understand what I need even if I don't tell him. He should get it. Get me. Because that's what happens when people fall in.... No.

"It's dumb," I whisper, and he presses our foreheads together. He must be developing a crick in his neck. I should get a step stool or something to help him out. Anything to avoid the rest of this damn conversation.

"Not to me."

And it's stupid. It is, but I think he cares. At least a little. And I've been carrying this grudge around for far too long for no reason. We might as well clear the air. We're married after all.

"That day your brother came to the rink for the first time. You didn't give me an interview." I feel him tense under the hands that are resting on his firm pectoral muscles. "I was told to get Erik to talk to us. Everyone thought you wouldn't say no to me."

"Tristan," He sounds shattered.

"I told you it was stupid. I'm being petty, but you didn't even say no. You just ghosted me for three days." *And I almost lost my job.* I got called into Chris' office and had to listen to him tell me that if I couldn't even get one basic interview, one measly video, from the man who says yes to everything ever asked of him, then I must not be trying very hard. I must not be cut out for this job and perhaps I should consider another career path. A week later, they announced that the position I'd been promised was given to someone else. A new hire. A man.

"It's more than that," he says, and I can't hold back anymore. I tell him about how it felt to stand in that office and get dressed down over something I had no control over, but how I couldn't just walk away from the job. My siblings count on me. Hayley has tuition payments. Max has a scholarship, but still needs housing and massive amounts of food. Joey keeps forgetting to get her oil changed and someone has to pay to fix her car every time it quits on her. I don't want to stay in social media forever but walking away after everything I'd put in felt like admitting defeat.

I let the words spill out of me, feeling dumb and gutted as his expression shifts from shuttered to devastated.

"Tristan." I shift my eyes away from his, "Oh no you don't, baby. Look at me."

I hold out for a moment, heart thundering in my ears, but it's useless.

"I'm sorry," he says, and I pull back, stepping out of his grasp. He doesn't haul me back, but he moves with me. "You did not deserve your boss to speak to you that way. Especially when the issue at hand was out of your control."

I squeeze my eyes shut and he tips my head up again. I can't see him, but I can feel his breath breaking over my skin, feel the vibration of each word through my chest. How did I end up here? Panting over a man I've been telling myself to stay away from. Panting over a man I don't even...

"I don't talk about my brother to the press. We don't give interviews."

"You asked me to plan his grand gesture." And there's the crux of the issue. The man avoided me when I needed him but he had no problem asking for help when he needed me.

"I don't talk about Erik, per his request." A hand slips around my neck to cradle the back of my head. I want to lean into the touch, to let this man hold me up so I can take a fraction of the weight off my shoulders. "When I asked you to help get his message on camera, that was because *he* requested it." A pause as he works my hair loose from its twist. "Erik was diagnosed with bone cancer right after we received our Junior invites, Tristan. He was the better player. Faster on the ice, better stick handling, he'd have gone pro for sure. We wanted to go together."

"Like the Lundqvists?"

"More like the Sedin Twins." Right, I'd forgotten the most famous NHL twins. "We wanted to play on the same team. The same line. Most people forget the Lundqvists are twins."

"Well yeah, because we all just think Henrik is attractive and we forget about Joel." I smile up at him.

"They're identical."

I shrug. "Maybe I like goalies."

"You like *me*," he says, the words pouring into my soul. And fuck... I do.

"Erik went through multiple rounds of chemo and

surgery and still lost his left leg right after we turned eighteen. Hockey had become my whole life, and it was the one thing he couldn't go back to. So no, we don't let the press get wind of how we could have been the sixth set of twins in the NHL if not for the tragedy of cancer. Erik and I could barely speak to each other for years. It was physically painful for him to attend games." Vic swallows hard and we're standing so close I can feel the motion of his throat. "It's the same reason I couldn't work with you this season until I had his okay. Things are better between us now. He and Quinn come to more games, but he still deserves his privacy if he wants it. I don't get to take that from him. I won't."

My heart aches, a sickly pulse under my sternum. I'm the world's biggest bitch. I've been holding a grudge over something he couldn't control. It's admirable—attractive— the way he holds this boundary to protect his family. For his brother. I understand loving your siblings. More than most.

"You could have just told me," I can't help the parting jab, because that's the part that hurt. I wouldn't have pushed if he'd just *told* me all of this. "You avoided me for days and then went on the road. You could have just said no. To me, or to Chris. He was so sure you'd say yes if I asked, and then I couldn't even get you to talk to me."

A deep laugh fills my tiny apartment, rolling over my ears like a rumble of thunder.

"Baby. Kitty cat. Tristan. That was the entire problem." He tips our foreheads together again. "I can't say no to you. I couldn't then and I can't now."

"Well," I sniff. "That sounds like a *you* problem. Might I suggest therapy if you struggle to hold boundaries and say no to people?"

Vic steps into my body again and my back comes up against my fridge. He's almost taller than it.

"I don't like to say no to people, not if I can help them, but I know how. I've said no about Erik before. It's *you*, Tristan. I wasn't sure I could say 'no' for my brother when the person asking was you."

"Why?"

"You know why, baby."

My heart is going to pound right out of my chest. My insides are liquifying as I try not to read into what he's saying. Try to hold on to a modicum of distance. Where are the walls I had built between us? I painstakingly laid each brick aside and now they are nowhere to be found.

Because you were wrong, my brain says. *You hated him because of how he handled one media request over a year ago, and now you know why. And it's a good reason. You can't help but—*

I shut my brain up.

"You know," I say, shifting my hips against his thighs. "I still have some regrets about Vegas."

"I'm sorry—" I press my hand to his mouth, halting the apology in place.

"I don't remember marrying you." I trace his top lip with the tips of my fingers. He tries to nip them and I move away, sliding my palm along his cheek to tangle in the hair falling across his temples.

His eyes close, but it's not the flutter of a man starved

for physical contact. It almost looks like guilt. That won't do.

"Tristan." I can't remember the last time someone said my name as much as he does. I like the way it sounds on his tongue. I want to hear more. "I have to tell you. We didn't—"

I press my mouth to the line of his jaw, scraping his stubble with my teeth, and I roll my hips again. Vic sinks against me, pinning me to the refrigerator, and I can feel the hot, hard ridge of his erection pressed into my belly. He's going to need to lift me for this to work, or we'll need to move. He pulls away.

"Tristan. In Vegas... you were... I thought you were..." His mouth drags across my temple. "Fuck. I thought you were drunk. We didn't... I would never..."

I'd wondered about this. Waking up with my panties still on. With his underwear too. The hold was proprietary, but there was no twinge of soreness, no sticky fluids dripping down my thighs. No condom wrapper tossed on the bedside table. But...

"I remember an orgasm." It's one of the few things I *do* remember about that night. I remember a hand between my thighs and coming like a freight train.

"It was you." He's given up the distance, chasing my mouth again. We aren't even kissing, just rubbing our lips together so they can touch. "You pushed me to my absolute fucking limit, stripping out of that little white dress—it pooled on my floor like water, Tristan—and then, while I was distracted by the curve of your tits and the perfect pink of your nipples, you had a hand down the front of your panties. I should have stopped you. I should have left the room. I should have done just about anything, but it was taking all the blood left in my brain to stop myself from reaching for you and giving you an orgasm you didn't have to work for."

I climb him like a tree. One minute my feet are on my linoleum floor, pressed up on my tippy toes to get as close to this man as I can, and then my legs are around his waist. We're face to face—almost—and his hand is cupping my ass as he crushes me between his chest and my refrigerator.

It feels like we might hurtle out of control. Tumble right off a cliff into an abyss with no end, but I can't stop the shiver in my veins or the rocking of my hips. I wouldn't want to, even if I could. This conflagration has been building for weeks. Maybe even years. One look, one brush of arms or fingers, one laugh, one nickname, one teasing joke, at a time. Smoothies, and naked chests and puppies and the way he looks, looks, looks, at me.

"Tristan," we're both panting. "I need to tell you—"

"Later," I say, tightening my legs around his waist. "I want that orgasm I don't have to work for. Maybe more with interest." And then I press my mouth to his for real, licking along the seam of his lips and swallowing his groan.

THERE'S something I'm forgetting. Something big. Something important. But I can't think past the feel of Tristan's mouth, her lips, her tongue swiping lazy circles around mine.

I'm not a man who folds under pressure. I have the highest shootout percentage on the Arctic. I win more face-offs than I lose. I've barreled onto the ice with seconds left on the clock aiming for that tie-goal to take us to over-time. I've held onto my mother as she sobbed over my twin's hospital bed. I have nerves of steel honed through years of practice. Shove all those pesky fears and doubts down. Smile and nod, shrug your shoulders, look friendly. Affable. Be in control.

But I can't stop my hands from shaking as I press Tristan into the stainless steel front of her refrigerator and cup my hands under the curve of her ass. I can't stop the sounds that wrench from the well of my chest. I can't stop, can't stop, can't stop kissing her. She tastes sweet and spicy as she devours me, like the tea I know she loves. Her arms press into my traps as she tries to boost herself higher, get a better angle. I press a knee to the fridge and help shift her up.

She throws her head back as she sucks in a breath, an audible thunk against the hanging calendar behind her. My mouth is already dragging across her chin, her jaw, down the long line of her delicate throat. She's gasping, rolling her hips against my abdomen, and I'm nipping at her skin with my teeth. My brain wipes clean, not a conscious thought to be had. Instinct guides me to leave quarter-sized marks along the column of her neck. My ring on her finger, my hands on her ass, my claim on her skin.

Fuck.

My hips jerk, seeking friction.

This woman has been starring in my fantasies for the better part of my Quarry Creek career. I love the dip of her waist. The trio of freckles at the base of her neck. I want to drag my tongue over both. I want to know the color of her nipples. My only goal is to make her come. As many times as she'll let me. In as many *ways* as she'll let me.

I can hold her weight with one hand, and I free my left to slide up her side. She shivers under my touch and I wonder if she can feel the ring on my finger even through the thick fabric of her dress. The same dress with the skirt hiked to her waist. If I dip my eyes down, I'll be able to see her panties. Her pussy. That visual will ruin my self-control, ruin me.

I barely survived in Vegas, watching her slide her hand down the front of a tiny pair of white cotton panties. Watching the small wet spot grow as her fingers found her clit and circled. She'd come hard and fast, which might have been the only thing that saved us both. Another moment of watching her stretch for that peak and I'd have hit my knees, burying my face in her cunt.

Her face presses to my chest, mouth panting a damp patch onto my shirt. The breath is sawing out of my lungs like I've never run a mile in my life. I'm a professional fucking athlete. I'm at my physical peak. We aren't even fucking naked yet. Zero items of clothing on the floor, and I can barely suck in enough oxygen with her finally in my arms.

My fingers skate over the curve of her tit and Tristan moans. The sound flows over my ears and sinks into the atoms that make up my muscles, my blood, my bones. I'm undone. Nothing exists outside of this moment. This kitchen. This woman. I need this dress pooled at our feet. I need to know she's in this with me.

"Tristan."

She doesn't hear me, or she doesn't react.

"Kitty cat."

Still nothing. I slip my hand away from her glorious chest and bracket her throat, tipping her head back so she has to look at me. Her cheeks are flushed, eyes a hazy blue behind wide-blown pupils. Her lips are kiss-swollen, still red even after I destroyed her lipstick. She wets them with her tongue and I almost forget what I'm doing, almost lunge for her mouth again.

"Baby." My fingers flex against her skin and her eyes roll back, lashes fluttering and fuck. She likes the grip I have on her throat. She likes the pressure. I put as much steel into my voice as I can, "Tristan, look at me." She does. "I'm going to get this dress off you. Do you want that?"

Her nostrils flare and she squirms against my chest, ankles crossing behind my waist. I can feel her arousal through the cotton of my shirt. I'm going to lose my fucking mind here. I can't resist the light kiss I press against her mouth. She tries to chase my lips as I pull back.

"I need words, baby. Do you want this dress on the floor?"

She nods, "Yes. Please. Yes—"

I'm pulling down her zipper before she's done. Her bare back touches the fridge and she flinches. It's easy to take two steps to my right and slide her onto her counter. She's lower than she was in my arms, harder to kiss, but her counter height is perfect. I pull her hips to the edge of the granite and rock my cock against her center. Her head falls back, and if I wasn't still gripping her throat, she'd have brained herself on the cabinets.

I fumble for the zipper at the back of her neck, and it's a miracle how I get her dress pulled down to her waist. Then I'm almost braining myself because her tits are free and utterly magnificent. I release her throat to cup them in my hands, rolling the weight over my fingers. Her skin is smooth and pale, each swell topped with a dusky nipple. I suck one into my mouth, unable to stop myself as my fingers find the other one.

"I've been waiting for this." I press the words into her skin, feeling the hitch in her breath and fuck me. This is the best I've ever had, and she's still in her underwear. I'm still fully dressed. "I swear you were created just to mess with my head."

Her fingers wind into my hair, pulling on the strands, and she shifts her hips. I need her naked now. I've been patient enough. I drop my hands to tug her dress the rest of the way down before I let it drop onto the floor. The fabric settles against my feet. Fuck. I didn't even get my shoes off. I switch sides, paying her other nipple some much-needed attention as I toe off my sneakers and kick them somewhere behind me. I'm not concerned about where they went. I'm hoping I won't need them for a long time.

"I haven't had a single thought that didn't include you in months." My hand slips to her belly. I can span the entire width of her body with my fingers outstretched. Fuck, she's tiny. I knew that. I'm hyper aware of every part of this woman, but sometimes she seems bigger in my mind. Her fire, her personality, her. It expands to fill any space it can. I'm achingly aware I could hurt her if I'm not careful.

"Please," her hands slip to the collar of my shirt, tugging in all different directions, too pleasure-drunk to get me undressed. I sacrifice my palm on her belly and reach over my neck to pull it off one-handed. Her fingers are on my skin before it can join my shoes and her dress on the floor. I groan, leaning into her touch. Her skin is chilled as her fingers slide over the curve of my pecs, threading through the fine hair on my chest. Her nails scrape my nipples and my hips rock into hers.

My control is in tatters. I have maybe three good pumps before it's game over.

"Tristan."

She pulls my mouth down and pushes her tongue past my lips and I lose myself in her taste, her smell, her feel. She's everything I hoped she would be, and nothing I could have ever imagined. My hand slips down her stomach again, fingers dipping below the band of her panties. Blue today. Blue lace. I love her in blue. She traces the lines of my abdominal muscles, counting out the six ridges, and my cock twitches. He's been hard since I walked into her apartment. Now he's weeping into the soft cotton of my team joggers.

Who the fuck am I kidding? He's been hard since Vegas. Hard since I passed a tiny puppy into her cautious arms. Hard since she walked right into my chest that first day in the head office. Maybe the first time Coach introduced her and warned us to play nice.

"I'm gonna make you come." I say and give her zero-point-two seconds to say 'no' before I push my hand down and cup her pussy against my palm.

She's soaked, dripping between my fingers and if her panties were off, I think there'd be a puddle on her countertop. It's the hottest fucking thing I've ever had the honor to discover. My kitty cat is as hot for me as I am for her. And I'm desperate, mouth parched like a man stranded in the fucking desert for weeks. I let my fingers trace her opening before circling her clit. Her hips buck, her tits shake with each gasped breath, her fingernails bite into my skin. Touching her is equal parts heaven and hell. She's every fantasy I didn't even know I had, and I know I'll never get enough. Not even if I live three hundred lifetimes.

Her eyes meet mine, bright but clear. "Do it," she growls, and I slide two fingers into the scalding heat of her cunt.

Her inner muscles flutter around me. Tight and hot and so wet I might embarrass myself. I curve my fingers, looking for that spot along the front wall of her pussy. Her hips grind into my hand and there... I press the tips of my fingers against the rough flesh, and she keens, her walls clamping down as she comes hard.

Nothing has ever felt like this. Nothing. Not getting my Junior's letter, or getting drafted. Not my first NHL goal, or my first hat trick. Not the first time I was the first star of a game. It's better than my own orgasms, watching my girl come on my fingers. Even better is the soft smile spreading across her face as she blinks up at me, holding onto my biceps as if she'll fall if she lets go. She won't. I wouldn't let that happen.

"Well, Victor Varg, you certainly live up to expectations."

I can feel the flush rising up my neck, and I can't help dropping my chin to my chest and letting out a bark of laughter. Fuck, she's amazing. She laughs with me and I let my gaze soak in the sight of the faint lines around the corners of her eyes, the wide curve of her mouth, the shine of her teeth. She hasn't seen anything yet.

"Set them higher and I'll do it again." I yank her back into me, letting her feel my aching dick. Honestly, it's a wonder I can form words or even think straight at this point. Her panties mold to her cunt and my mouth waters. "But first I'm going to eat this pussy until I'm fucking full, Tristan." She shudders, biting into her bottom lip and my voice goes hoarse. "Then I'm going to do it again before I feed you my cock, inch by damn inch, until you are."

The fucking vixen. She raises one blonde eyebrow, slips a hand down the front of my pants to fist my erection through my underwear, and bites her teeth into my obliques. I cup the back of her head, drawing her even closer just as she lets go and looks up at me from under her dark lashes.

"Yes, captain." She says with a wink, and my brain whites out as I lunge to suction our mouths together, her hands letting go of me to shimmy out of her panties. "But you already made me come, so I want to suck you first."

This time I have to fist my cock myself, gripping the base tight enough to halt the sudden and imminent release. That wasn't what I'd meant when I said I'd feed her my dick. I imagined looking into her icy eyes as I guided myself between her legs. I hadn't imagined, hadn't dared even think, about her lips closing around my shaft and sucking me into her throat. I won't make it to the grand finale if we try that. I won't. I know my limits, and this will end me. I've been waiting too long for her.

I haven't had an orgasm that didn't come from my hand since... well, since before my brother met Quinn. Since I first stepped foot into the main office to sign some paper-work and meet the head honchos, and clapped eyes on a tiny blonde tapping away on her phone. Even before I knew who she was, I wanted her. And apparently nobody else.

I'm in over my head. I need to get my mouth on her now. Two or three more orgasms and coming the minute I push inside her tight pussy won't be as mortifying. And maybe, just maybe, she'll let us do this again. And again. And again and again and again. Not that I think the edge will ever come off. Not with her.

Tristan reaches for my pants again, and I circle her wrists to stop her. I can feel the fine bones under my grip, and I loosen my hold. I don't want to hurt her. I just need to maintain some semblance of control.

"No," I say in the voice I use on Spags and Pelé when they're being complete idiots.

"No?" She tries to pull back, but I don't let her do that either.

"If you get your mouth on my dick, this is going to be all over, baby. I'll come down your throat so fast I'll drown you."

She licks her lips. "Yes, please."

Demon.

My brain glitches again and she takes advantage of the momentary weakness in my grip to reach for my drawstring.

"Tristan." I regain my hold and pull her wrists up to my chest. "Kitty cat." I press my forehead to hers. "Baby, I want to feel you come on my cock and drag me over the edge with you. The first time, at least. I'll let you suck me off as many times as you want after that."

Our gazes hold for a heartbeat. Two. Three. Then she nods, slipping her hands up to twist in the hair at the nape of my neck. I thought I was just about ready for a pre-play-offs haircut. But now I want it longer. I want to feel her grip and pull as she comes apart in my arms.

I kiss her again. Lost for eternities against her mouth. I twist my tongue around hers and we trade breaths back and forth. I could live forever in this moment. Right here with the taste of my...

Fuck.

I was going to call her 'my wife.'

But she's not.

That's what I was supposed to tell her. The part I was trying to say before she sucked my soul out with her lips and tongue. The right thing to do would be to tell her now. Clear things up before we take this irrevocable step. There's a reason annulments can't happen after a marriage is consummated. Not that this is a marriage. Just a pretend one. Just one she's already told our boss about and gotten his stamp of approval for. His congratulations. His fucking check. I pull back.

"Tristan."

"I need you," she breathes against my mouth. "Please, Vic."

My conviction falters.

"Wait," I say, "Hold on,"

She shakes her head, trying to pull me back in.

"I don't want to wait. I've been waiting for you for ages,

Vic. Please." Her legs are strong and she draws me right back into the heat of her. I'm lost. If there's a Hell, it's being this close to Tristan Grant when I shouldn't take advantage. I hope if there's a higher being out there, that they're seeing the effort I'm putting into slowing this down. Slow us down. Just until I can tell her about that night.

"Tristan. In Vegas... we didn't—"

"I know," she smiles up at me, sweetness and light, and a devilish gleam I already know is bad news... except... what?

She knows?

"You—"

"Yes," she says, "It was obvious."

I think I should fight this more. I think there's something still getting lost here, but to be honest, there's zero blood in my brain right now. I don't even know how my body is continuing to function without it. I think it must be some sort of reflex, like a chicken without its head.

She works my pants down with her feet and then my erection is between us, hard and leaking right against the bare skin of her pussy. I'm shivering, my teeth chattering out of my head as I hold back the urge to press forward and bury myself to the hilt.

"Fuck me Victor." She presses a kiss over my heart and I'm losing it. I can't hold out. The wet heat of her brushes my cock head and I jolt like I've been struck by lightning. "Please," she says and rocks her hips forward, wedging me against her entrance.

Fuck it.

It won't change a damn thing, not after what we've

already done. Not after what everyone already assumes. I have to believe that. I have to, because if I don't have this woman now. Right now. Now. Now. Now. I might have an aneurysm. A stroke.

She slides her hips along the counter again and I push in another fraction of an inch. She hisses and I groan. I want her mouth. I lean down to get it and we have a problem.

I can't kiss her without arching my back, a move that will pull me out of her cunt. I'm not willing to do that, but I need her mouth, her lips, her tongue on mine. Our height difference is massive. I knew this, but I didn't think about the potential pitfalls. I liked the idea of being able to hold her, protect her, carry heavy objects for her.

I meant to draw this out. I promised to feed myself into her, but desperate times and all that. I scoop her forward, impaling her on my dick. Her pussy contracts and she moans at the sudden stretch. My vision goes hazy. She's tighter than compression shorts made three sizes too small, her walls pulsing as we pant against each other.

"Sorry," I mumble into the top of her head. I slur the word, my brain sluggish. What was I doing? Her head lolls back, lips parted, and I lean down to fasten my mouth to hers, only to slide back out a few inches. That's right. I can't kiss her like this. Not if I want to stay inside her glorious cunt.

"Vic," my name is a wail as the head of my cock slides over the slick inner walls.

"Hold on to me, baby." I say and slide my hand under her ass, lifting her off the counter. Her couch isn't too far. My fingers brush the place where we're joined and I falter, my knees going weak at the visceral reminder that I'm here. Inside Tristan Grant. The woman I've been dreaming about for months. Years. Possible eternities.

She winds her arms around my neck, and the move pulls her up and off me before she slides back down until I'm seated fully inside her again. We might not make it to the couch. I could just lift her and kiss her every time I pull out.

"You're too big," she pants against my chest and that's the bolstering I need to regain my composure.

"I've got you Tristan. I'll always have you. Give me one second and I'll make it better." I'm pressing promises into her hair. *Forever. I'll take care of you forever. Just let me. Please let me. Marry me. Don't let anyone inside this pussy, but me. Please Tristan. Please. Please. Please. I lo—*

I let myself sink back into the purple velvet of her microscopic loveseat and pull her knees to either side of my hips. She's squeezing me tight, deep inside, and the woman must do pelvic floor exercises morning, noon, and night because I'm hanging on by the barest of threads.

"So good," she groans, finally able to reach my mouth. She bounces on my lap, as if gauging how far and fast she can move. I grit my teeth as my balls draw up tight, willing myself to relax. I know I said three pumps max, but I don't want those pumps to have been on the stagger to her couch.

"We're doing this." I say to her, in awe that she's here. I'm here. Inside her. Feeling her muscles clench with each move as my thighs tremble below her. Fuck, I put us on the couch so I could kiss her. Why am I not kissing her?

I still have to dip my head, but she tips her chin up and then we're pouring gasped breaths and muffled groans into each other's mouths as she rides me in her sun-drenched apartment. My hands grip her hips and I pull forward on each downstroke, letting the base of my cock rub right against her clit. She breaks the kiss to suck in a breath, incoherent streams of words leaving her mouth. It sounds like, *Oh god. There right there. Fuck Vic. Fuck. Yes. More.* And I can't hold out any more. Lava pours through my gut as every muscle in my body locks down.

I grip a tit, rolling her pretty pink nipple between my fingers. I suck her tongue into my mouth. I keep up the grinding pulse. And there. There. There it is. Her body bows and her walls clamp down so hard I see stars. And then I'm pouring everything that I am into the tight sheath of her pussy.

We lie together for long moments, catching our breaths in tandem. Then she presses a soft kiss to my mouth and shifts back to my knees. Cum drips out of her, painting my thighs, and I grimace.

"Fuck, condom. Tristan. I'm sorry. I didn't—"

"It's okay." She leans over the mess between us and kisses me again. "I'm on the pill. I'm clean, and I've seen your medical records."

I'm pretty sure that's some type of HIPPA violation, but I don't care. This girl can have my blood type, my social, my account numbers. Anything. My cock twitches at the thought and I stare at him, shocked. I don't think I had this recovery time even as a teenager. God, this woman.

"Again?" Tristan grins at me and if she keeps smiling like that, then yes, I'll be ready in less than a minute. I nod.

"Good," she says. "Let's go take a shower and then I want to see what your mouth can do. Husband."

I'LL ADMIT that I knew things were going to change, but I didn't realize how much. I guess I thought faking an actual relationship would be harder. Or maybe easier. Either way, the changes come fast.

We agree not to put out a formal statement. The gossip raised by our viral photos keeps the focus on us even without joint interviews or an official commentary. I guess I naively thought that would be it. We could tell the organization that we were together, that we were in love, and that would be the end. We'd live together, maybe, for a few months so the team wouldn't get suspicious, and then file for a quiet divorce after playoffs. And maybe it would have been if we hadn't been seen. If we hadn't been photographed. If I hadn't pounced on my husband like he was a wounded baby antelope and I was a starving predator.

As Madison would say, I was clearly delusional.

When Vic came home from a practice with a change of

address form, I told him to put my name down and fill it out with his address. I assumed I could pick up any mail sent to Vic's and stay at my place, but he walked through my apartment, smiling at my duck-yellow curtains, and told me he liked the space.

It took me precious moments to realize he meant he'd be listing my address. Even longer to realize he was planning to move in for real. The next day he showed up with a duffle bag full of his clothes and toiletries and it did something funny to my insides, seeing his shampoo in my shower, his razor in my bathroom cabinet, his massive shoes by my front door.

"Are you sure this is necessary?" I'd asked as I shouldered my purse for our trip to the grocery store. "Living together?" If I thought my siblings ate a lot of food, they had nothing on my new... on Vic. This was our third trip in as many days. He was covering the bill, so cost wasn't an issue, but I didn't have the space to store the massive quantities of dry goods and produce and lean meat that he ate.

"There are three photographers waiting in the parking lot," he'd said with a grin, sliding on his shoes. "Act besotted."

I heard the telltale clicks from some interestingly dressed landscapers as he handed me into the front seat of his Mercedes, pressing a panty-melting kiss to my cheek as he shut the door in my face.

"I thought you had a chef," I said as he added a fifth box of pasta to the shopping cart he was pushing through the organic grocery store I usually avoided based on the cost alone.

"I do." He looped an arm around the curve of my waist and pulled me into his body. "But now that I'm not living with mommy anymore, I figured you could—" he was laughing before the sentence ended, ducking my half-hearted swat to his chest.

"Kidding." He held his hands up in mock surrender. "I'm kidding. I took the chef when the team sent him over, but I can boil water and chop veggies with the best of them. Besides." He leaned down to press a kiss to my jaw, and I sucked in a surprised breath. "I thought we'd give the press something to talk about, even if it's just farfalle and chicken thighs.

I'd frowned as he ran a thumb over the jut of my chin. I knew we'd slept together, and he'd moved in, but since when were we the touchy-feely kind of couple? And then we'd rounded the corner into the dairy section, and there was a camera pointed our direction from under someone's elbow.

Then I frowned because when did Vic get better at understanding the press than I did?

That first night in my home, he tried to take the couch. I took one look at the loveseat that could barely handle *me*, stretched out, and pulled back the ruffled pink comforter on my bed, patting the mattress. My little brass bed frame creaked as he settled in next to me, but I'd be lying if I hadn't loved the way my body rolled into the dip he created in the mattress and the possessive hand that cradled my hip as he wrapped around me. Or the tongue that woke me in the morning.

If I was worried about what my siblings thought of

Vic's sudden and unavoidable presence in my life and in my apartment, I shouldn't have bothered. The first time Hayley and Joey let themselves in unannounced, Vic asked if they wanted dinner and doubled the pasta he was boiling. He also asked if he should clear out to give us some family time. My sisters were smitten within minutes, and my husband won Max over with conversations about conditioning drills and team dynamics.

"Don't be a dummy," my brother said to me as he shepherded our sisters out the door. "Lock that man down for good and blow him every night."

"I think marrying him locked him down, thanks. Always knew I could count on you for love and support," I'd responded with an eye roll.

"This is both," Max said, pressed a kiss to my cheek. "He could be the best thing that ever happened to you. He wants to take care of you and god knows you deserve someone to handle your wants and needs for a change. Let him."

I'd never actually tell my baby brother, but I did exactly what he suggested and followed Vic into the shower that night, hitting my knees and gladly swallowing him down from root to tip. He moaned his appreciation into the stream of water, holding my hair back in a tight fist.

The Arctic hits the road for a five-game spread after that, and it surprises me how much I miss my... Vic... even after only a few days. I blame his size for the emptiness in my seven-hundred square foot apartment. A pair of sneakers by the front door. His team hoodie hanging in my closet. The mug he's commandeered for coffee every morning—"Okay, so you're a hockey player... that don't impress me much."—still sitting next to the sink. One of his sticks leans up against the end table next to his side of the bed.

Fun fact, Vic's stick is taller than I am. A whole inch taller. Something that makes Palmer snort milk out of her nose when she finds out. It also leads to some interesting jokes I will forever pretend my baby siblings don't understand.

I make it through the first four games before I cave and drive to the gated neighborhood I've visited exactly one time before. I park my car in the circular driveway and ring the doorbell. My heart is trying to escape, thundering against the curve of my ribs. What am I doing here? This is insane. I have only a few more days without him. I've survived longer trips. I've survived entire off-seasons. If I'm this desperate, I can distract myself with work, or call Palmer to whip my ass into shape on a run from hell, or... or I can go back to my couch and curl up in a cozy blanket and obsessively watch all the film footage I have of Vic. Dammit.

For all I know, nobody's home.

"Tristan?"

Right. Too late to bail now without looking like an idiot.

"Hi." Shit, I don't know what to call her. Maria? Ms. Varg? I know Vic told me his parents aren't together. What if her last name isn't Varg? Why didn't I think to ask? "I hope I'm not interrupting anything."

"Of course not, sweetheart." She enfolds me into a firm hug, right there on the stone steps. "Come on in."

She's tall. Not as tall as Vic—few people are—but tall enough that I have to reach up to pat her shoulder. I'm not sure what else to do. I can't remember the last time someone hugged me. Vic touches me constantly too, but it's not the same when it's a precursor to sex. Or while sharing my slightly too-small bed. Even my siblings run in with the one arm kind, a squeeze into their sides and a quick 'thanks' before we step back.

"Thank you..." I trail off.

"Maria," she supplies with a wink. "Although as my daughter-in-law, you are always welcome to call me mom."

A vice tightens around my chest and my arms drop limply to my side. It's too late to turn around and walk away. That would be rude, suspicious. Also, not a move that calm, cool, collected Tristan Grant would make. The last time I was here, and she opened the door to let me in, I didn't crumble into a mess of feelings on the front stoop. Of course, I was a little focused on murder at that time.

I need to regroup. Coming here was a bad idea.

"Oh honey, Vic warned me you were a little skittish, and here I go making things awkward from the start. Come in, come in. I'll make us something warm to drink."

I follow Maria into the house on autopilot. Without rage blinding me like last time, I can take in the ornate swirls carved into the grand staircase—the man has a grand staircase—the crystal chandeliers dripping from the vaulted ceiling, the slick shine of the marble floor. Why the hell is the man staying in my too-small apartment when his house looks like this?

The kitchen is bigger than my apartment and my neighbor's put together and I think his island has more prep space than all my countertops combined. Although we put my counters to good use the other day. Not a thought I should have in front of the man's mother. I blush and catch the tiny smile as Maria ducks her head.

She puts an honest-to-god kettle on the stove and clicks on the gas burner before sliding a wooden box toward me. There are more types of tea than I know what to do with and several fancy-looking hot cocoa packets.

"Chai is in the upper right-hand corner." She points and I fish out a packet. "I'll steam some milk. Vic mentioned you prefer a latte."

I don't know what to say to that. I knew Vic remembered my drink order. Robbie let that tidbit slip, but it's one thing to buy me one at a coffee shop. Stocking his kitchen with the ingredients? In a home I've been to exactly one time to yell at him? Telling his mother how I take my preferred caffeine? That's different. Right?

Maria is waiting for my response, so I nod. "I do. Thank you."

An awkward silence descends over both of us as we wait for the kettle to boil. I didn't realize how involved making tea could be. I usually stick a pod in my brewer or make a pit stop on the way to work. Although it's not the waiting that's weird. It's the fact that I'm here at all. Aside from seeing her at games, and that one fateful trip I made here weeks ago, well, I don't know Maria Varg at all. It's ridiculous that I barged in here needing... something.

"I'm sorry for interrupting your day," I say, my voice smaller than I intended. I give myself a mental shake. Time to pull up the big-girl panties and buckle up the armor.

"Oh honey, don't worry about that." Maria adds the water and my tea bag to a shiny white mug with the Arctic team logo on the front. Vic's number is on the back. Her own mug has a tiny chip in the rim and a green shamrock on the front. There are two numbers on the back, twenty-five and twenty-six written in chunky block print. "I would have texted you, but Vic said to give you some time to settle in. That's the *last* time I listen to my idiot son. You take oat milk, right?"

I nod, trying not to choke on a laugh as Maria pulls a carton out of the massive fridge and adds a healthy pour to a small black frother.

"The first time is always the hardest. It doesn't get *easier*, but you learn ways to manage with them on the road."

My eyes snap to hers and she's offering me another soft smile, one I recognize from her son. "I'm sorry?"

"His first road trip since he moved in. It's harder when you get used to them being underfoot." She pours the hot milk over my tea and hers and then pushes the cup toward me. "I'm not a chef, by any means, but it'll warm you up a bit." Another smile.

"Oh, I'm fine," I say, finding the bravado that was missing just a few minutes ago. "I'm used to the trips. I've been with the Arctic for a few years now. The guys travel all the time and I typically stay here..."

Maria shakes her head. "It's not the same, honey." She moves toward the large wooden table at the back of the room and sits down, patting the bench next to her. I sink into it, my knees feeling weaker than I realized.

"I just..." I take a deep breath, sucking chai scented air into my lungs. I study the rim of my mug, tracing my finger around the smooth edge. I don't recognize the Shamrock's as a team and I know Erik never made it to the juniors. That means the mug is from before the boys turned sixteen. What must it be like to have a mug for that long? To have a parent that kept it for as long as Maria did? She didn't even toss it when it chipped. She still brings it out and uses it. The way it's cradled in her hands, I wonder if it's her favorite.

I don't think my mom ever kept anything of mine.

"I'm just a bit all over the place," I say and take a sip, feeling the tea warm me deep into my chilled bones. I didn't realize I was cold. I think I've been cold since Vic pressed a kiss to my temple on his way out the door to the airstrip.

"I know a thing or two about that," Maria says and sips her tea too, she closes her eyes as she swallows and even if I didn't know she was Vic's mom, I'd see it in their matching smiles, the curve of their ears, the line of their noses. "Do you want to talk about it? Or did you just need to feel close to him again?"

I don't know. I'm not sure what there is to talk about. I feel this stretching pull in my chest when I see his things in my space. My throat feels scratchy, like there's something stuck that I keep trying to swallow when he doesn't walk through the door. We've lived together for less than a week and I can't fall asleep without my face pressed into the pillow that smells like him-and even then it's not a good sleep. I'm tossing and turning without his body crowding me to the edge of my mattress, without his heat warming me more effectively than a down comforter. I can't dream without seeing his hazel eyes and smiling face and cheeks flushed as he reaches for me. When did that happen?

"Can I be frank, Tristan?" I swallow another mouthful of tea the wrong way and I come up sputtering for air. Maria's hand is on my back, rubbing soothing circles between my shoulder blades as she reaches for a napkin. "Sorry, sorry. Didn't mean to startle you, honey." I wipe my mouth, feeling splotchy, and ridiculous, and out of control.

Tristan Grant is a force to be reckoned with. I made sure of that. She's capable and confident and she doesn't take bullshit from anyone. She doesn't *need* anyone. *They* need *her*. So why am I falling to pieces without a man I thought I couldn't stand? Why do I feel better with his mother's fingers pressing lightly into the sore knots of stress that I carry at the curve of my neck?

"No, it's fine." *I'm fine.* I am. I have to be. In a few months, we'll say our goodbyes and go our separate ways. I must just be reacting to the thought of losing someone all over again. It's never gone well for me in the past.

"I know that this wedding and this marriage came on faster than either of you expected. I might be a momma who wants to see her babies settled, but I'm not completely blind to what's in front of me. I know things between you two weren't like a fairytale romance. I know this step was probably one that you both jumped into headfirst, with your eyes screwed shut."

This is it. The moment she drops the nice and tells me what she really thinks. I've trapped her son. I'm a gold digger. She's watching me. She's on to me. Don't get comfortable. How dare I steal her baby away from her? I brace for impact.

"And I'm so glad you both did."

Wait.

What?

"Vic has spent far too long worrying about other people. That's my fault." Her laugh is watery, stuck in her throat. Her eyes focus on the far wall of the kitchen, and I feel a little like she's about to share something deeply personal with me and maybe I should stop her. Maybe I should wait and let Vic tell me this stuff himself, but I want to know.

I've spent a long time thinking he was just a superficial jokester. One who made light of every situation put in front of him. One who enjoyed the attention that being helpful brought his way, but one I couldn't count on when it mattered. I was wrong. About all of it. I *know* that now, which hasn't helped my teensy tiny little crush one bit. But now I want to know more.

"When Erik was diagnosed, I did not handle it well," Maria says, and I instinctively reach out and grip her hand.

"I'm not proud of the mother I was for those years. It was just me and the boys. Anna was off at school, and I refused to let her give that up. The kids' father hasn't been in their lives since the boys were barely walking. So it was me, just me, listening to treatment plans and rates of reoccurrence, and giving everything to Erik. And I let Vic slip through the cracks."

She turns her gaze on me, and I can see the tears forming in the corners of her hazel eyes. Eyes that look just like her son's.

"He doesn't ask for what he wants." Maria's hand is squeezing mine like a vise. I think I can feel my knuckles grinding together under my skin. "He puts his own needs last. My baby was going to give up skating in order to help around the house. To be there for me and Erik if we needed anything. Robbie's the one who fixed it for him, did you know that? Robbie Oakes? The boys grew up together. He contacted the commissioner. Something I should have done. Something I will always regret I didn't do."

I feel cold and hot at the same time. Sweat beading along my upper lip and the back of my neck. I'm not sure where she's going with this conversation, but I think it's going to devastate me. I want to cover my ears, ask her to stop, run from the room. I don't.

"I saw the way my boy looked at you in those videos. I heard the way he talked about you to his friends, his teammates."

"Like I was a thorn in his side and he wanted me far on the other side of an Olympic-sized ice rink?"

"Like you were the one ray of sunshine he was willing to keep all for himself, even if he knew he couldn't."

I can't breathe. I can't think beyond every interaction I've had with Victor Varg. The way he held my gaze, read my mind, cupped my elbows, followed my lead. The way he smiled at me, tugged at my hair, called me kitty cat.

"Putting a ring on your finger was the first time I've seen Victor take what he wanted in years. Consequences be damned. So thank *you,* Tristan, for bringing my boy back to life. For being someone he wanted to live *for* rather than without."

FIVE GAMES on the road translates to close to two weeks. In the past, that never bothered me. Jet-setting city to city, sleeping with a neck pillow and noise cancelling headphones, hitting the opposition's ice for practices. It was fun, exhilarating. This time feels different and I won't pretend that I don't know why. I feel itchy under my skin, like I need to peel off the layer of team captain, of professional athlete, of hockey powerhouse, and go back to just being Vic. Vic, who made a home for himself in Tristan's bright little apartment.

I've always been all-in with hockey. Once I went off to the USHL, I had little choice. How could I let the gift I'd been given, my opportunities, my talent, fall by the wayside when my twin would never play again? How could I do anything but focus all my fear and frustration into becoming the best I could be? You don't look a gift horse in the mouth and all that jazz. I know it wasn't just hard work and talent that got me here. It was a shit ton of good luck, too. I couldn't, wouldn't, squander it.

The first game on the road was okay. I put up two assists, one for Robbie and one for Ahlstrom, but I couldn't connect my shots to the back of the net. I winged one off the post more than once and even Ullmark, the opposition's goalie, looked at me, shock visible behind the cage of his yellow and black helmet. The team pulled out the win without me, and I helpfully avoided the look Robbie sent my way as we stripped out of pads and guards and gear.

The next game was worse. I put up no points whatsoever. But it was the third, when we let Buffalo score shorthanded, when I realized how deep my distraction ran. Nothing had put me off my play before. Not my twin, not cancer, not the time I fractured a finger, or had blood leaking into my eyes from a high-stick I took to the face. I've skated on a sprained ankle. I've run miles in a torrential downpour because conditioning just couldn't wait and I couldn't let Erik get in more distance than me for the week. But slipping a shiny gold band off my finger felt like cutting off my oxygen.

"Get your head in the fucking game," Robbie growled at me, pulling me aside after the loss. I knew Noris was on a tear, knew he was going to hand our asses to us. Fried up. With potatoes.

The rest of the guys filed past us as Robbie gripped my elbow pad. He'd taken off his gloves and hooked the tips of the fingers around the elastics holding mine in place. It halted my mission to get past him, too. I tried to shake him off, but he tightened his grip.

"Stop," he said, words shifted around the mouth guard between his teeth. "God fucking dammit Vic. Just listen for two fucking seconds. 'Kay?"

I make a production of glowering at him.

"Yeah, yeah, yeah. I'm an asshole, I know, but you're tanking yourself here."

"It was just a bad game," I lied.

"The kids are already whispering about your good luck charm." Robbie let go, but I didn't make a move to leave our secluded corner. "Look," he said, "I don't know the full story between you two, how you went from nothing, to something, to married," he holds up his hand "and honestly I don't want to know. It's your business, not mine."

"So back off." I tried to push around him, but he held me firm. I have a few inches on Robbie, but I can't match his muscle. It's a wonder he was never pushed into playing defense.

"You're making it my business, stinking up the ice." He glowers. "You're playing like a fourth string rookie. In the juniors." It's a low blow, but he's not entirely wrong. "I know you miss your pretty little woman, but playing like shit won't change the fact that we have two more games to go. Look, if Spags has a shit game, the guys will TP his gear. If you keep having shit games, then we all lose our mojo. There's a reason you're the captain. So get your head screwed back on and then go home and screw your wife blind."

I slap a gloved hand across the back of my neck. "It's not real," I tell my best friend. My teammate. "We need everyone to believe it's true so she can keep her job. I guess Seever told her it was me or her, so..."

"So you made it we. Got it." Robbie waves it off. "The question is, if she's a distraction for you on the road, how long before you think they can her, anyway? Or trade you?"

Cold knifes down my spine.

"Play for her, man," he grins. "Not to mention, she's watching you make a fool of yourself for sure."

I shake my head. "Doubt it."

"Oh, she is. She has to. It's literally her job, idiot. And today, when you were supposed to put another goal on the books, you let a twenty-two-year-old kid, on a team that only kills eighty percent of penalties, score. Pull your head out of your ass and be the flashy, cocksure bastard I know you can be."

So that's what I did. I lifted my head off my chest and threw myself into games four and five like my life depended on it. Or like Tristan's did. We took game four to a shootout loss, but I scored once in regulation and once again during the head-to-head with Sorokin, the New York goalie. Five was a barn burner, both us and New Jersey throwing up three goals apiece by the end of the first period. We traded goals back and forth for the second and most of the third. Then Spags pulled out a dumpster fire of a goal that no one saw coming. And that was the end of the road trip from hell.

I turn my car toward the modest apartment buildings without even thinking about it. I didn't text her when I landed. My phone was nearly dead, and I wanted to focus on getting my gear, hearing the debrief from Coach, and getting home to my almost-girl. The gift I secured for her is wrapped and buckled into my leather passenger seat. I waffled over getting it. Wondered if the strings I pulled were too much, but it's too late to change my mind. Although I don't *have* to give it to her. I just want to.

I second-guess myself as I turn into the parking lot. Thirteen days is a long time to be away from anyone, and the limited messages between us stayed more superficial than I wanted. I wanted phone calls, video messages, more than words on my screen as she asked how a flight was, told me the dentist called to confirm my appointment, I'd gotten a package.

I miss you. I wanted to say.

I wish you were here.

I'm worried I need you more than you need me.

If Tristan missed me at all, she gave no sign. I would have told her to raid my dresser drawers. Sleep in my shirt, Tuck herself in to one of my hoodies.

Maybe I should have called her first. Told her we'd landed, that I'm heading her way. Headed home. Maybe she thought I was going to my mom's—I mean, my— house. Geez, I almost forgot that my name is on the deed.

She opens the door before I can knock, her eyes wide at the sight of me, and I drink her in from head to toe. Even in the short time we've lived together, I've never seen her this casual. She's in a pair of Arctic sweatpants and an old t-shirt that has my middle school travel team logo on the front. A green shamrock wearing a pair of sunglasses and holding a hockey stick, teeth clenched in a grimace. The Fighting Shamrocks. I haven't seen that shirt in ages. It hasn't fit me in almost two decades. I didn't know I still had it.

"You're home," she says. It's not a question and the edges of her lush pink mouth curve into a small smile. "Hi."

"Hi," I can feel my smile spreading across my face, my cheeks aching from the stretch. She's still staring at me in my rumpled suit, duffle slung over my shoulder, when I ask, "Can I come in?"

She shakes herself, like she needed to be sure I was really here, and then steps back. "Of course." She holds the door as I step over the threshold onto her bright pink welcome mat.

I toe off my shoes and drop my duffle to the floor. Anything to stop from hauling her into my arms. We've been sharing a bed, acting out a marriage for everyone's benefit, but that doesn't mean I have a right to pull her to me just because I couldn't handle a few days on the road. It's not like there's anyone hiding behind her gauzy curtains with a telephoto lens. She's twisting the hem of her shirt—my shirt—in her hands, shiny white teeth worrying her bottom lip and for a moment I wonder if I walked into something I shouldn't have.

"Everything okay?"

There's a muffled thud from the bathroom.

"Yep," she says, her voice tinny and too bright. "Actually, no. I think I did something dumb." A nervous laugh.

"Really dumb. It was a spur-of-the-moment thing, and I remembered what you said, and I just. I don't know. I'm feeling kind of stupid here. Because I thought I had this all figured out, how hard could it be? Right? I only raised five siblings. But I might be in over my head."

This time the sound from the bathroom is a crash and Tristan flinches. It's instinct to step into her space, cup the curve of her cheek, stroke the soft skin under her eye. She relaxes into my touch, just briefly. Her eyes flicker closed, and I can feel her sigh break over my chin. I'm going to kiss her. It's inevitable. It has been since the moment she opened her door. Since the moment our plane touched down. Since the moment the final buzzer sounded during our fifth game.

I wait.

"I have a gift for you. Want to open it?" Maybe I can take her mind off her rising panic. Or maybe I just want her to have it. Them.

Another crash and this time some sort of scrambling sound. Is my mother hiding in her bathroom? I'm not really sure what else it could be, unless a raccoon broke in through a window and she's waiting for animal control. I don't think that's what's going on here. If it was Hayley, Palmer, Madison, Max, or the elusive Joey, I'm pretty sure they'd have barged into the living room to watch our reunion. Probably with snacks and their version of the director's commentary.

"You brought me a gift?" Her head tips to the side like a puppy encountering something new. "Why?"

Why did I get her a present? I *want* to say because she's

my wife, but I can't. She isn't. And I still have to clarify that one little detail, even if I've been putting it off. I'm selfishly eating up every second we have together. I didn't want to say something before I left. I don't want to ruin this moment now that I'm back. The news that we didn't actually take the legal steps to bind ourselves together doesn't change the fact that we need the world—and our bosses—to think we did. And maybe a selfish part of me hopes that if I wait to tell her, her desire to stay with me, to make this work, will overpower the anger I know is going to arrow straight for me.

"Because I thought of you every minute while I was gone," I say instead. "Because I counted seconds until that plane touched down." I snake my hands into the mess of hair piled on top of her head and tip her head back. "Because I dreamed of your mouth." My lips touch hers. "Your tits, your hips, your eyes, your heart." I press my tongue into her mouth and kiss her, sucking her air and her taste into my soul.

Her arms slide up my chest, her wrists resting on my shoulders, and I help lift her higher so she can twine them around my neck. She sighs into my mouth, her tongue taking over the role of aggressor, twining around mine as she kisses me and kisses me. Until we're not even kissing anymore, just panting, our lips still fused.

Tristan's cheeks are flushed and I can feel the heat in mine, the tension in my abdomen as my dick stiffens in my pants. She's hot against me, fire in my arms. Forget the gifts. Forget whatever, or whoever, is in the bathroom.

Forget everything but how fast I can get this woman to come and then get inside her.

Thud.

"I missed you," Tristan says, "and I want to open my present, but I don't think yours is going to wait any longer."

My present? She wriggles out of my arms and slides down my body. I bite back my groan at the friction over my desperate erection. The momentary distraction is enough to let her turn toward the bathroom door. And I bite back a snort at the sight that greets me. Plastered across the back of her sweatpants are the words "VIC'S CHICKS."

"Nice ass," I say, and this time I do laugh as she drops her hands to cover the curve of her butt.

"There was a fundraiser," she says, like that explains everything. "They were selling Arctic gear to raise money for the youth hockey program."

"Arctic gear that says Vic's chicks?"

Her blush deepens. "As your wife, I figured that made me Vic's number one chick. I had to support the cause." And yet she still put them on tonight.

It's cute. Adorable. It has my brain growling '*mine*'. While my animal instincts try to recover, she pushes open the bathroom door.

I'm looking at human height, not at the floor, so I miss the little black ball until it's launched itself at me from the top of the sink. Tiny claws attach to the front of my shirt and my hand automatically comes up to cup the back end of a tiny kitten. It's fuzz-soft and I can't help stroking the line of its spine, feeling the bumps and grooves under my fingers. Narrowed green eyes look up at me, and it hisses even as it kneads my chest like I'm a ball of biscuit dough.

"A kitten?" My chest feels tight. "You got a kitten?"

"For you." Tristan nods. "Well, I meant to get you a kitten. I think that's some form of tiny demon. I've been calling her Hell Spawn as she's attempted to destroy everything in this apartment."

Come to think of it, the living room had looked a little disheveled. It was hard to notice anything other than Tristan.

"She?" I say as the kitten blinks slowly up at me, a tiny purr beginning to vibrate her whole body. "You didn't have to do this, Tristan. She's adorable, but I'm already imposing on your home and I know you aren't comfortable with pets."

"You told me that day at the shelter that you'd always thought about getting a cat. You're allowed to ask for what you want, Vic. I've made all the decisions for us until now. Actually, adopting the demon was my decision too, but you're allowed to have things you want."

My eyes are burning, my throat feels sticky and thick with something I can't quite swallow down. Because she's right. I *did* think about getting a pet, especially after meeting Erik and Quinn's fur babies. It just didn't feel right when my mother would have ended up taking care of any animal I brought home. That felt like a decision that should include her, and she's already taking care of the house when I should be taking care of her.

"You don't mind her staying here?" I ask, because as

much as I don't want to inconvenience my mother, Tristan's comfort is my priority. My latent desire for a pet will not stop me from making this arrangement between us permanent.

"If you try to take her away from me, I will end your family line." She leans in and runs a single finger over the head of the tiny cat. A growl whines out past an itty bitty set of sharp fangs. "She's a bitch, but I'm a bigger one. We have an understanding."

I look past my fake wife into the destroyed bathroom. The blinds at the window are bent at a ninety-degree angle. Toilet paper has been unspooled and shredded. An assortment of bottles roll around the tile floor.

"Okay, well, we *will* have an understanding. She's better when she has a run of the whole place, but I wanted to surprise you."

Can she hear the way my heart is hammering in my chest? Can she read in the depths of my eyes how much I love her?

"It's a great surprise, baby." I lift the little kitty until she can curl up on my shoulder, settling against the warmth of my neck. Her purr is a rumble in my ear. Soothing like white noise.

I press a kiss to the top of Tristan's head.

"Do you want your gift now?" I ask her and when she'd nods, I go back into the living room, kitten still perched on my shoulder, to grab the wrapped present.

"It's not much," I say as she carefully peels back the paper. "I just wanted you to have them." Tristan pulls out the Arctic jersey with my name and number emblazoned across the back. *I want my name on you, Tristan. I'd tattoo it on your forehead if you'd let me.*

"Vic," she's smiling as she says my name. I want her to do it again. "Why are there six jerseys in here?"

"Home, Away, Classic." I shrug.

"That's three."

"And I got a set that says Grant, just in case you didn't like Varg." I pointedly glance down, "Of course that was before I realized you were one of Vic's Chicks."

She swats me in the chest and the kitten rumbles a warning at her.

"Oh hush you," Tristan says, and from her tone it's clear she and this little cat have been trading conversation back and forth for a while now. "You're all talk. We both know you sleep with me every night."

Another grumble from the kitten and I rub a finger under her chin until she settles.

"I think we should name her Hela." I say, and Tristan's eyebrow raises.

"I was mostly joking about calling her Hell Spawn." No, she wasn't. "Okay, no I wasn't. But you can name her anything you like. She's yours, Vic."

"Hela is the Norse goddess for the dead. She's basically the ruler of Hell."

Later that night, as I pull Tristan into the circle of my arms, tucking the comforter around us as Hela grumbles at the top of my pillow, I can't help but ask, "So where'd you get the shirt from, baby?"

Tristan stiffens in my arms, then turns so we're lying face to face, her blue eyes bright even with the lights off.

"Your mom gave it to me," she says. "I might have gone to visit her while you were gone. She mentioned that keeping things of yours close would help the time go faster."

I smile as I pull her closer, because this sweet and prickly girl missed me as much as I missed her. And that's a start.

IT SHOULD BE a forgone conclusion that between my siblings and my proximity to a team of professional athletes, I'd have a healthy dose of skepticism when someone grins at me, holds out a hand, and tells me to trust them. It should also go without saying that the better looking the conspirator, the more suspicious their motivation. Or maybe that's something I'll eventually need to unpack in therapy.

Despite all of that, I still end up here. On the ice. Wearing a pair of white figure skates, and clutching the wooden boards so I don't fall on my face. In front of my husband. The man who does this for a living. Allowing myself to look like an idiot in front of him should be obvious proof of my trust.

I give him credit for trying not to laugh as one of my legs slips out from under me. He bites into the plush pink of his bottom lip as I wobble, clutching the boards even harder. When he reaches out a hand, clearly meaning to slip it around my waist, I glare. Hard.

"I said I can do it myself." I recenter myself on the pockmarked ice.

"The perk of being here with a professional is that you don't have to." His grin is infuriating. *He* is infuriating.

"Look, I'm trying really hard not to tell you how much I hate your stupid sport and your stupid ice. That should count for something."

His laugh comes from deep in his chest.

"You like hockey just fine," he says, as if I don't work for the same damn team he plays on. That's different. "And I've seen you on the ice before."

"Not on skates, and I don't have to risk broken bones to watch you play."

"Stop trying to insult me," he laughs again. "It's not working. You know I won't let you fall."

"Remind me why we have to do this again?"

And okay, yes, I want off these metal death traps, and I want back on less slippery ground, but mostly it's fun to quip at him like this and have him blind me with his grin every time I do. I've never met someone—other than my siblings—who didn't crumble when I let my bitch out to play. Maybe it never bothered me when he gave it all right back. Maybe I've always liked it and Palmer was right when she asked if this was our form of foreplay. It's working.

"Because I have a day off and you had nothing planned for this afternoon." He leans into my face, close enough that I can see all the blues and greens and browns in his eyes. "And because I'm a professional hockey player. It seemed criminal that you don't know how to skate."

"Oh, I know how." I say, using my arms to turn and face Vic. I lean back against the boards. "In theory. I just don't have much practical application."

"You're pretty cute for a smartass," he says as he lets his lips ghost over mine. "Besides, we have an audience and we're supposed to be showing everyone that we're in love."

I try to turn my head to glimpse the audience he's talking about. There are only a handful of people still taking advantage of the outdoor rink. It closes at the end of the month, but the temperature has been all over the place and I think spring is finally here to stay. It's been near fifty all week. I don't spot anyone before Vic's hand cups my chin and draws me back to him. I'm not complaining as he kisses me again.

"Come on kitty cat," he teases, "I know the Haine scandal has mostly gone away and we don't need to film anymore, but let's give them a show, anyway."

I can't say no to this man, not anymore, which is why I end up nodding and letting him draw me off the boards and into the firm curve of his arm. There's no more wood to hold on to, not as he pulls me toward the center of the oval, but my feet are barely on the ground at all. Vic is literally holding me up as we glide over the slick surface. I know he's big. I know he's strong. But I'm still impressed.

Give them a show...

This whole thing was my idea. Well, not the ice-skating but being a couple. Pretending we are so head over heels, we couldn't resist shackling ourselves together when the opportunity arose in Vegas. That rather than making rash decisions, we're a beacon of love, family values, and responsibility. I said that. I pushed that.

When did it stop feeling like it was all an act?

When did I stop remembering that it was supposed to be for show?

The first time we fucked? When I learned how wrong I'd been about the avoidance and the interview all those months ago? If there's one thing I can understand, it's protecting family. And Vic was right, my anger with him was misplaced. He didn't let me down. I'm not entitled to his time. That I felt so betrayed by his decision to avoid me? A clear sign I had some kind of draw to this man even then. I felt like I wasn't a priority. Something even I know is absolutely ridiculous. We were barely even colleagues. Not friends. Definitely not more.

Maybe that was the actual beginning of my heart's slow slide into loving this man, because I do. I love him. Even if it's messy and complicated and I shouldn't, I do. And it's as easy as breathing to trust him. With my body as he carries me across the ice, solid against his side. With my heart as he smiles down at me and the warmth spreads through every atom of my being.

And, if I'm reading Victor Varg correctly, he loves me right back.

An hour later, my hockey player is kneeling on the cold rubber floor covering and unlacing the skate he has propped on his over-developed thigh. His lips quirk as he smiles up at me from under the smudge of his lashes. A smile that tells me he knows I had fun, even if my legs are made of pudding, and I'm still grumbling about the cold.

"I told you I wouldn't let you fall," he says again, and I roll my eyes because catching me around the waist and carrying me around the ice under his arm like a football seems to violate the spirit of his promise. Even if *technically* I didn't hit the ground. "This is the rink where my brother first stepped back onto the ice."

My own grumblings are immediately forgotten as Vic slips my boot back on and switches my legs. He loosens the other set of laces and my ankles scream in relief. I know Vic said they had to be tight, but I don't think I'll need to worry about broken bones or wrenched joints if I've lost circulation.

"I didn't know you could skate on a prosthetic," I say, watching the different emotions flicker across Vic's face.

"I didn't either. I don't think even Erik knew for sure. He brought Quinn here on a date while he was trying to convince her to give them a shot. He hadn't wanted to try before."

And I get it. Why he brought me here. It's not about his profession. It's not about smiling for the cameras. It's about giving me a date. A real one. A moment in time where this thing between us is real and tangible. He brought me to a place that held a special meaning for someone who means the world to him. It's beautiful in a way. And I feel guilty for bitching most of the time.

"Thank you," I tell him as he slides on my second shoe. "For bringing me here. For planning this."

His grin is huge as he meets my eyes, tossing both my

skates and his over his broad shoulders. I can't resist a quick peck to his lips. His mouth chases mine and I pull back, panting. Vic's eyes squeeze shut, and he blows out a breath, the warm air breaking over my chin.

"Come on," he says. "Let's get you a hot chocolate and a chance to walk out the stiffness in your legs."

"My legs are just fine," I say as he hauls me to my feet, looping an arm around the top of my shoulders.

"They're better than fine." Smooth asshole. "But I also know you were tense the entire time we were out there and you kept locking your knees. You're going to be sore if you don't loosen your muscles up."

We leave the rink and walk down one of the smaller alleys. I know we're headed to the coffee shop along the other main road, but being here, in the shadow of two tall buildings, I have the urge to take advantage of being alone. I angle my body, pressing Vic into the stone wall behind him. And okay, it takes a moment for him to realize what I'm doing and to allow me to move him where I want him, but then I'm up on my tiptoes as his arm drops to my waist and I'm pressing my mouth against his.

His mouth opens under mine and his tongue sweeps past my lips. He's everywhere. His scent in my nose, his taste on my tongue, his hand gripping my hip as the other slides up to cradle the back of my head. His fingers spear through my hair and I feel the tension, the tug, between my thighs.

He groans into my mouth, a sound I've grown used to hearing even if this part of our relationship is still new. I want him naked. Now. I want skin, and heat, and—forget my legs—I want the thick slide of him stretching out every one of my feminine muscles until they're the ones sore and trembling. My fingers have a mind of their own, pushing down the collar on his sweatshirt, trying to stroke whatever part of him I can reach.

Vic spins us, pinning me against the wall. The hand buried in my hair cushioning my head from the stone. His hips push between mine, holding me in place with the bulk of his body and those fingers that were leaving tiny bruises along my side slip up under my sweater, tracing patterns against the skin of my stomach. Never have I ever been so grateful that I forewent a coat. I shudder against him as his hand cups the weight of my breast and I roll my hips into the hard ridge between my thighs.

"Tristan. Kitty cat. Baby." He's panting between each word. "We can't do this here. Come on, I promised you cocoa."

His hands haven't moved from my hair and my breast, so I shift my hips again and he buries his face against my neck and grunts into my flushed skin.

"Forget the drink." He's hitting the perfect spot, and I keep the steady roll of my lower body against his. "Warm me up like this."

He curses against the column of my throat, but the hand in my hair tenses.

"This is what I thought about doing outside the wedding chapel," he says. "And in the shelter parking lot. And at the smoothie place. I thought about pressing you down to the benches in the locker room. Or the couches in the lounge. I wanted to take you over Seever's desk. That's what you do to me, Tristan. You look at me with those big blue eyes and I forget that we're in public, that we could get caught. I forget, and I lunge for you, anyway."

I whimper, picking up the pace as he pushes back, telling me all the things he's imagined doing to me. With me. All the places he pictured us together as he gripped his dick and brought himself off. I'm close from his words alone. I'm keyed up, and I can just see the edge of oblivion. Even now. Fully clothed. Then Vic stills.

"Holy shit." A voice says from either right behind us or a million miles away. "Victor Varg getting lucky in a dirty alley. Who'd have thought."

His muscles are stone against mine, and his grip is bruising in its intensity. He's holding me still, his jaw clenched, and this is bad. We've been caught, sure, but I'm pretty sure Vic's about to blow.

"Not a good time, buddy," Vic says, but he's still looking at me, eyes flashing fire. I'm sliding down the front of his body, tippy toes touching down on the sidewalk, but my husband doesn't step back.

"Come on," the guy says. "Can't you spare a minute for your biggest fan? I'm sure your girl isn't going anywhere. Who'd want to miss out on a fuck with the Victor Varg?"

I don't have time to be offended, but Vic explodes into action. He spins, keeping me firmly behind him against the wall, and I can see the knuckles on his hands turning white and he clenches his fists.

"What did you just say?" His voice is low, deadly, But apparently our interrupting audience has zero sense of self-preservation, or he doesn't know Vic the way I do.

"Chicks, am I right?" The guy laughs loudly, and it's the wrong thing to do. Made even worse when he says. "I was hoping for an autograph, but I wouldn't mind sharing your sloppy seconds. I bet she'd take both of us if you asked her real nice. A bit of screaming makes it more fun."

In less time than it takes to blink, Vic has the blade of his hockey skate pressed to the other man's throat. I peer around my husband. The man he's talking to is only a few inches taller than me, and round in a way that tells me he is *not* a professional athlete. He has a receding hairline and glassy, bloodshot eyes that, along with the flushed face and smell, tell me he's drunk. And Vic looks ready to murder him.

"What the fuck did you just say about my wife?"

Does it make me a sick puppy that his words send a rush of warmth through me? I'd assumed being caught would dampen my libido, but it's doing the opposite. I'm ready to clock this asshole myself and fuck my husband over his unconscious body. Watching Vic defend me is doing something twisty to my insides.

"Shit man," the guy says. "I was just messing around. It was a joke."

"I don't get the punchline." Vic says, and I can hear the growl coating his words. I guess we're both going feral.

"That's because it wasn't funny," I say, slinging my arms around Vic's waist. I rest my head between his shoulder blades, smiling into his sweatshirt. It feels good. Having someone stand up for me. I can eviscerate this toad myself, but with Vic, I don't have to. In fact, I'm feeling so grateful I may send this jerk a fruit basket. Or some Arctic merch. At least a thank-you note.

"Beautiful and smart," Vic presses his palm over the back of one of my hands, pressing my touch deeper into the firm plane of his stomach. "I suggest you leave now," he tells the other man, "Before I get really mad."

Whatever is on Vic's face, the other guy must realize that he means business because he steps back, hands up in the air—I'm peeking around Vic's middle because I'm nosy —eyes wide and darting from one end of the alley to the other.

"Hey man," he says to my avenging angel, "relax. You can't do anything to me, anyway. I'll call channel five and ruin you."

Vic sucks in air and his stomach goes rock hard under my hands. I'm torn between disbelief and laughter. Vic is beloved on and off the ice. His reputation is squeaky clean. He's a man any parent would love to have their kids bring home. I don't think I've ever seen him throw a punch. Not even during on-ice brawls. I also know we're a trending topic with a mostly positive reception. There are very few people who would believe this drunkard's version of events even if he strolled into the newsroom with a black eye and footage of Vic clocking him.

But I also know that Vic isn't worried about his reputation.

He's worried about mine.

Or, more accurately, the existence of my job if he and I end up on the news. Again. The trembling in his muscles, the flex in his jaw, the fist wrapped around his skates with the knife-sharp blades... He's protecting me. He's frozen because he can't figure out the biggest threat.

"That's a great idea," I step around Vic and face down the man myself, "We can take a walk downtown together and tell our side of the story, too. In fact, we can go right to the police station and file a report with whomever is on duty." I lean into Vic's side, feeling his body heat clear through all my layers.

"What's even better," I say, "Is that I got that whole conversation recorded." I wiggle my phone at the man. He's turning an interesting shade of gray. Maybe we should contact Pantone and see if they'll let us name it "Fear of Repercussion." Gray. "I'm guessing Vic might get a pass for basically telling you to walk away after you asked him to help you rape his wife."

"I didn't—" the man is gasping for air, mouth gaping like a fish out of water.

I wiggle my phone at him again. "That's not what this will say." He loses even more color. "And let's think for a moment, who do you think people are going to believe? A misogynistic drunk? Or a decorated professional hockey player with video and audio evidence on his side?"

I'm bluffing. I haven't recorded a single moment of this interaction. I was too busy melting over my husband's fierce protectiveness, but I'm betting that our friend here will believe it.

"You—you can't record me without asking!" He's switched from gray to purple. It's not a better look for him.

"Actually, I can. This is a single party consent state. And I consented to it." I smile my shark smile, the one

Mads says sends people running for cover. "I know these things. My job is social media, after all. So maybe I'll delete this when you walk away and leave us alone. Without an autograph."

"Right." The man nods. "I'll just be going now. I'm sorry. So sorry. Sir. Ma'am. Fuck."

Vic presses a kiss to the top of my head as the man disappears down the alley, moving faster than I'd have thought possible.

"You," he kisses my temple. "Are magnificent."

My heart is pounding, thundering away inside the cage of my chest, and I twist my fingers in the hem of Vic's sweatshirt. Heat is pouring through my veins, I'm panting, and I know this is the adrenaline talking, but I'm about to drop to my knees to thank my husband properly.

Has anyone ever stood their ground for me before? My parents certainly didn't. Not the neighbors, or my teachers. Not the foster system that tried to separate all of us. Not even my siblings. They care about me, love me, but I've always been the one to fight their battles for them, not the other way around. They just quietly—and not so quietly—assume I can handle anything. And I can. I've learned how. But it's nice to have someone do it for me.

It's nice that Vic cares enough to do it for me.

"I don't think I want hot chocolate anymore." I tell him, towing him down the alley back to where his car is parked. The poor man looks completely shell-shocked.

"Are you okay?" He asks me, cupping my face in his hands. "What that man said—"

"I'm fine, Vic." I reach into his pocket for his keys and click open the doors of the Mercedes.

"I didn't know what to do," he says, tangling his fingers into the strands of my hair.

"You did exactly right." I wrench open the back door.

"What are you—?"

I shove Vic into the backseat, watching him hit ass first and tumble back against the far door. God, he's big. Could his legs span the entire width of the car? I climb in after him, straddling his thighs as I push my hands up to frame his face.

"Thank you," I say, staring deep into worried hazel eyes. "For standing up for me. For caring enough to do it."

"Of course I care about you," Vic says. He's frowning even as his hands cup my hips.

I'm insanely grateful that I wore a skirt. Despite cursing my choice when we first got to the rink, now I lift the hem up and try to wiggle my tights down over my thighs. It's not working. Not if I don't want to brain myself on the roof of the car.

"Tristan?"

I give up on my tights and focus on his jeans, ripping open the top button and pulling the zipper down. He hisses as my fingers trail over the bulge of his erection. I pull him out and he drops his head back to the headrest, cursing as I wrap my fingers around his swollen length. He's hot and hard in my hand, pulsing in time with my heartbeat.

There's so much I want to do to him. With him. But I'm

desperate here. I've been revved up since we were on the ice and I can't wait. I can't. Not another second longer.

"Fuck, baby," He says the words against my mouth and I swallow them down, greedy for more.

"Yes, please." Am I whining? I might be. My core is contracting on nothing, clamping down so hard I might already be coming.

"I've got you, Tristan. Always. I'm never going to let you go." And then his hands are between my thighs and he's tearing the tights apart—they were supposed to be un-rippable. I paid top dollar for that feature—pulling me forward until he's notched at my entrance, and I sink down on him, taking him inside me to the hilt.

"I'M GOING to miss you after we get divorced."

Forget the fact that we're in the backseat of my car half dressed. Forget the fact that I'm still buried deep inside her and just roared my release into her neck. Her words hit me like sliding headfirst into the boards at breakneck speed.

My fingers spasm on her waist and I feel like she's slipping out of my grasp, dripping through my fingers like water as I try to hold on. There was a reason I didn't tell her the truth before. A reason I held back. We aren't married. We never were. Pretending it won't change anything, not when the photos leaked, and she already told our boss, is a weak justification.

Now... I can't lie to her face. Not when those eyes are warm with pleasure, her limbs loose from her orgasm. Her full weight is cocooned against my chest, our hearts beating in tandem, and I can't keep it back. I can't pretend that what I should have told her won't matter. It will.

I tuck my nose into her hair, breathing her in one last

time before I ease her off me. Citrus and ice and her. Like a pine tree covered in snow and orange slices. Christmas.

"We should head back," I say, because we need to have this conversation about the legality of our marriage, but I don't want to do it here. Not now. Not like this. This moment is too raw, too vulnerable. I want to have this conversation in our space, not out in the open, waiting to be popped for indecent exposure.

Tristan shifts, her head tipping back so she can look up into my eyes.

"Everything okay?" Her brows tip together in a frown, and I can't breathe. Can't suck in air. I'm drowning in the backseat of a Mercedes. Not how I ever thought I'd go.

I move my hips back, slipping out of her. My lap is a mess and I ignore it as I pull my pants up and over my softening dick. There's not much I can do about it right now, anyway. Tristan pulls her skirt down, still frowning, and slides to my right. She twists, pressing her back into my leather seat, but her eyes are still on me. Questions swirl in them. She's not dumb. I'm not subtle.

"We don't want to get caught out here," I say, like an idiot. Instead of *I love you. Marry me for real. Please.*

"Right." She pops open the car door and I wince against the sudden light and chill. Tinted windows made me almost forget where we were and why we shouldn't be doing what we were doing. She slams the door and I wince again, watching her shimmy her tights into a manageable position. She's in the passenger seat and buckled in before I get out of the car, but message received: get moving.

I drive us back home on autopilot, secretly wishing for

a detour, construction, anything to prolong the inevitable. She's going to be furious, and rightfully so. I always knew this house of cards would tumble when she found out. I had hoped to build a foundation strong enough to rebuild us stronger than before. Either way, I've wound up for this shot and now I have to see it through.

She's out of the car before it's in park and the door to the apartment almost closes before I get my foot over the threshold. She's speeding away from me, as fast as she can, and I almost plow into her body as she whirls in her living room, squaring up against me like we're meeting in the face-off circle. Jokes on her. My win percentage is just over sixty percent. I intend to win this one too.

"Just spit it out," she says, eyes on the center of my chest. "Say what you want to say. I know I basically forced you into this, but if you want out, then I'll give you an out. It would be worse staying married when I—"

She's gnawing on her bottom lip, and twisting her hands around and around, and something inside me snaps. The kind of break I'm not sure I can fix.

"There isn't going to be a divorce," I say, and dammit, that is *not* what I was supposed to lead with, and definitely not with that tone of voice, but I'm all instinct now. I'm barely cogent around this woman on a good day, let alone when tears well up in the corners of her eyes.

"You asshole." Her hands are on my chest and she's pushing me back. One step, two. I let her propel me until I bump up against the door. *Still on this side, kitty cat. Good luck getting rid of me that easily.* "You let me think..." she hiccups as a tear breaks free. "I thought... I thought you were breaking up with me. Or something. That you wanted out. You Jerk."

And dammit, dammit, dammit, I need a time machine right now. I need to dial back the last twenty minutes and say something, *do* something, *anything*, because she has the wrong idea. Tristan thought I had one foot out the door. She's doubting me, and I've never felt pain like this before. Not when I fractured bones, or dislocated my shoulder, or got nasty concussions, or Erik, or anything. Ever.

"I thought you were done with me." The words stick in her throat. "I wasn't serious about getting divorced. It was a joke. A one-off. I thought you'd hold me tighter and tell me it wasn't happening. I-I haven't even thought about it since Vegas. Not really. But then you said nothing. You pushed me away and—oh god—"

I don't know which one of us moves, but her hands fist in my shirt and mine cup her cheeks. Tears slip over my fingers. I might be crying too.

"I'm not going anywhere," I say the words like a promise. An oath. I will die before I break this one. Slit my throat with my skate blade. Let the ice grow sticky with the red of my blood.

"I'm sorry." She sobs. "I shouldn't be crying. This is stupid. It's—"

She thinks I'm going to leave like her dad. She thought I *was* leaving.

"I'm crazy about you Tristan." It's not enough. She needs more and I can give it. I want to. "I love you."

She's frozen in front of me and my heart is trying to

slam its way out of my body and into the living room with us. Hela is twining around my feet, mewling for attention, and I have none to give. Every fiber of my being is focused on the woman I love. The woman who thinks I could ever consider walking away from her. I can't.

"I love you Tristan Grant." I give her the words again. "I love your work ethic and your drive to succeed. I love your patience and your care for your siblings and the team. I love your willingness to do things that scare you, to better yourself day after day after day. I love that you let everyone think you're ice cold, but your heart burns brighter than anyone I've ever met. You love more deeply. Care more."

"You've spent your whole life feeling like you have to take care of everyone around you, but no one ever returns the favor. I'm just an average guy who plays above average hockey, and I'm begging you to let me be the one who takes care of you because I love every tiny piece of you. You aren't getting rid of me. Not today. Not after the season. Not next year. Not when our first kid is twelve. Never."

She's shaking, or maybe I am.

"Marry me." I beg. "Please, kitty cat."

I feel her smile under my palms before it splits her lips. She laughs, eyes still watery as they dart away from my face.

"What, like again?" Her eyes touch mine and dart away again. Like she's afraid of my answer. "Like renew our vows? Have a fancy party and a cake?"

"No," I shake my head, "Like for real this time. Marry me for real."

I see the moment the words sink in and I let my hands drop from her face as she shifts back. It's not even a full step, but she feels miles away.

"What?"

This is it. The moment I knew would come. The one I've been avoiding since that morning in Vegas.

"We aren't married," I tell her, and it takes an effort to keep my voice even. "We never were."

It's like the oxygen leaves the room. Sucked out so fast, we both lurch in response. Now's the time to explain. To tell her she was so excited to see a real Vegas wedding chapel, to watch couples profess their love for eternity in front of a man dressed up in gold and white leather. A man with sideburns covering half his jaw.

I could tell her that her feet hurt, so I boosted her up on my back. That I thought dirty, inappropriate thoughts as her thighs closed around my torso. That she weighed almost nothing as I carried her the twenty minutes to the little white chapel, her skinny heels looped in my fist so they wouldn't smack into my chest. I've carried hockey bags heavier than her.

I could tell her how bright the little space was, with a small selection of jewelry in a big glass case. How she wiggled her way down my back and skipped toward the case, her smile rivaling the fluorescents overhead. How her hair fell in a silk curtain around her shoulders. How between her white dress and my slacks we looked like we fit right in. I could tell her anything about that night, but I don't.

"We aren't married." The words aren't a question, she's repeating, letting the meaning sink into her bones. "Not legally."

I shake my head as a flush climbs up her neck.

"But I told—You didn't—" She blows out a breath, hair fluttering around her face. "You didn't think this was information I deserved to know? I almost torpedoed my career. You're... stuck... here with me. All because of a lie?"

"I'm not stuck anywhere." She also didn't exactly give me a chance to tell her anything prior to the story breaking or talking to Bob, but that's not the important part right now. This isn't about being right or wrong. This is about the look of betrayal on her face.

About the fact that she didn't give me those three little words right back.

Everything I did in Vegas and since we came home has been about giving this woman what she wants. What she needs. My every action has been carefully calculated to cause the least damage. To protect. And yes, it's all exploded in my face like a nuclear warhead. But I'm not sure that, given the chance, I'd have done anything differently. Are mistakes less regrettable when they happen for the right reasons? Except maybe, just maybe, if I'd known how off-kilter she actually was that night, how she was going to wake up with gaps in her memory, I'd have pushed to take her back to the hotel.

"Tristan." I hold my hands out, palms up. No threat, nothing to hide. "I know you're angry—"

"You lied to me." Her voice is eerily calm and fuck, I'd

rather have her yell, scream, throw things. Anything but look at me with cold, dead eyes. Like the fight has gone out of her.

It's not the time to split hairs about omission versus outright untruths. I kept this from her. I might have been pushed into it at first, but it was a conscious choice I made for the last few weeks. My only excuse is that I didn't want to lose her. I didn't want us to end up here. I wanted us on solid ground before this detail came to light. I wanted us to be in a place where a fight was a relationship adjustment, not an automatic end. The truth is, I was scared. No matter how I try to justify it, I was afraid to lose this woman.

"Yes," I say, swallowing down bile as my stomach heaves.

She blinks once, twice. Arms loose at her sides, and I want her to glare, to spit, to hiss, to fight. Something. She's looking at me like I'm a stranger. The calmer she gets, the more I panic. I might actually throw up right here on her welcome mat.

"Are you even going to tell me why?"

I want to.

I want to give her every single reason this went on as long as it did, but she's not ready to hear it now. She's ready to get the answers to the questions she *thinks* she should ask, to get some semblance of closure, and then pack me neatly into a box and act like this never happened. And god, that thought is terrifying, because I know she'd succeed. Even if she shattered both our hearts in the process.

"Would you believe me if I did?"

She looks away from me. The only sign that she heard what I said is the white lines bracketing her mouth.

"I don't know if I can," she says, and that's that. My heart is careening through my body, slamming down through my stomach, my intestines, my legs. It's crashing through her hardwood floor and shattering into grains of sand that slip and slide into the cracks between the boards.

"I'm sorry Tristan." I owe her at least this much. "For what it's worth, I didn't mean for it to end up like this. And..." the organ in my chest stutters, stalls. "None of it changes the fact that I lo—"

"Stop."

I swallow the rest of the words back.

"I think you should go," Tristan says, but her calm is cracking. She's not meeting my eyes anymore. And suddenly hope is blooming in my chest again, like those tiny sponge animals that expand when wet. The kind we put in Spags' water bottle during his first week of practices. Every time he filled the thing, the sponges expanded, soaking up all the liquid until there was nothing left for him to drink. The hope is there, expanding into every space between my atoms, because I can't crack indifference, but hurt means she still cares.

"I'll go because you're asking me to." *And I'd do anything for you.* "But I'm coming back for you, Tristan. I'm coming back for us. Okay? What's between us is real. It's important. You and me, kitty cat. I'm going to fix it."

She can have all the space she needs. Now that I know

she cares. She was originally terrified I was leaving. Scared at the prospect of losing this. She's mad. She has a right to be, but I'm not going anywhere.

And when the door shuts in my face, and her eyes flash with threats of my dismemberment, I try not to smile.

MAYBE IT'S A TRAUMA RESPONSE, but my siblings descend on my apartment late the next afternoon. I don't call them, or text, but I know they know something's up because they're all piling out of Palmer's eco-friendly sedan and cramming onto my couch. I'm used to them showing up unannounced, but it's rare to have all six of us in the same room when it's not a birthday or a holiday. They've also cut back on their unannounced visits after Joey told the group chat that she saw Vic doing unspeakable things to their sister-mom.

That's how I know it's some form of sibling ESP. Madison comes loaded with face masks and it takes thirty minutes for everyone to be coated in sage green goop, Max included, as we sip hot cocoa doctored with a heavy dose of amaretto for most of us. I pretend to look away when Joey and the twins add the liquor to their cups, too. After getting high and drunk and fake married in Vegas, I'm the last person who has a leg to stand on about underage drinking. Although I didn't break any laws. Just saying.

I haven't heard from Vic since I sent him away yesterday, and my phone is locked in my bedroom so I'm not tempted to check it every five minutes. I know it's ridiculous to be mad at him for giving me the space I asked for, especially when I was already mad at him, but I can't help but feel abandoned and pissy. I don't know what I wanted, but leaving when I told him to wasn't it. Is it too much to ask for him to read my mind? Anticipate my every need?

And maybe he'd have a chance of doing that if I knew what *I* wanted.

"So are we going to talk about where Golden Hubs went?" Joey asks, wiggling her toes on my coffee table. She picks up the nail polish and swipes another coat of lime green over her big toe.

"Maybe he's just giving us space to have sister time." Hayley looks at me, brows raised.

"Hey," Max protests from my fridge, where he's sourcing one of the local beers Vic brought with him.

"Yeah, yeah, yeah, suck it up, buttercup," Palmer waves him off. "Except we didn't tell them we were coming."

"They have a game tonight." Mads says, looking up from her phone. She waves the device in the air, team schedule outlined in blue. "Is he already at the rink?"

Considering the game starts in less than two hours, yes.

"Nah," Joey stares me dead in the eye, dark brows scrunched together. "Something happened. She looks like a cornered cat. Spill."

I have no intention of saying anything, but the words bubble in my chest, rising up and out without my control.

"He's gone. He left."

For a moment, my apartment is silent. Quiet enough that I can hear my pulse thundering as my eyes burn. Then Max, my sweet, kind, baby brother, the one who rarely opens his mouth during sibling sit-downs, starts to laugh. Not just a chuckle, either. He's laughing so hard that he's bent over at the waist and I think I see tears in his eyes.

"I told you we should have left him at home." I catch Madison's eye roll before Max increases in volume.

"I can't believe you're laughing right now," Hayley says, voice shaky, "Tristan is devastated. The love of her life just walked out."

Max laughs harder. He slides down the cabinets to sit on the floor of my tiny kitchenette, legs stretched out in front of him, dark head thrown back against the cupboard that holds my assorted Tupperware.

"Now hold on," Palmer says, "When you say he left, do you mean left left? Or like he had to travel again and will be back later?"

I love my siblings. I do. With my whole heart and soul... but right now I'm having serious fantasies about dropping them one-by-one into the garbage disposal and going back to bed.

"I'm pretty sure she meant he left her, like it's over," the ever-tactful Joey adds. "Why else would she be here all depressed and mopey?"

"She's always kind of depressed and mopey." Madison. "Besides, she's still wearing her wedding ring."

"And it's a home game," Palmer.

I glance down at my hand. It hadn't even occurred to me to take it off. Should I? The wedding was fake, but everyone thought it was real. Do we have to keep pretending? Come clean? Do things ultimately change now that I know the truth? I've already blown the news to my boss's boss's boss. I cringe at the thought of having to go tell him it was all a misunderstanding. I'm pretty sure his heavy office door would slap my ass on the way out. What do we do about the ten-thousand-dollar check from Bob?

"Of course she is." When did Hayley start crying? "Because she loves him. She's heartbroken."

Am I?

I'm angry he lied to me. I can feel it bubbling in my gut like lava, ready to ooze out and destroy everything it touches. I'm embarrassed he let me full steam ahead on a fake relationship. I yelled at him, cursed at him, I slept with him. All the while, he was keeping this from me. But am I heartbroken?

"Stop laughing," Palmer barks at our brother. He's wiping tears from his cheeks as his chest heaves. He's gasping for air, trying to swallow down the next bout of guffaws.

"You guys are all idiots."

My sisters gasp as I cross my arms over my chest. Max might outweigh me by almost eighty pounds, but I'm the one who used to push his hair back when he was sick, make his birthday cakes, ground him when he skipped school.

"He didn't leave," Max says. I open my mouth to

protest, but my brother bulldozes on, "That man is gone for you. He's head over heels. You had a fight. He's giving you the space we all know you asked for, and he'll be back. He's probably strategizing how to deal with moody mcmooderson here, and he has to work. A game he has to win even if you get to mope about in sweatpants."

"He lied to me, Max. He fucking lied and then he left."

"And you didn't ask him to leave, right?" Max rolls his eyes so hard I'm tempted to tell him they'll stick. "You didn't ask for space?"

Maybe I did.

"He lied to her." *Thank you Mads,* "Are we forgetting that part?"

"Right, because you've never lied to her? I haven't? Palmer? Hayley? Joey? Everybody lies about something," Max says, "Anyone who says they don't *is* a liar. The real question is why? What was the reason? What did he stand to gain? And was it something you can understand and forgive?"

Five sets of eyes—six, if you include Hela from her perch on the windowsill—swivel to me. I take a fortifying sip of cocoa and look down at my ring again. The one still on my finger. The one I haven't taken off since that first morning in Vegas. Not when I was furious with Vic. Not when I was panicking about my future. Not when he was trying to talk to me and I wouldn't let him get a word in edge-wise.

"We aren't actually married," I say into my mug, hoping the words are muffled enough to get lost, but also clear enough that I don't have to repeat myself.

Max laughs again, but Hayley and Madison suck in air in a gratifying gasp.

"Explain," Joey says.

"We went to the chapel, we picked out rings, but it wasn't a legal marriage." My chin quivers for some inexplicable reason.

"And why does that upset you?" Max asks. "Did you want to marry him?"

Did I want to? Did I head to Vegas intending to come home married to Victor Varg? Of course not. Except...

Except when I saw the ring, it wasn't the prospect of being married that horrified me. It was the potential impact it would have on my job. My career. Moving Vic in with me wasn't a hardship. Having him here, in my space, has been fun. It's nice to share my home with someone I don't need to take care of. Vic washes his own laundry, makes the bed, cleans toilets. He cooks.

"Do you want to be *not* married to him?" My brother winces. "You know what I mean."

I think of that torturous ride back to the apartment. The hollow silence between us after I opened my big mouth and mentioned divorce. The fear that ate through my spinal cord when I thought he wanted out.

"Okay, so she wants to be married to him," Palmer says, "But he still lied about it."

"Motivation," Hayley says. "Why would he lie about being married?"

"What did he say when he told you?" Joey.

"He said 'we aren't married. Not legally.'"

"No, you dummy. What did he say when he lied and told you were married?"

That gives me pause. I'm not sure I remember. It must have been when we woke up in his hotel room... except it wasn't, because I fled like my ass was on fire. To be fair, if I knew then what I know now—about Vic's sexual talents—I probably would have stayed and made us late for the bus.

I made it to the lobby without noticing. Oakes bought me a drink—no. Vic did. Robbie picked it up—and then I noticed? No. Robbie wanted to talk to me. Weird. When I first started working with the guys, Robbie Oakes set up a meeting specifically to tell me he was not a fan of social media and while he was willing to work with me, he was not going to "shake his ass" for the internet or the team. Robbie didn't tell me either.

I noticed... when the team did.

"He didn't actually tell you at all, did he?" Max grins at me as I rifle through my memories. "That's fantastic. Man, he's good."

"Good?" Madison shrieks the word, scaring Hela off her perch. "It's still lying."

"He apologized," I say, but they don't hear me. I barely hear me.

"Is a lie of omission really the same thing?" Joey asks and three yeses chirp back at her. "Okay," the baby regroups, "maybe this situation is a big deal, but overall? I don't think they're exactly the same."

"Listen, miss philosophy," Palmer says, "let's save this conversation for another day. Okay? Right now, we're educating Max that our darling fake brother-in-law is a lying bastard."

"Wait a minute," Max crosses his arms across his chest. "Let's be realistic here. What are the odds that our darling big sister didn't give him much of a chance? No offense, Tris."

"That's not exactly her fault," Madison points out. "The tabloids had the news by the next morning."

"And what was he supposed to do after that?" Max has the same look on his face when he knocks a pitch out of the field. Smug satisfaction. "As far as the world was concerned, they were hitched."

I feel like I'm at a play, watching the actors on stage volley quick lines back and forth. I'm literally just a spectator in my own apartment, watching my sisters and my brother debate the actions of my husband—No, fake husband.

"So that absolves him, then? He doesn't have to tell her?"

But he *did* tell me, I remind Madison.

She raises one dark eyebrow at me. "You said he told you he didn't fuck you."

Not for the first time, I wonder if I need to share less of my personal life with my siblings.

"Technically, that's another plus," Max says with a shrug. "Not taking advantage of you and all that, since he thought you were drunk."

"Drunk?" Palmer gives me a look. "Do we need to have a talk about responsible fun?"

Technically, I was high, too, but I don't think sharing

that tidbit will help in this situation. In fact, hadn't I been pissed off that he'd married me even though he thought I was too out of it to have sex? I'd been mad that he hadn't taken care of me. Turns out he had. The whole time.

I could kiss my sisters for their willingness to be on my side every time, no matter what we're facing, but I can't shake the feeling that my brother might be right. I was so angry, spitting mad, like Hela when she fell in the sink. I lashed out every time Vic was within spitting distance.

And yes, he still should have told me. He still should have found time to say, "Hey, Tristan. Just so you know, we didn't *actually* get married." But I think he might have tried. More than once. And I think, right now, that I'm mad at him, but I also want him back. I want to cry and yell and have him fold me into his arms. I want him.

I love him.

"I'm not saying he didn't fuck up." Max levers himself off the floor to wrap his arms tight around my middle. "Just that I don't think this is a relationship ender, and I don't think Vic has any intention of letting you go."

"And you know this from your vast experience with women?" I tease.

"Hey," he ruffles my hair, "I do have five sisters. But no. I know this because his stuff is still here. His clothes, his toothbrush, his cat, his girl." He digs his phone out of his pocket. "And because he may have sent me a ticket for you for tonight."

"Max, you asshole. Why didn't you lead with that last part?" Madison smacks her twin on the back of the head. "Save us a bunch of heartache."

But I know why. I wasn't ready to hear it at first. I was mad and hurt and still missing Vic like a piece of my soul. I couldn't see the forest for the trees, couldn't see the truth past the lie, because Vic didn't tell me right when he should have—and part of that is on me—but he also didn't wait to be found out. There was no way this could have stayed a secret forever. Even if we'd gotten to a point where divorce was off the table—and to be honest, I hadn't thought about it much in a long time—the truth would have come out during tax season or any other time where legal became involved.

And yet... Vic didn't wait until it was out of his hands. He had to know my response wouldn't be good, and he still offered me the information when I was upset. Not to distract, but to offer comfort, reassurance. I was standing here, stomach twisted into knots, thinking he wanted out, and he asked me to commit to him for real. He gave me the information, not to hurt, but to help. It was misguided and dumb, but his heart was in the right place.

Just like it was in Vegas when he took care of me, let me live out my little Elvis fantasy, and then brought me safely back to the hotel and didn't make a move. Even when he admitted he wanted to. He put my needs and my priorities first. Has anyone ever done that before? I love my siblings, but they have always assumed that I'll give and give and give. Vic put me first.

He showed me over and over and over again. I just didn't pay attention.

"Max," my voice catches on my brother's name. "You said Vic sent you a ticket?"

He grins. "He did."

I hold out my hand and my brother slips the phone into my palm. I type in his passcode and there it is, an email from Vic.

> ‹ All Inboxes   ∧ ∨
>
> **VV** **Victor Varg**
>   To: Max Grant
>
> **Please Read. Please.**
>
> Hey Max,
> It's Vic.
> I know I messed up, but I love your sister, and I'm willing to do whatever it takes to get her back. I know she isn't big on going to games, but will you let her know there's a seat with her name on it for every home game from now until the end of the season? I'm going to give her the space she asked for, but when she's ready for me to grovel, please tell her to come to a game. I'll look for her in the stands.
> Take care of my girl for me.
> Vic

There are tears burning in my eyes. I can't stop swallowing despite the dryness in my mouth. I check the clock over my microwave. If I get dressed fast, I can be at the rink just before puck drop. Do I want to? Am I still mad? Maybe a little, but not enough to leave him hanging. It'll be close, I'll have to skip my normal routine. No time to wash and dry my hair. I don't think I'll have time for my full makeup. I won't have time for much of anything.

I could skip this game. They have another home game the day after tomorrow. I could prepare. Get my brows waxed, exfoliate, do my skincare. I've been doing nothing for the past twenty-four hours but sitting around in my Vic's Chick's sweatpants and eating ice cream out of increasingly large bowls. The only useful thing I did was feed Hela, and that was almost entirely out of self-preservation.

"Go get dressed kid," Max says, like I'm not almost a decade older than him, "I'll drive you to the Stand for the game." He looks around the room at our sisters. "I think I'm the only one who didn't enjoy the cocoa."

I bolt to my room.

"I NEED THE PEP TALK." I crowd Robbie up against the boards, trying to block out the sounds from the crowd.

He glides a few feet away, stopping to prop his stick across the top of his thighs.

"No," he says, "You don't."

I follow him, ignoring the warmup, because I do. I really do. I need the reminder to get my head screwed on right now. I'm coming off a shit road trip. I need to be on top of each minute I spend on the ice.

I didn't expect Tristan to show up, not tonight. I figured she'd need more time, but Max gave me his email after I offered to do some off-season conditioning with him, and I saw a chance to let her know I wanted her here without bothering her. Mom gave up her ticket for the rest of the season. She'd be watching from the box, agreeing that the grand gesture was putting Tristan in the stands. On the bench. Somewhere I could interact with her, grab a kiss as I walked out of the tunnel, at least see her face.

Of course, Mom had made her opinions of my intelligence known before agreeing to spare the seat.

"How did you get to be this old and this successful and this stupid?" She'd asked, scrubbing a non-existent spot on the bathroom tile. I have a full-time cleaner, but mom has always scrubbed when angry or stressed.

"It would have been inappropriate to marry her when she couldn't consent, mom. You raised me better than that."

The long-suffering sigh and the nose pinch told me I should have kept my mouth shut. Her question had been rhetorical.

"Not *that* part. I'm actually proud of you for that one. I know how much you love that girl, so how could you not tell her? Were you that willing to risk everything?" Mom paused. "How could you not tell *me*?"

I'd never intended to tell my mother at all. I'd let myself into my own house with my own key and assumed she'd leave me alone. She hadn't. Where was my wife? What had I done? Didn't I know I needed to go grovel? Women like Tristan Grant—who are willing to put up with men like me—only come along once. Maybe twice if she included Quinn, my almost sister-in-law, but Erik was not cocky and arrogant and difficult the way I was. Erik wasn't followed around by fame and a hoard of women with "Vic's Chicks" painted across questionable parts of their bodies.

She'd stalked me from room to room in my overlarge house, waiting for me to cave. When I had, the story tumbling out, she'd pulled out the bleach and bristle brush and gotten to work on the perfectly clean grout lines.

Why had I kept it from Tristan? Mom had wanted to know. Why hadn't I just pinned her down and come clean?

Maybe because the last thing I thought about doing when I had my wife—fake wife—pinned down involved talking. My mouth had other ideas. Maybe because, contrary to current popular belief, I wasn't actually dumb. I knew the conversation would end here. With Tristan and Hela in our sun-soaked home, and me puttering about my mausoleum of a house alone. No, in this instance, my mother didn't really count. I had tried to tell Tristan at first. It was my mission to hunt the woman down and make her hear the news that the rings were just decorative, but she didn't let me near her. I admit I didn't try too hard because my mother was right. I enjoyed being married to Tristan. I wanted to make it real.

Even she'd warned me that Tristan might skip this one. Given the length of time between our fight and the game.

"You are in the wrong here. You do not rush her willingness to hear you out," Mom said. But I still looked for her as we marched through the tunnel and took the ice.

My twin and his fiancée are sitting in their seats. I can see Quinn's shock of red curls from almost anywhere, and I know there's still time before the puck drops, I know I have to focus on the game and my teammates, but I can't stop looking at that empty aisle seat wishing I'd see the bright blonde of Tristan's hair or even the ice blue of her eyes. I see neither.

"I do," I say again to Robbie as the buzzer goes off and

we file back into the locker room. "I fucked everything up and I'm going to keep fucking up if I can't get my head in the game."

"Do I want to know?" He asks, and I shake my head.

"Probably not."

"I don't know, man," Robbie grins at me. "If you fucked things up with your social media manager, maybe you want to play like shit on a stick. Maybe she'll feel sorry for you and come running back."

And maybe pink elephants will fly out of my ears and dance the cha-cha at center ice.

"Robbie." I close my eyes against his knowing look. "How do you put Vera out of your mind before a game?"

"Fuck," he says, and yes, it was a low blow, but desperate times call for desperate measures.

The seat is still empty as we take the ice for the anthem. I try to focus only on the flag, but my eyes keep darting back to the spot behind our bench. Maybe it's a good thing she isn't here. Maybe Max hasn't shown her the email yet. Maybe she already had plans. I saw new content on the team socials. Not that I went looking, I just—okay, I went looking.

She'd shared a video about superstition and good luck charms in the hockey world. There was Spags talking about his lucky socks. Gagey saying he calls his dad on the way to the rink, even on the team bus for away games. Ahlstrom saying he and his three kids eat chocolate chip pancakes as their pregame ritual. Pelé does yoga and takes a bubble bath. Robbie glowered and told the camera that pregame rituals could be deeply personal and he didn't feel like sharing, but anyone who's watched a game has seen Robbie's in action.

She'd put this video together right after Vegas, inspired by her new nickname. When it had been my turn, I'd smiled directly into her camera lens and told the truth.

"I give the puck to my good luck charm."

She'd lowered the camera. "A ritual, Varg. You've done that once."

"And I played the best game of my career," I countered. "A new ritual is still a ritual."

She'd left me in the video, the last one up, smoldering at the camera. The comments had gone wild. Everyone knew I'd meant her and apparently the public approved. I want to take it as a sign, but I know she lines up a lot of posts ahead of time. It could mean everything or nothing to see myself still on my phone screen. It didn't mean she'd forgiven me, or that everything could go back to the way it was, but I couldn't resist letting that twenty-second clip give me a sliver of hope.

Maybe there'd been time to change the video after our fight, but she'd chosen not to.

My eyes go to the empty seat again and my twin nods as Quinn waves. I drop my chin in acknowledgement, kicking my skates back and forth over the smooth ice while the Canadian anthem begins.

Maybe it's a good thing she's not here. If Tristan had made it to the game, I'd spend all my time looking at her, looking *for* her. I'd let my teammates down for sure.

I see the line breaking apart, a sure sign that the singing is over and it's time for the puck drop. I missed the entire anthem. Tristan's seat is still empty, and that's okay. There's always the next game. I knew this was a long shot. I'm not giving up. Not this easily.

I'll just have to win tonight and then send her the game puck. Maybe some flowers. I can leave stuff at her door every single day until she's ready to hear me out. I'll ask Erik to sit down and do an interview with me—he's less opposed now than he used to be. I can do this. The Arctic is the odds-on favorite tonight. Our offense is better than their defense, our goalie more confident and consistent.

Robbie takes his spot at center ice opposite the Toronto player. I take my spot behind the hash marks, getting ready for the drop. My mind is still on my—not-wife, but the beauty of my position means the bench is at my back and I can't stare at her empty seat. Not this period. It'll be harder in the second, when the spot is still empty and directly across from me. Hopefully by then I'm in a groove. Robbie waits for the other player's blade to touch the ice before dropping his own stick. Usually, he likes to lift his opponent's stick and swipe the puck back to one of our defenders, but if there's a scrum, or a fight for possession, he'll drop it to me.

The puck hits the ice and gets lost under the sticks and skates of Robbie and Toronto's center. I'm moving in close, angling my stick to give Robbie an open target. The ice is a little softer than I like and I'd bet my contract that's why my teammate hasn't taken possession yet. If it's too soft for me, it's too soft for him. I cut to the left, losing the man guarding me like his life—or job—depends on it, and there, out of the corner of my eye, I see something.

For a moment I think I imagine it, the flash of blonde hair and baby blue. I don't have time to take a real look. I don't know if I want to. The puck hits the blade of my stick and muscle memory takes over. I pull it in towards the bulk of my body, and then slip around the Toronto player trying to steal possession back. Ahlstrom is racing across the ice, giving me a wide-open target for a pass right there in front of me.

I should take it. We're moving faster than Toronto and we could probably make a break for the goal and put one on the scoreboard right off the draw. It would be good for morale, good for momentum, jazz up the crowd, but as I angle my hips to box out the opposition, I see it again. The bright shine of light blonde hair.

She's here.

I blink, shake my head, and when I open my eyes, she's still there.

Tristan.

My wife.

It's instinct to pump my legs, powering my body towards the Arctic bench and my little blonde with her hand pressed against the glass. She's smiling. I'm close enough to see the curve of her mouth. Her bare mouth. No lipstick or gloss, just soft skin and bright eyes. Hair falling in soft strands around her flushed cheeks. It's a miracle I still have the puck. A miracle I'm still upright as relief courses through me.

She's here. She came. I'm not down and out just yet.

I scoop the edge of my stick under the puck and lift it into the air, watching it sail over the glass and down into the lap of my wide-eyed wife. And as the whistle blows and the ref calls a two-minute minor for the delay of game, I skate to the box grinning because Tristan Grant is in my arena, watching my team, and wearing my jersey.

That's worth two minutes in the sin bin any day.

THERE'S a puck in my lap.

There shouldn't be, not in the middle of regulation play, not on *purpose*, but here it is. Smooth and solid and a little wet from the ice, it sits in my lap like a cinder block. I had tried to make it to the rink before the game started, but I had forgotten how awful the traffic could be on game days. I had also forgotten my badge and credentials, which could have let us into the back lot. So after sitting in traffic for fifteen minutes, I'd opened Max's passenger door and run the last few blocks.

Besides having no makeup, unbrushed hair, a pair of threadbare leggings and an oversized Arctic jersey slipping off my shoulders, I'm also sweaty and gasping for air. I can't remember the last time I looked this disheveled in public, and now the whole arena is staring at me as the Jumbotron zooms in on the woman who got golden boy Victor Varg to break the rules.

Because that's exactly what he did.

It's one thing to be his good luck charm and have him flip a puck over the glass during warmups. There are dozens of rubber discs bouncing around as each team takes shots as the clock counts down to game time. It's another to send the puck up and over during play.

My eyes move from the gift in my hands to the man on the ice. He wears a half shield on his helmet, but the small strip of polycarbonate doesn't hide the wink he sends me. A wink that ends up larger than life on the screen. He holds eye contact, lips pulled up in a crooked grin around his mouth guard. My insides free-fall, stomach flipping and intestines twisting, and I bite down hard on my lower lip so I don't do something mortifying like moan.

"Am I allowed to say something now?" A man says to my left and I turn to come face to face with Vic. Well, Vic's face.

"You must be Erik and Quinn." I hold out my hand to shake, but I'm still holding the puck. "Sorry," I laugh and switch hands.

"Quinn told me to wait to introduce myself," my... Vic's brother says.

"So you wouldn't ruin the moment." Quinn smacks his chest, and he smiles at her, hearts in his eyes.

"Also, because Vic might have warned us not to scare his wife off during his grand gesture."

That answered several questions I had brewing and raised a few more.

"He told you about..." I wave my hands around the rink and the crowd, my wedding ring catching the low light in the arena.

"Yes," Erik nods, "but don't worry. It's because I needed help with something similar last year. And I remember pulling strings after a panicked message from Vic so the team could help this man get his girl. Even then, I told myself that I had used my contacts because the publicity was good for the team, but I'm pretty sure I pulled in all my favors in Chicago just because it was Vic who asked. Even if I wasn't talking to him much back then. I think it's possible I've loved him a lot longer than I want to admit.

"Of course," Erik is still talking. "He didn't tell us he was going to get himself thrown in the penalty box. He's going to get reamed for that one. Did it at least work? Could be worth it if it worked."

I turn the puck over in my hands. It had already worked. I'm here, aren't I? Across the rink, the door to the penalty box opens and Vic powers back onto the ice. Robbie slaps a pass in his direction as he blazes across the blue line and breaks for the net.

"Erik," Quinn has a soft voice and a kind face, but even I can hear the steel in the name. "Stop ruining this. We are *helping*, not trying to sabotage Vic."

Erik gives me a sheepish smile. "Sorry, twin instinct to rib him, but Quinn's right. We're just happy to meet our sister-in-law."

"Well, our sort of sister-in-law." Quinn bites her lip.

And there it is. I knew it was probable that Vic told his family the whole truth. They know we aren't married. My anger flares. Did everyone know before I did? Does the team know? Was everyone laughing behind my back?

"I'm not quite your sister-in-law yet," Quinn blushes as

she takes her fiancée's hand, the diamond on her left ring finger almost blinding me.

"I would marry you now," Erik tells her, leaning over to press a kiss to her neck and her blush deepens. "You know the piece of paper doesn't matter. You're mine and I'm yours. Forever baby."

Wait... the "sorta" wasn't about me?

"Did Vic tell you? About me?" I'm not sure I want the answer, but I have to know.

"Of course he did." Quinn laughs. "He adores you. I feel like we've known you forever, Tristan. I'm sorry we didn't get a chance to meet before now, but we thought we should give the newlyweds some space."

It's my turn to blush.

"He doesn't shut up about you." Erik adds. "Tristan is so smart. She graduated top of her class with a dual degree while working full time. Her soul is bright like a rainbow but her favorite color is a deep indigo. She wears fuzzy bunny slippers and giant socks at home but can run in stilettos. She loves scrambled eggs but not omelets. She's smart, she's generous, she loves harder than anyone he's ever met. She's the only one who can keep the team in line. To be honest, I'm half surprised you're a real person and not a figment of his imagination. I thought for sure no one was that cool."

Quinn narrows her eyes at him.

"Except for you, baby." He loops his arm over her shoulder, pulling her back against his chest.

"He said you were gorgeous, too," Quinn says. "And you make the best pancakes. We stock chai tea at our house and oat milk if you ever want to come over." She winks and I can't help but laugh.

Warmth is flooding my veins. I'm hot. Burning up here in this plastic seat and oversized jersey. Because he didn't tell them about our fake marriage, he told them about *me*. He knows *me*. What did Erik say to his fiancée? A piece of paper doesn't matter. Not when we belong to each other?

That resonates deep in the dark untrusting pit of my soul. It doesn't matter if we got married or not. It doesn't matter because I'm his. And I think he's mine.

"It's working," I say and Erik grins.

"Then the trouble was worth it. Especially if he can play the rest of the game like that." Erik nods at the ice, and Quinn and I turn our attention to the game in time to see Vic pull his stick back and slam the puck into the back of the net. The buzzer blares through the arena, the red light behind the net blinding as Vic pumps his fist into the air. He heads to the bench for a shift change and our eyes meet as he steps off the ice.

I blow him a kiss and he lifts a gloved hand to catch it out of the air and press it against the C embroidered on his chest.

I'm a goner. I don't think I can even pretend to be mad anymore. I just want to wrap my arms around him. I want to fold myself into the solid wall of his chest and burrow in for eternity. I want him to come back so Hela has someone else to stalk through the apartment. I'm sick of drinking coffee in the morning because I made it for him by mistake and don't want to pour it down the drain. I've only done that once. He's only been gone a day, and I'm over it.

Coach Noris puts a hand on Vic's shoulder and he turns away from me, smile dropping as the coach says something into his ear. I can't make out the words, but the facial expression tells me it isn't anything pleasant.

"Tell me about the trouble," I say to Erik.

Erik is watching his twin get a lecture, too, Vic nodding even as his eyes follow the moving puck on the ice.

"He deliberately drew a penalty," Erik says. "He put the team at a disadvantage."

"He's tossed me a puck before." I say. Vic settles into the bench, tuning to meet my eyes before he grabs a drink of water.

"Sending the puck out of play is considered a delay of game. There are situations where it's unavoidable, or the penalty is worth the chance to regroup, but showing off to one's wife doesn't count as either of those. Not to the coaching staff or the team or anyone in the NHL."

"Why would he do that?" I ask. The ticket was enough. I was already here. He'd already won this round. But I already know.

Vic thinks I'm worth it.

"I'm guessing he knew the Arctic's penalty kill was stronger than Toronto's power play," Erik says, which is a good point. "And that goal went a long way to helping him out."

"You know why he did it." Quinn smiles. "You're his good luck charm."

I am. I will be.

I can make this easier on him. On us. It takes less than a minute to pull up Chris's contact information and send off a quick text. I slip the phone away before I get a response, but twenty minutes later after Vic's second goal of the night, my video plays across the Jumbotron and the whole arena sees my husband say that tossing me the puck is his lucky charm. He pauses his slow circuit of the ice to point first up at the screen and then at me, and the crowd goes wild. Quinn and Erik scream louder than almost anyone else.

My heart beats against the cage of my ribs, my blood fizzing in my veins like champagne, popping each time Vic's eyes meet mine.

The buzz of my phone draws my attention as both teams set up for another face-off. And there, in writing so I can see it again and again and again, is a message from Chris.

"Great call on the video. Let's talk next week about how to incorporate more of your ideas into actual game time."

This is it. The break that I hoped for. A grin splits my face and still I tuck my phone away without answering, because Vic is streaking over the boards and back into play, and there's nothing I'd rather turn my focus to than this moment. Than him.

The game is blowout, Ólaffson blocking every single shot that comes his way. Erik says he's "standing on his head" and it's an appropriate description. I didn't even know people could bend the way the Icelander does. Robbie Oakes puts up two goals and Spags scores on the power play. By the end of the third period, Erik tells me and Quinn that the Arctic is playing keep-away, not even trying to up the score anymore. Every time Vic leaves the ice or passes the bench, we lock eyes and he smiles.

I am yours and you are mine.

There are only a few minutes left on the clock when he takes a pass from Ahlstrom and Erik whistles low under his breath. The puck seemed to find Vic's stick by magnets or magic or some greater force. Hockey gods maybe.

"He's going to do it," Erik says. If this was a closer game, the whole arena would be standing, watching Vic break for the wide-open net.

"Do what?" Quinn asks and Erik doesn't answer. I don't blame him because I see it too. "Seriously," the redhead asks as Vic's eyes dart right to left. He's alone. Just him and the puck and the second-string goalie Toronto put out for the start of the third period. "What's he—"

Erik shushes her. "Sorry baby," he says, eyes glued to the ice and his twin. "Take the damn shot, Vic. He's weak on his left side and we all know it's your best—"

Vic's stick pulls back, his hips square up, and the puck sails right past the wide-open glove and into the back of the net. Goal.

A hat trick.

His first of the season.

I'm on my feet along with half the arena, hats pouring down onto to ice to celebrate. The game is almost over, but there's no way the fans would miss this chance. He points in my direction as Erik, Quinn, and I bang our fists on the glass. The arena is so loud I can't hear myself screaming, but my lips form the words, anyway.

I love you.

Vic points at me, blowing a kiss in my direction, and the volume around me increases. He scoops a hat off the ice and tosses it to the bench as both teams regroup while a group of teenagers flit across the ice with shovels and large trash barrels.

"Do you know how to get to the bench?" Erik asks as the noise settles. Most of the fans file out of their seats. The game's conclusion is obvious, and they'd rather beat the traffic.

I nod. "Yes, but I don't have my badge."

"I don't think you need it," Quinn smiles at me. "Your husband's the captain of the team and the guy who just scored beaucoup goals."

I scramble out of my seat and up the concrete steps, grateful for my size and sneakers as I dodge around other fans. Quinn is right and they let me down the back stairs with no problem, just a wink and a smile. For a moment, I wonder if we need to tighten up security and if I should let Chris or someone know, then I'm sprinting down the steps and bolting for the tunnel like my life depends on it.

I reach the end as the announcer calls the final score and I know the teams are headed onto the ice to shake hands. I stop, torn. Do I go out there and make a spectacle of us? Throw my arms around his neck and kiss him? Do I wait here?

I stay where I am. I want there to be no doubt about my actions, my choice. I'm here because I want him back. I am his and he is mine, not to put on a show for anyone else.

The guys file past me. They're buzzing with energy,

dripping sweat. There's a testosterone funk that comes with them, muted by the frigid scent of the ice. I smile at Oakes, Spaeglin, and Ólaffson as they pass. Offer congratulations on a well-deserved win. I take the good-natured ribbing and the lucky charm nickname as I crane my neck, looking for one tall, blonde-haired, hazel-eyed captain.

He's the last one off the ice—of course he is—and my heart races as I catch sight of his broad shoulders and helmet. His hair is dark with sweat and he has a cut above his right eye from a high stick during the second period. He stops when he sees me. The last couple of guys between us exchange grins and hurry the rest of the way down the tunnel until it's just me and Vic staring each other down.

"I thought you left," he says, and my heart aches.

"I'm sorry I was late. Max didn't tell me about the ticket until I was in the middle of a clay mask."

"No. I'm sorry," he says, and I shake my head.

"I'm sorry about the penalty."

"I don't care about the penalty." He drops his stick to the rubber flooring and peels his gloves off. "I don't care that you were late. I'm sorry that I lied to you."

He steps into my body.

"I'm sorry that I didn't marry you that night because god knows I wanted to, but I'm also not sorry because my aim was to protect you. I'm sorry I didn't tell you the truth sooner. I meant to, but I thought I had more time. And then I didn't, and I was terrified of losing you. I made some bad decisions. I've done a lot of things in my life that I regret, but none of them comes close to how sorry I am for letting you doubt me. Doubt us. I love you, Tristan. I will spend the rest of my life showing you that you can trust me. That I'm all in. You can have all the time you need to see I'm not going anywhere. That you are my number one priority. Always."

His big body trembles. I can see the movement even under the bulk of his pads and uniform.

"I love you," I say, pressing my hand to his sticky cheeks. Tears and sweat making them wet against my palms. "Did I get a chance to say that before?"

His eyes close as he leans into my touch.

"I love you, Victor Varg. I'm not happy you kept something like our marital status from me, especially when you knew how much it was going to upend our lives, but I still love you. I don't have to like what you did to recognize the part I played in our fight."

"You what?" His voice is hoarse, like he was the one screaming into the mass of people.

"Okay, maybe I had some help to see my part in it. I shut you down every time you tried to tell me anything. I gave you hell for your role in our marriage, and the reality was I was hurt. I thought you'd protect me, keep me from being stupid, because even then I loved you. Trusted you."

"I don't care about any of that." Vic presses his forehead to mine. He's pumping out heat like a furnace. "Say it again. Please."

"I love you." I say, and he fuses his mouth to mine. It's not a real kiss, not with the way our mouths fall open, inhaling each other's breath, but it's everything all the same. "I love you Victor Varg. I love you. I love you. I love you." I press each word to his lips and he swallows them down like they're the air he needs to live.

"I would give up my life to make you happy, Tristan. God, I love you so fucking much, kitty cat. I want to be yours. I want you to wear my ring for real. I want to live in your cozy apartment surrounded by our cat and our siblings. I want to wake up every morning with my arms around you, and I want to call you every night that we spend apart. I want to hold the Stanley Cup over my head and have you run out to kiss me at center ice."

"Let's not get ahead of ourselves." I say, smiling until my cheeks hurt. "You know how I feel about skating."

"Marry me. For real this time." Vic says as I throw my arms around his shoulders and he boosts me up into his arms. In skates, the man is a behemoth, and his pads are cutting into odd parts of my body as I wrap myself around him like a koala, but I'm not letting go. I don't think the jaws of life could pry me free. "I love you, Tristan."

"Let's not get ahead of ourselves." I press the words into the sweat-soaked mesh of his jersey.

"Right," he says, "I need to earn it."

"I think it's time for you to come home and we can sort through what comes next. I missed you. So does Hela."

His nose skates down the line of my cheek.

"You just want her to have another moving target to attack."

"I do," I say, "But I want you back more."

Vic doesn't bother grabbing his stick or his gloves, he just carries me down the hall, headed for the locker room. I have no intention of letting go. He can drop his pads and uniform off and grab his keys and we can shower together at home. Water conservation and all that. It's only been a day, but it feels like a year.

"Hey Vic?" I say as the locker room comes into view and I can hear an excited team stripping down and getting ready to see their families. "Ask me again soon. I'm pretty sure I'll have a different answer."

"You got it, kitty cat."

VEGAS

He thinks the night air is probably too cold for her, especially with so much creamy skin on display, but she doesn't seem cold. He's had his fingers along the curve of her spine and her skin was smooth and warm to the touch. That might have something to do with the fizzy pink drink she'd commandeered from him. And the yellow and orange one he bought for her afterward. That one came with a tiny umbrella that she'd tucked behind her ear like a paper hibiscus flower.

It's easy to turn and offer his back as she reaches down to unbuckle her fancy shoes. Her slim hands wrap over the top of his shoulders, sliding across the bulge of his trapezius muscles. He has to bend his knees so she can reach, careful not to lean his chest forward. The sharp points of her heels bang against his pecs as they dangle off her fingers.

Her thighs are smooth under his palms as he helps boost her up. It takes a few tries. She's giggling into his shirt as he counts down from three. Lagging as he tries to help and she jumps too late. Finally he lifts on two, her weight slight enough that he has her high on his back before she can think to help.

His hands drag down the length of her legs and he knows he's probably taking advantage of the situation but her skin is like silk against his fingertips and her quads tremble under his touch. He has to help her wrap her legs above his belt buckle, pushing his hips back so her heels don't touch the bulge he's trying to will away.

"Please," she whispers against the shell of his ear, her arms tightening until he can barely breathe, and he wouldn't change a second of this moment, not for all the air in the world. Anything that is in his power to give... it's hers. He'll find a way.

It's a short walk to the chapel and he wishes it were longer.

"I just want to see one." She'd said in the club, tugging on his shirt sleeve until he leaned down so her breath could break over his skin. "With Elvis."

So here he is, letting her slip down the length of his body as he hands her tiny shoes to her and holds open the old wooden door. The paint is chipped and there are only two cars in the parking lot, and even if it weren't the closest place to their hotel, he thinks it's probably the best choice because no one will see them here.

Not that he's embarrassed, but he's pretty sure she would be. He doesn't want to think about that at all. It makes his stomach hurt. An aching coil of ice that slowly wraps around his intestines.

The chapel is dated but clean, and there's a small woman standing behind a glass counter with beige curls that add at least four inches to her height. She's snapping bubblegum, as she scrolls through a phone in a sparkly pink case. A small bell announces their arrival and he assumes she'll look up at the couple who just walked in, welcome them, try to upsell luxury rose petals, something, but she doesn't lift her eyes from the screen.

"You boys are in luck," she calls out, still glued to a game with matching candy pieces, swiping, swiping, swiping with a tap tap tap of lime green nails.

He's doesn't even think about correcting her. Mostly because they aren't looking to enter wedded bliss with Elvis at the helm of the ship. No matter what she says into the skin of his neck, no matter how big her eyes get as she looks up from under her thick lashes, no matter how much he likes the idea of branding her with his name so everyone who looks at her will back right off. She is drunk. He is going to keep his dick and his name away from her because he told himself he'd take care of her. It feels like his most important job.

Even last season, his biggest dream was to hoist Sir Stanley's cup over his head as he took a victory lap around the ice. Now... dreams change. He doesn't care about the win, or the ring, or the cup, unless she's at the center line to press her mouth to his in congratulations. With his name draped across her back in big block letters.

But the woman isn't talking to them, she's talking to two very familiar faces peeking around the white door that leads to the chapel and, hopefully, to Elvis.

"Cap?" The kid says, eyes wide. "What are you doing here?"

"We're getting married by Elvis." She slips her arm into the crook of his elbow and he swallows down his urge to agree with her. They aren't doing that. Not today. He'll fly her back tomorrow if she changes her mind. He'll fly Elvis to them. He will research marriage licenses and requirements. But not tonight. "Ooh, rings."

She's pressed over the top of a glass display case, eyes shining down at the glittering gold bands like a kid on Christmas morning. Given her history, he wonders if she ever had memories of happy holiday mornings. He knows her dad left when she was twelve, but a family has to be fundamentally broken before that. Right? Did she have twelve years of joy and presents and hugs around a Christmas tree? He half hopes she did. If anyone deserves a little bit of joy, it's her. The other half hopes she doesn't. You can't miss something you've never had.

"These boys are volunteer witnesses." The woman at the counter says, eyes still on her phone. "You need two for any legal marriage. You can use them, or we can provide some." Her voice is the monotone of someone who works a night shift that sees very little action. It must be Hollywood that made him think that getting married overnight in Sin City would be popular. Maybe he should be glad that it isn't. He wonders how many people who get hitched on a whim in Vegas make it long term.

"We don't need them," he tells the chapel worker, trying not to laugh as his teammates' faces fall. They don't want to miss the good gossip. "No one's getting married tonight."

To the hockey players he adds, "We have an early flight. Head back to the hotel."

Two "yes, captain"s and a longing look toward the jewelry case, and the bell over door chimes as Tyler and Jack walk away. That's about the same time Tristan comes skipping back to him, her hand outstretched with two plain gold bands nestled in her palm.

"I like the matching ones. How about you?" The rings clink

together as she shakes her hand back and forth. He's not sure what she's doing, honestly, but the open joy on her face is intoxicating. He could barely say no to this woman before. Now it's going to be next to impossible. "I think it's important that they match." She says, the rings reflecting in the sky blue of her eyes and he catches himself nodding at her. "Do you have an Elvis?"

She's turned her attention to woman behind the counter and he has a moment to look his fill. Her cheeks are flushed, her pupils wide, and he wants to lean down and slot his mouth over hers. More than he can remember ever wanting anything, and he's had some big dreams in his life.

The older woman is saying something, nodding at the interior doors, and his blonde is throwing them wide open, a charmed squeal breaking out of her as she spots the King of Rock 'n Roll standing under a gravity-challenged arch that seems to favor the left side.

"Oh my god this is my dream," he hears her say as she trails her fingers over the fabric petal of a grayish synthetic rose.

He doesn't point out that her siblings aren't there. That he's sure she'd want them there for the real thing. He learned a long time ago not to tell a woman what she wants. Maybe the solitude is exactly that. Maybe she wants someone willing to choose her first, over and over, someone who wants her with such a burn of longing that they would jump at the chance to keep her. To never let her go.

Instead he hears himself ask, "How much to have a ceremony but not a marriage license?" And if he expected the chapel worker to push back, insist they have to go through the proper channels, well he would have vastly underestimated the indifference of someone working the night shift for minimum wage.

The service itself is less than ten minutes. Later he'll barely remember the bad accent, the limp bouquet of daisies she holds in her pale hands, or the musty smell of the maroon carpet. He'll remember the way her hair shone under the lights like polished silver. How she wet her bottom lip with the edge of her pink tongue before repeating the vows fed to her by fake-Elvis. He'll remember how her hands didn't shake, but his did, as he slid a gold ring past her knuckles.

He'll remember stopping just outside the chapel doors, crowding her back against the stone as he pushed a strand of hair behind her left ear. His own band shining in the glow of the neon sign above them. He'll remember that it was softer than the silk of her little white dress as he cupped a hand around her hip and drew their bodies together. How his gaze fixed on her mouth and he felt drawn in as if she had a gravitational pull he couldn't escape.

How at the last minute he remembers himself and presses a kiss to the hollow below her earlobe, and the sound of her quick inhale would fuel his fantasies for decades to come.

He carries her most of the way back to the hotel, her legs again wrapped around his waist, and his hands helping hold down her short skirt. No one gets a show. No one.

He takes her to his own room, trying not to shiver as she asks ridiculous questions against the skin of his neck.

"Do you know you're really tall?"

"Do you and Erik communicate through telepathy? Because I think my twin siblings do."

"Is anyone actually real? Or are we all some computer simulation, or a growth on some alien child's science project they left in the back of a closet?"

348

"Can you hear the way my heart pounds every time you touch me?"

He sets her down carefully, putting her shoes near the desk in his single room. The king-size bed takes up most of the space and he leaves the curtains open because she keeps looking out at the night lights with awe-struck wonder. He steps into the bathroom to grab her a cup of water and finds her with her nose pressed to the window.

She asks him to untie her dress and he pauses, wondering if he should. If his control will hold. If it's taking advantage if she asked him to, and he won't go any further, he won't. He won't. Definitely won't. But she's untied the knots herself and the dress is sliding off her shoulders as he slams his eyes shut.

He counts to ten, lids squeezed tight, because if he doesn't see her then he can pretend she's not naked in front of him. Maybe not naked, but close enough to make no difference. Especially silhouetted against the sixteenth floor windows. He doesn't think he could handle seeing the shimmer of the lights against her skin.

He's doing well until she makes a sound. A breathy moan mixed with a laugh. His eyes snap open and it was a mistake. His brain is screaming warnings, alarms and lights blaring in the recesses of his mind, because there is the smooth line of her back and the round curve of her rear covered. Her panties are plain white cotton, not particularly fancy or provocative, but all the blood in his brain rushes south so fast he goes dizzy.

Her head is thrown back, hair brushing the edges of her shoulder blades, and she moans again. He can see her breath fogging up the window. His fists are clenched so tight he might break a finger, but he doesn't care. His throat is dry, each breath agony. He once played in a playoff game that went to a third overtime and even then he wasn't as starved for oxygen as he is now.

She spins against the window, and he can't figure out where to look. Or not look. Not at her breasts, tipped with rose petal nipples. Not at the movement of her fingers under damp cotton. And maybe he should close his eyes again, look away, turn around, but he's caught in her web. Stuck. Spellbound. He won't touch her. He won't. But it would take the force of the entire US military to make him stop watching her.

"Please."

The tendons in her neck stand out in sharp relief, her stomach quivers. She's close. He knows she is.

"Please, Vic."

And goddamn. His name on her lips is a prayer, a siren song. He will not have sex with this inebriated woman. He won't. But maybe...

He wants her to move her panties, let him see the damp pink of her pussy, but if she does his control will shatter like glass. He'll break every promise he's made to himself. He'll break every rule. He won't even care.

"I can't." Her words are a whine, desperation teasing each syllable. "I need you, Vic. Oh god."

He can't either. Can't touch, can't taste... but maybe he can talk? If he keeps every part of himself over here, away from the gravitational pull of her body and voice?

"I've got you baby," he says. His voice sounds like ten miles of bad road and he clears his throat twice.

"Please," she whimpers again.

"Those aren't your fingers, Tristan. They're mine. I'm the

one. Circling your clit. Do you feel me? Harder baby. Pinch that little nub and twist."

She follows his directions, throwing her head back to thunk against the window. He almost steps into her. Almost lets his hand cup the back of her head. Just to make sure she's okay, but it's a trap. If he touches any part of her it will be game over.

"Yes," she says, and he's glad she's coherent but he also wants her lost to pleasure.

"Bring your free hand up to your tit, kitty cat. Do you like your nipples played with? Show me."

She does and he could come from watching her alone. His cock aches and he wants to fist it, pump his hand up and down until he can release some of this tension and heat and want. But no. He's going to maintain some control here. If he touches himself, he reasons, that's crossing the line. Then it's sex. He won't do that. He presses both hands to his eyes then braces them on the top of his head. As far from his erection as they can go.

"Good girl," he says as she pulls on her swollen nipple. He wants to bite into the curve of her breast like it's a ripe apple. He wants to leave a mark. He wants to brand her as his. He wants the world to know.

Another keening wail and his hips jump on their own, even as he stands five feet from her.

"Slide two fingers into that dripping cunt, Tristan. Slide my fingers deep and rub the heel of your hand against your clit."

He has to close his eyes as her hand starts to move.

"Fuck yourself on my hand," he says.

She shatters with a wail. His name pulled out of her in a never-ending stream of sound. Her panties are almost sheer with her come and there isn't enough air in this room. Not enough to keep his head from spinning.

She slumps and he lunges toward her, his arms banding around her waist as she loses her footing. Her head nestles against his chest. Eyes closed and a sleepy smile curving her lips. Her cheeks are stained red and her mouth is swollen as if he had devoured her lips for real, and not just in his fantasies.

He lays her down on his big bed, tucking her under the covers in her underwear. Her eyes are closed and her breathing slow as he steps back. He'll sit in the armchair. He'll wait and when she wakes up, sober, they'll talk about what happened. He's done staying away from her. They'll need to make this work.

She begged him for relief.

She called his name when she came.

Rules be damned, she's his.

"Where are you?" She mumbles, one arm sliding out from under the covers to reach for him. "Come back."

And he's sliding in next to her before he realizes he's moved.

She plucks at the buttons on his shirt.

"Off," she demands, sounding every inch of a queen even with her eyes shut and hair is tangled mess.

He didn't pack pajamas. He doesn't share a room on the road and never wears them. But he can't ignore her request any more than he can stop his heart from beating or the sun from rising every morning.

He's still sporting a massive erection. It's tenting the front of his boxer briefs, but he can keep it away from her. If he maintained control through her orgasm, he can handle this too.

He strips down, leaving his clothes in a muddled pile by the *bed, and climbs on top of the covers. He'll stay up here, she'll stay under them, and it will be okay. It has to be.*

And it is until she nestles into his side, fighting the down comforter as she tries to work her arms free, and helping her get free is instinct. One slim thigh comes over his stomach and he shifts so his dick won't poke her, even as she presses her mouth to the skin over his heart. The organ that's pounding a concerning, unsteady rhythm inside the cage of his ribs.

Her body goes limp, loose, pliant. Her breathing steadies, even as her lips touch his skin. And this is okay. This is fine. They haven't technically broken any rules. Not yet. He'll just stay awake and everything will be fi.........

THE ARCTIC

On Ice

(Keep an eye out for more of our favorite players. Coming soon)

———

OTHER TITLES

The Trope

Mother Knows Best

The Escalation Clause

ACKNOWLEDGMENTS

If Ali Hazelwood can bullet point her Thank You's, then so can I (mostly jokes, but also I wrote the 90k words in this book and my brain is now goo oozing out of my ears).

———

The Love of My Life: Thank you for answering a million questions about your sport, allowing me to interrupt live games to ask more questions, and for taking the kids so I could write/edit/draw. I love you endlessly. And I have more questions. Sorry.

Thing 1 and Thing 2: If someday you choose to read these, I hope we never talk about it. Thank you for letting mommy's laptop become a member of the family. I love you both more than words.

Mama: Thank you for your love, support, and proofreading prowess. I know it hasn't been easy this past year, but I couldn't do this without you. I love you.

Octopus: Thank you for holding my hand in my darkest moments, and making me truly believe that I can do this author thing. I love you.

Moonbeam: Thank you for holding me together when my insides feel like they're falling out. Thank you for being there every day even when I try to hide, and showering me with love always. I love you.

Starlight: Thank you for being my forever hype woman, giving me external validation whenever I need it, and showing me how to self-care properly. I love you.

Soul Sister: There will never be enough words. Thank you for keeping me sane in every other aspect of my life. And always supporting my dream. I love you.

Writing Soulmate: Thank you for making me laugh, listening to me cry, and supporting every step I take, even when things were hard. Keep going. Don't stop. I love you.

My MA Book Babes: I adore each and every one of you and would not have made it this far alone. Literally. Cam can attest to watching me try to sign in with my legal name at FILNE. I am so thankful to have a little local author family.

My Therapist: Seriously. Thank you isn't enough.

To all my booksta/booktok baddies: Endless *Thank You*'s for hyping this book, this team, these characters, and my awkward self for the last year and a half. I am forever grateful.

To my readers: Thank you for reading my stories. I appreciate you more than you know, and I can't believe someone wants to see the silliness inside my brain.

———

Thank you, Stella✦